Journey's of the Heart

HISTORICAL CHRISTIAN ROMANCE

VIVIAN BELLE

STERLING RIDGE PRESS LLC

Cover designed by Sterling Ridge Press LLC

Published by: Sterling Ridge Press, LLC www.sterlingridgepress.com

ISBN: 978-1-966093-26-8
Printed in the United States of America

First Edition: May2025

For permissions, contact: support@vivianbelle.com or visit www.vivianbelle.com

Dedication

For those who have loved and lost,
yet found the courage to journey onward.
The trail may be steep, the path uncertain,
but sometimes the longest journey
leads to the most beautiful destinations.
Vivian Belle

About The Author

Vivian Belle is a talented author known for her sweeping **Historical Christian Romance** novels set against the untamed beauty of the American frontier. With a deep love for history and storytelling, she brings to life **resilient heroines, steadfast heroes, and faith-filled journeys** in the vast, rugged landscapes of the past.

Nestled in the **majestic mountains of northern West Virginia,** Vivian finds endless inspiration in the rolling hills, winding rivers, and boundless sky that mirror the spirit of her stories. When she's not writing, she enjoys **kayaking on tranquil waters, hiking through breathtaking mountain trails, and, of course, getting lost in a good book.**

Vivian's novels capture the heart of **faith, love, and perseverance**—where strong women and honorable men overcome life's trials to find hope, home, and happily-ever-after. Whether she's exploring the great outdoors or crafting her next frontier romance, Vivian's passion for adventure and storytelling shines through in every word she writes.

You can find out more about Vivian and her latest releases at www.vivianbelle.com or follow her on social media for updates and behind-the-scenes glimpses of her writing process. Stay connected—you won't want to miss the heartfelt stories of love and family she has in store!

Also by Vivian Belle

Where the Heart Finds Home
Faith on the Frontier
Love in Hopewell Creek
Abigail's Promise
Beneath Montana Skies
Rocky Mountain Promise
Hearts Unbroken
Beneath the Oregon Pines
Journey's of the Heart

Contents

Chapter 1

The silence pressed against Emily's ears, suffocating and absolute. Not the peaceful quiet of an empty room, but the hollow absence left by voices forever stilled. Four months, and still the faint smell of carbolic acid lingered beneath the scent of beeswax and lemon oil. Four months since she'd scrubbed every surface until her hands cracked and bled, as if cleanliness could somehow reverse what had already happened. As if anything could.

Emily forced herself to move, each step requiring deliberate thought. She crossed to the mantel, where four daguerreotypes remained in their silver frames. Her parents posed stiffly, but with kindness in their eyes. Margaret at sixteen, and Mary at eighteen, before typhoid had stolen the blooms from their cheeks forever. And Thomas—dear Thomas—on their wedding day two years ago.

She reached toward Thomas's image but stopped short of touching it. Such indulgence would only weaken her resolve. Instead, she turned and strode toward the hallway. The distinctive click of her boots against the hardwood echoed through the deserted rooms, announcing a departure no one remained to witness.

The house at 412 Franklin Street had once been filled with conversation, music, and laughter. The comfortable hum of a family. Now each room held only ghosts—at the dining table where they'd shared meals, in the study where her father had maintained his accounts, and beside the hearth where her mother had taught her to knit.

Every corner contained memories that threatened to pull her under like quicksand.

Emily paused at the base of the staircase, one hand resting on the newel post Thomas had repaired the summer after they wed. The third step still creaked—he'd promised to fix it, but his legal practice had kept him too busy.

Upstairs, two trunks stood packed and secured with leather straps. One contained practical needs—clothing suitable for the journey west, and a few personal items she couldn't bear to leave. The other held her medical texts and supplies. Emily refused to abandon her training, despite how thoroughly it had failed her when it mattered most. Perhaps in Oregon Territory, those skills might serve some purpose beyond reminding her of her inadequacy.

Emily reached for the leather-bound Bible on the bedside table. The gilded edges caught the light as she lifted it. Inside the front cover, her mother-in-law had inscribed a verse from Psalms in elegant script: "He will cover you with his feathers, and under his wings you will find refuge."

The words struck her like a physical blow. Where had God's protective wings been when the fever ravaged her family? Where was divine refuge when she worked until her body screamed for rest, applying cold compresses, administering what medicines were available, and praying desperately for intervention that never came?

Emily's fingers clenched around the Bible, a momentary impulse urging her to abandon it altogether. Yet, she knew Thomas would have wished for her to take it on her journey. Despite the bitterness simmering within her, she couldn't bring herself to leave it. With deliberate care, she nestled it between folds of clothing in her trunk.

From behind the door, Emily retrieved her traveling cloak, the wool heavy across her shoulders as she secured the clasp at her throat. Her fingers brushed against the silver locket hidden beneath her high-necked blouse, and she paused, drawing it out with trembling hands and opening it. Inside, miniature portraits of Thomas and her family gazed back at her.

"I don't know how to live without all of you," she whispered. "I don't know how to be in a world where you don't exist." Emily closed the locket with a decisive snap and tucked it back beneath her clothing, feeling its weight against her skin.

A knock at the front door startled her from reverie. The small clock on the nightstand showed precisely ten o'clock. Mr. Peterson, the driver she'd hired, was punctual.

"Coming," she called.

Emily descended the stairs carefully, one gloved hand sliding along the banister her father had installed when she was still a child. The knocking came again as she reached the bottom step.

She opened the door to find a weathered man in his fifties standing on the porch.

"Mrs. Wilson?" he asked.

"Yes. The trunks are upstairs. Two of them. Last door down the hall on the right." Her voice sounded distant, as though someone else spoke through her.

He nodded. "I'll fetch them straight away, ma'am."

As he lumbered up the stairs, Emily found herself drawn back to the parlor, to the shrouded piano. She pulled the sheet back, exposing the polished rosewood that had once gleamed in the candlelight during evening gatherings. Margaret and Mary's beloved instrument. Her sisters had played beautifully—hymns on Sundays, popular ballads in the evenings. Emily traced her fingers across the keys without pressing them.

"I have to go," she whispered. "I can't breathe here anymore."

No answer came, of course. Just the hollow echo of a room that held too many memories and not enough life.

Emily replaced the sheet carefully, smoothing it over the curved top. Then, with deliberate steps, she walked through each downstairs room one last time. The dining room where they'd shared their last meal together. The kitchen where her mother had taught her to make bread, kneading the dough with flour-dusted hands. The small study where her father had worked on household accounts and studied by lamplight. She paused before the bookcase where he had kept his medical texts. She'd already packed those she thought might be useful to her in Oregon. Her fingers brushed the spaces on the shelves where his books had stood.

"Dr. Franklin Beaumont," she murmured. "Devoted husband and father. Skilled physician." The words caught in her throat. "And in the end, none of it mattered."

By the time Mr. Peterson had carried both trunks to the waiting wagon, Emily stood in the empty front hall, medical satchel clutched in one hand, a small valise containing immediate necessities in the other.

"Ready, ma'am?" Mr. Peterson asked from the doorway, clearly uncomfortable with her stillness.

Emily nodded, though readiness had nothing to do with her state of mind. Ready implied preparation and anticipation. She felt neither—only the desperate need to escape this house before the memories smothered what remained of her will to continue.

She took one last look at the hallway, at the staircase, and at the small watercolor of the James River that her mother had painted last summer. Then she turned her back on it all and stepped onto the porch.

Mr. Peterson offered his arm, but Emily pretended not to notice. She negotiated the steps alone, concentrating on each movement with excessive care.

The wagon appeared sturdy enough. A basic conveyance with two horses and a covered bench seat. Her trunks were secured in the back with rope. Mr. Peterson climbed up and took the reins, waiting as Emily settled herself, arranging her skirts with meticulous precision.

"Richmond station, correct?" he asked, flicking the reins to set the horses in motion.

"Yes. The train departs at noon." Emily kept her gaze fixed ahead, refusing to turn for one last glimpse of the house. Behind lay only ghosts. Ahead lay... nothing she cared to contemplate. It was enough simply to be leaving.

The wagon wheels crunching against the packed earth of Franklin Street. They passed familiar buildings that now seemed strangely remote, as though viewed through clouded glass. Spring had transformed the city—dogwoods and cherry trees bloomed along the boulevards, their blossoms a stark contrast to the colorless existence Emily now inhabited.

"Fine day for traveling," Mr. Peterson said.

Emily made a noncommittal sound. The weather held no significance to her anymore. Rain or shine, what difference did it make when one's internal landscape remained barren?

They passed St. John's Church, where she had once attended services faithfully. The white steeple rose against the April sky, drawing the eye heavenward as intended. Emily looked deliberately away. Her last visits had been for funerals—Thomas's, then her father's, then Margaret's three days later, then her Mother's and then Mary's.

As they turned onto Broad Street, the bustle of Richmond's commercial district surrounded them. People moved purposefully along the sidewalks. A woman laughed at something her companion said. Two children chased a hoop down the street while their mother called after them to be careful.

Life continuing as though nothing had changed. As though the world hadn't ended four months ago in the house on Franklin Street.

"Almost there now," Mr. Peterson said as they approached the station. "Train should be ready for boarding soon."

Indeed, the Richmond train station loomed ahead, its brick façade bustling with midday activity. Porters moved luggage on wheeled carts. Families embraced in greeting or farewell. Businessmen consulted pocket watches before hurrying toward their platforms.

The wagon halted at the passenger drop-off area. Mr. Peterson climbed down first, then circled to help Emily descend.

"I can manage," she said, gathering her skirts and stepping down without assistance.

"I'll see to your trunks, ma'am." He tipped his hat. "And then our business is concluded?"

Emily retrieved her purse and counted out the agreed-upon payment, adding a small additional sum. "Thank you for your services, Mr. Peterson."

"Very kind, ma'am." He pocketed the money, hesitating. "Are you certain there's nothing else? No message to be delivered to anyone in Richmond?"

"There is no one," she repeated, finality in her tone. "If you'll see to my trunks, I'll wait inside."

The station's interior hummed with voices and movement. Emily found a bench against the wall and sat with precise posture, hands folded over her valise. Her medical satchel rested at her feet.

Nearby, a young mother bounced a fretful infant while two older children circled her skirts in endless, energetic orbits. The woman caught Emily's eye and offered a weary smile, an unspoken solidarity from one woman to another.

Emily looked away, a sharp pain lancing through her chest.

Once, she would have smiled back. Might have offered to hold the baby while the woman corralled her energetic offspring. Might have noted symptoms if the infant seemed truly ill rather than merely overtired.

That version of Emily Grace Wilson—the doctor's daughter, the lawyer's wife, the sister, the woman of faith and compassion—had died alongside her family. All that remained was this hollow shell moving through the world.

"Cumberland train now boarding on platform three," called a uniformed attendant. "All passengers for Cumberland, Martinsburg, and points west, platform three."

Emily rose, gathering her belongings. At the ticket counter, she presented her pre-purchased fare and received directions to her assigned car. A porter appeared with her trunks on a wheeled cart, following her to the platform where the great steam engine waited, hissing occasionally like some impatient beast.

Emily settled into her seat by the window, placing her valise and medical bag on the empty space beside her—a physical barrier against potential conversation. Through the glass, she could see other passengers saying farewell to loved ones on the platform. Handkerchiefs waved. Children were swept up in last embraces. Promises to write were exchanged with visible emotion.

She turned her face away from them.

Minutes later, the train whistle sounded, piercing and insistent. Emily felt the slight jolt as the engine engaged, and the cars began to move. Slowly at first, then with gathering momentum, as the train pulled away from Richmond station.

Buildings and trees slid past the window, gradually giving way to the Virginia countryside. Green fields stretched toward distant hills. A winding river caught the light, its surface rippling with movement. Farmhouses stood amid freshly plowed fields ready for planting.

Emily registered these details with detached observation. Beauty, like joy and hope, belonged to a past she could no longer access.

From her valise, she withdrew a small leather-bound notebook and pencil. She had planned this journey with methodical precision, plotting each stage carefully. Now she reviewed her notations, confirming connections and timetables.

Cumberland by evening. Overnight there, then a stagecoach to Wheeling by the following afternoon. Steamboat to Cincinnati, then another to St. Louis, and finally a stagecoach to Independence. Each step taking her further from what had been.

The notebook also contained a letter of introduction to a Dr. Simmons in Oregon City—a former colleague of her father's who had moved west years earlier. Emily had written to him after making her decision, and his response had been prompt and kind. Too kind. His sympathy had scalded her, and she had nearly burned the letter. Instead, she had folded it precisely and tucked it away, another obligation to fulfill in a life that had become a series of mechanical motions.

Emily closed the notebook and returned it to her valise. Then, almost against her will, her hand crept to the locket beneath her blouse. Through layers of fabric, she traced its outline, feeling its shape against her skin—the one tangible reminder of Thomas and her family she permitted herself.

The train rounded a bend, wheels clacking rhythmically against the tracks. Each revolution carried Emily further from everything familiar, every landmark of her previous life. By autumn, she would arrive in Oregon Territory.

Or she would die trying.

Emily caught her reflection in the window glass, superimposed over the passing landscape. Twenty-four years old, with a lifetime of grief etched into her features. Behind her eyes lay memories she could not escape—Thomas's hand, burning with fever, clasped in hers as he spoke in his final moments of lucidity. Mary's blank staring eyes as she slipped away. Margaret's delirious cries for water that no amount could quench. Her mother's rattling breath. Her father's dignified resignation to his fate.

She closed her eyes, shutting out both the reflection and the view beyond. The rhythmic motion of the train became a peculiar lullaby, rocking her toward whatever awaited to the west. Not salvation—she had abandoned that hope. Not happiness—she had forgotten its meaning. Just distance. Space between herself and the graves she had left behind. Room to breathe without inhaling memories with every breath.

The train whistle sounded again as they approached a crossing, long and mournful in the afternoon air. It echoed Emily's unspoken farewell to Richmond, to Virginia, to the life that had shattered beyond repair.

She leaned her head against the cool glass of the window, allowing the steady vibration of the train to seep into her bones. Her body ached with a weariness that sleep could not cure. The exhaustion of grief carried too long alone.

In her pocket lay a small pouch of lavender her mother had sewn the previous spring. The scent had faded, just as her mother's voice was fading in Emily's memory. Soon, she feared, she would forget the exact timbre of Thomas's laugh, the precise shade of Margaret's eyes.

Were they fading already, her loved ones, becoming less distinct with each mile that separated her from their graves?

The thought produced a panic that clawed at her throat. Emily pressed her hand against the locket again, feeling its solid form through her clothing. No. She would not forget. Could not forget.

She closed her eyes. The train's wheels kept their steady rhythm beneath her, carrying her forward into uncertainty. For the first time in months, Emily felt something stir within her besides grief—not hope, but perhaps the faintest shadow of possibility.

That somehow, somewhere beyond the boundaries of all she had known, she might find a way to breathe again.

Chapter 2

The rising hum of voices competed with the creaking of wagon wheels and the insistent clang of a blacksmith's hammer. Dust hung thick in the air, coating every surface with a fine, gritty layer that found its way into eyes, mouths, and clothing. Independence, Missouri, teemed with a restless energy—the last clutch of civilization before the vast wilderness of the Oregon Trail stretched westward.

Weston Reynolds moved through the chaos, his stride purposeful as he navigated between wagons, livestock, and the sea of hopeful, anxious faces. His deep blue eyes missed nothing—a loose wagon wheel here, a team of oxen hitched incorrectly there, and supplies piled haphazardly and vulnerable to the first heavy rain.

"Mr. Croft," he called, spotting Silas examining the lead pair of oxen. "Those beasts need to be rotated with the younger pair. They're showing signs of strain, and we haven't even departed."

Silas Croft straightened his back and nodded. "Noticed that myself. The left one's favoring his front hoof."

"We need them strong for the crossing at the Kansas. Switch them with the younger pair in the morning." Weston's voice carried authority without arrogance—the voice of a man who had seen the trail take lives for smaller oversights.

"Will do, Mr. Reynolds."

"Weston," he corrected, as he had a dozen times already. "Out there, formalities waste breath, and breath is precious."

A half-smile creased Silas's weathered face. "Weston, then."

The wagon master continued his rounds, pausing to check harnesses, examine wagon covers for tears that would invite disaster in the first rainstorm, mentally cataloging each family's readiness for the brutal months ahead. He couldn't fix everything. The trail would demand sacrifices from each of them, but he could prevent the most obvious calamities.

As he neared the blacksmith's makeshift forge, the steady rhythm of metal striking metal intensified. Samson Early, broad-shouldered and perpetually solemn, hammered a glowing strip of metal into shape, each blow precise and purposeful.

"How's the supply?" Weston asked, not bothering with greetings. Samson wasn't a man for unnecessary words.

Samson dunked the metal into a water barrel, unleashing a violent hiss of steam before answering. "Nails enough for repairs. Three spare wheels banded. Extra pins for all the wagons." He wiped sweat from his brow with a forearm. "Still waiting on the Finch wagon. The axle needs reinforcing."

Weston nodded, mentally adjusting his departure calculations. "I hope to leave just after dawn in the morning, noon at the very latest. After that, we start to lose our advantage over the weather."

"It'll be done," Samson replied, already turning back to his forge.

A small figure darted between two wagons, momentarily catching Weston's attention. His posture softened imperceptibly as Matthew, all of six years old and vibrating with the restless energy of childhood, zigzagged through the camp. The boy crouched in the dust beneath the shadow of their wagon, intently drawing patterns with a stick, his tongue caught between his teeth in concentration.

Something in Weston's chest tightened, as it always did when he looked at his son. The boy's mop of dark hair and serious brown eyes were all Susannah, a ghost of remembrance that could still steal his breath six years after her passing. The familiar ache surfaced—grief's echo, duller now but never truly silent.

He walked to the wagon, dropping to one knee beside his son. "What have you found to keep you busy, Matthew?"

The boy looked up, his face brightening. "I'm making a map, Papa. Like yours." He pointed to the lines etched in the dirt. "This is the big river we have to cross. And these are mountains."

Weston's hand rested lightly on the boy's shoulder. "That's good thinking. A man should know where he's going." He studied the rudimentary lines. "But remember, the real trail has surprises no map can show. That's why we travel together."

"Is that why you're the wagon master? Because you know where the surprises are?"

"I know some. God knows all of them. I just try to listen closely to His warnings."

Matthew nodded with the solemn acceptance of a child raised to understand that some answers lay beyond human reach. "I prayed for the journey. Like you showed me."

"Good boy," Weston's voice roughened slightly. "Now, stay close to our wagon. There's too many people making poor decisions with their animals today."

As if summoned by the thought, a commotion erupted near the supply wagons. A man's voice rose above the general din, sharp with complaint and self-importance. Weston sighed, recognizing the tenor before he even saw the speaker.

"Impossible prices! Highway robbery, that's what this is!" Ezekiel Vance's nasal complaint carried across the encampment. His finger jabbed toward a harried-looking merchant. "Ten dollars for what I paid six for in St. Louis!"

Weston felt the tension creep into his shoulders. Ezekiel Vance had been a thorn in his side since the man joined them two days prior—a businessman from Chicago with money enough, but sense too scarce, in Weston's estimation. The type that believed his urban success entitled him to special consideration on the trail, where such illusions were dangerous.

"Stay here," Weston instructed Matthew, striding toward the altercation.

Ezekiel's face was flushed with indignation, his neat beard quivering as he berated the merchant, who stood impassively behind his goods. Several onlookers watched with the wary curiosity of those assessing whether this drama might affect their own preparations.

"Mr. Vance," Weston said, his voice pitched to carry without shouting. "Is there a problem?"

Ezekiel whirled, his expression shifting from anger to a transparent attempt at camaraderie. "Reynolds! Good timing. This fellow thinks I fell off the turnip wagon yesterday. The prices here are—"

"The prices in Independence have been the same for a year now," Weston interrupted, his tone level. "High, yes. These men make their living supplying the last necessities before a journey with no markets for a thousand miles."

"But it's extortion! You're the wagon master. Surely you can negotiate better terms for your people."

Weston's expression didn't change, but something in his eyes hardened. "My responsibility is to guide this company safely to Oregon. Not to bargain for luxuries that'll be discarded at the first river crossing when the weight becomes too much." He studied Vance, noting the man's fine boots that would be worthless once the mud claimed them. "Buy what you need or don't."

Ezekiel's mouth opened and closed, caught between indignation and the awareness of an audience. Finally, he sniffed, straightening his waistcoat. "I'll take my business elsewhere, then. Come, Mrs. Vance."

A thin woman who had been hovering uncertainly behind her husband moved forward, her eyes lowered. Weston noted the nervous twist of her hands and something in his expression softened minutely, the flicker of compassion quickly replaced by professional detachment.

As the Vance's retreated, Weston nodded to the merchant. "Might want to add a dollar for the entertainment," he remarked dryly.

The man chuckled. "Not the first, won't be the last."

Weston turned, scanning the sprawling encampment with a practiced eye. The day was waning, creating long shadows between the wagons. Nearly forty wagons now formed his responsibility, each carrying the dreams, fears, and futures of families who had committed their lives to his judgment.

His gaze cataloged the key members of his company. The Crofts, Silas and Martha, sturdy folk with their son Caleb in tow—a quiet, watchful boy of ten who seemed old beyond his years. The Billings family—George, Liz, and their son Luke, who was near Matthew's age—already demonstrating the cohesion and adaptability that would serve them well. The Calkins, Zach and Lavinia, young and clearly nervous, their wagon too neat, too perfectly packed, betraying their inexperience.

Elara Jenkins, a solitary woman of perhaps thirty-five who kept to herself but demonstrated more practical knowledge of wagon repair than most men. Samson Early, the blacksmith whose skill would prove invaluable when wheels failed and axles cracked. All different threads being woven into the fragile fabric of a community that must hold together through hardship, fear, and the indifference of the wilderness.

A slight movement near the Holloway's wagon caught his attention. Reverend James Holloway, a dignified man in his forties with kind eyes and a perpetually serene countenance, helped his wife Mercy down from the wagon seat. Beside them stood a figure that gave Weston pause.

The woman was dressed plainly, her black dress a stark contrast to the color surrounding her. Even from this distance, Weston could discern the profound stillness about her—not the peaceful quiet of contentment, but the frozen immobility of grief so deep it transformed a person into something like a shadow among the living. Her face, partially obscured by a bonnet, revealed little, but her posture told everything—shoulders slightly curved inward, a physical embodiment of emotional withdrawal.

His eyes narrowed, recognizing the outward signs of inward devastation. Reverend Holloway had approached him two days prior about taking on a solitary traveler who was looking to join the wagon train. A widow from Richmond that had no wagon or oxen of her own. This must be her—Emily Wilson. The reverend had shared a few details, but respected the woman's privacy.

As if sensing his appraisal, the woman looked up; her gaze sweeping across the camp before briefly meeting his. The distance was too great to discern the color of her eyes, but the empty desolation within them needed no proximity to recognize. Weston felt an unwelcome pang of recognition—that particular quality of loss, the hollow weightlessness that follows when a life is shattered beyond restoration.

He knew that look. He'd seen it in his own mirror for quite some time after Susannah passed.

The realization struck deeper than it should have, like a physical blow that momentarily stole his breath. Her sorrow, visible even across the distance, mirrored something in himself he had worked for years to bury. He recognized the weight she carried—the invisible burden that bent her shoulders, the effort each step cost her.

Weston turned away abruptly, unsettled by his reaction. It wasn't just recognition; it was the dangerous tug of empathy, of connection through shared grief. He had made that mistake once before, allowing a widow's pain to draw him into emotional entanglement, only to discover that grief shared didn't halve the burden—it multiplied the complications.

"Not my concern," he thought firmly, deliberately reinforcing the boundary between professional duty and personal involvement. "My responsibility is to guide, not to heal. To lead, not to restore."

He had spent six years building a careful life for Matthew, with structure, predictability, and security at its foundation. Emotional entanglements threatened that foundation.

When Reverend Holloway had approached him about adding Mrs. Wilson to the company, Weston had hesitated. Experience taught him that those running from grief often lacked the resilience the trail demanded. But the reverend's steady assurance that she possessed unexpected strength, plus the Holloway's' impeccable reputation, had swayed his decision. He had accepted the risk, against his better judgment, with the explicit understanding that she remained the Holloway's responsibility.

"Papa!" Matthew's voice pulled him from his thoughts. The boy stood by their wagon, small hands gripping a battered tin cup. "Mrs. Croft gave me water for you. She said you looked thirsty."

Weston accepted the cup, his expression softening. "Did she now? That was thoughtful of her." He drank deeply. Martha Croft had a way of noticing needs before they were spoken, a gift that would serve the company well in the months ahead.

Matthew's small fingers hooked on his father's belt loop—an unconscious habit when the boy felt uncertain. "Are we leaving tomorrow?"

"That's the plan." Weston set the empty cup on the wagon's edge, scanning the darkening camp. "Most are ready. The rest will have to catch up or stay behind."

"Mr. Vance was shouting again."

Weston glanced down at his son, measuring his response. "Mr. Vance has a lot to learn about the trail. Some lessons come easier than others."

Matthew considered this with a child's solemn perception. "Is he a bad man?"

"No," Weston said. "Just a man who believes his voice should carry farther than it does." He ruffled Matthew's hair. "Let's get some food."

As they walked toward their cooking fire, Weston felt the familiar weight of responsibility pressing on him. Forty wagons, nearly two hundred souls, looking to him for guidance through some of the most unforgiving territory on God's earth. Each decision he made would ripple through the company, bringing consequences he could only partly expect.

"Lord, grant me wisdom and clear sight," he prayed silently. *"These people have trusted their lives to my judgment. Help me be worthy of that trust, especially when the hard decisions come—as they surely will."*

Barnaby Cobb, an older man with a weathered face like a dried riverbed, sat near their small fire. One of the few in the wagon train who had made the journey before, Barnaby had attached himself to Weston's camp with the quiet understanding that his experience might prove valuable. He nodded companionably as they approached.

"Evening, Cobb," Weston said, setting out provisions for a simple meal. "How's that knee of yours today?"

Barnaby grimaced, rubbing the offending joint. "Same as yesterday. Tells the weather better than any almanac." He glanced up at the clear sky. "Rain coming in two days. Not enough to trouble us, but enough to lay the dust."

Weston nodded, accepting the forecast as gospel. Barnaby's predictions had proven unnervingly accurate since they'd met three seasons back, when Weston first took on the role of wagon master.

"Been watching the travelers arriving," Barnaby continued, accepting a plate of beans and salt pork with a nod of thanks. "Good mix, mostly. Couple might not make the first river crossing."

"The Calkins?"

Barnaby chewed thoughtfully. "Them for certain. Young and scared, but willing. They might surprise us." He jerked his chin toward the far side of the encampment. "The Vance fellow, though. He's the kind that makes trouble when the hard days come."

Weston didn't respond immediately, aware of Matthew's attentive ears as the boy sat cross-legged with his own plate. "Every train has one," he finally said. "Usually sorts itself out by Nebraska Territory."

"One way or another," Barnaby agreed cryptically.

They ate in silence for a time, the deepening dusk transforming the camp into a constellation of cooking fires, each a separate island of light in the growing darkness. Voices murmured across the encampment—prayers being said, children being settled, and last preparations being discussed. The immensity of the undertaking seemed to press more heavily as night fell, as if the absence of daylight emphasized the vastness of the wilderness waiting beyond Independence's boundaries.

"Papa," Matthew said, setting aside his empty plate. "Will it be like last time? When we went to Fort Kearney?"

Weston considered his answer carefully. "Some things will be the same. The rivers, the prairies, and the mountains. But each journey has its own character, son. Its own joys and hardships."

"Because of the people?"

"Yes. Largely because of the people."

Matthew nodded, satisfied. "I like the boy with the Billings family. Luke. He has a slingshot."

"That might come in useful," Weston said. "For rabbits, when fresh meat runs low." His eyes moved to the Billings' campfire, where the family sat close together, George's arm around Liz's shoulders. A good family, solid. The kind that understood the value of sticking together when hardships came.

His gaze drifted beyond them to where Reverend Holloway led the evening prayers with several families gathered around. The widow, Emily Wilson, sat slightly apart, her head bowed but her posture suggesting detachment rather than devotion. Even in the communal act of prayer, she remained isolated, wrapped in grief like a burial shroud.

A memory surfaced unbidden: himself after Susannah's death, going through the motions of life with mechanical precision, protecting Matthew, fulfilling duties, but feeling nothing beyond the vast, echoing emptiness where his heart had been. The recollection was uncomfortable, and too intimate. He pushed it aside firmly, just as he had pushed aside all that threatened the careful structure of the life he had built for Matthew.

"Time for bed," he told his son, gathering their plates. "We rise before the sun tomorrow."

After settling Matthew in their wagon, Weston made a final circuit of the camp. The familiar ritual helped calm his mind and assured him that the company was as prepared as possible for departure. Most fires were banked now, the camp settling into the quiet rustle of sleep and anticipation.

As he passed near the Holloway's wagon, he paused. Mercy Holloway was speaking softly to Emily Wilson, whose face remained in shadow. The older woman's hand rested gently on Emily's arm, a gesture of comfort that seemed to emphasize rather than bridge the profound isolation surrounding the younger woman.

"...find that the journey itself brings a certain peace," Mercy was saying, her voice carrying just enough for Weston to overhear. "When all else is stripped away, sometimes we can finally hear God's voice again."

Emily made no response that Weston could see, but something in her posture tightened ever so slightly. Mercy seemed to sense it too, patting the younger woman's arm before withdrawing.

"Try to rest, dear. The first days on the wagon train will be the hardest," she said.

Weston continued past, not wanting to intrude, but found his thoughts lingering on the exchange. Mercy's words held truth—the trail had a way of reducing life to its essentials, of burning away pretense and revealing a person's true character, for better or worse. He'd seen the journey transform people, breaking some and tempering others.

Which would it do to Emily Wilson? The depth of sorrow she carried was evident even in the way she stood, and the way she moved—as if putting one foot before the other required conscious effort. People carrying that magnitude of grief could become liabilities on the trail, where survival demanded resilience, adaptability, and a fierce will to continue despite everything.

Yet, there had been something in her bearing, a quiet dignity beneath the sorrow, that suggested strength of a different kind. The Holloway's were shrewd judges of character; they wouldn't have taken her on if they believed her incapable of the journey.

It had been that confidence, coupled with Reverend Holloway's earnest assurance, that had swayed Weston's decision to accept her into the wagon train. Against his better judgment, perhaps, but God often worked through unexpected vessels. Still, he would watch carefully. The well-being of the entire group of travelers depended on each member carrying their share, in heart as well as in labor.

He continued his circuit, checking that wagons were secure, animals properly picketed, and no hazards left unaddressed. The camp felt different on the eve of departure—tense, expectant, and humming with nervous energy that even sleep couldn't fully quiet.

By the time he returned to his own wagon, the moon had risen, casting the sprawling camp in pale light and deep shadow. Weston paused, taking a moment to appreciate the profound stillness of the plains at night, broken only by the occasional stamp of a restless animal or the crackle of a dying fire.

Climbing quietly into the wagon, he checked on Matthew, who slept peacefully, one arm thrown across his small chest, his expression serene in the faint moonlight filtering through the canvas. The sight provoked the fierce rush of love and protectiveness that had defined Weston's existence since the moment he'd first held his son, tiny and wailing, even as Susannah's life slipped away.

"I'm doing this for him," he reminded himself, a mantra repeated countless times over the years. Every hardship endured, every risk

calculated, every decision made—all for the sake of giving Matthew a future beyond the grief that had marked his beginning.

Settling onto his bedroll, Weston's thoughts drifted again to Emily Wilson before he could redirect them. What had brought her to the Oregon Trail, alone and wrapped in such profound sorrow? What future was she seeking, or what past was she fleeing? The questions circled briefly before he firmly dismissed them.

His experience had taught him the danger of emotional entanglement on the trail. Six years ago, overwhelmed with grief and the responsibility of an infant son, he had allowed himself to befriend on a young widow traveling in his company. Her own loss had seemed to create a bridge of understanding. That bridge had proven dangerously unstable, collapsing into complications he couldn't afford, not with Matthew depending on him for stability and security.

Never again, he had promised himself. The walls he had built around his heart were necessary, not just for his protection, but for Matthew's. For the entire wagon train was now committed to his care. Emotional clarity was essential for the decisions that lay ahead, decisions where lives would hang in the balance.

"Lord, grant us safe passage," he prayed silently. *"Keep the water crossings manageable, the weather favorable, and sickness at bay. Watch over Matthew with Your protection. Give me wisdom when decisions must be made, and the strength to lead these people through whatever challenges await."*

He paused, an unbidden image of Emily Wilson's grief-hollowed eyes rising in his mind.

"And Lord...for those carrying heavy burdens of the heart, grant whatever measure of peace they can find on this journey. But please keep me clear-eyed and focused on my duty to all."

As sleep began to claim him, Weston made a silent recommitment to the principles that had guided him since taking on the role of wagon master: Focus on the practical, not the personal. Make decisions based on facts, not feelings. Maintain distance—emotional, professional, and personal—from those under his guidance. The trail was hard enough without complicating it with attachments.

Tomorrow they would leave civilization behind and commit themselves to the vast, indifferent wilderness of the Oregon Trail. His responsibility was clear: guide them safely through it, whatever the cost. Everything else, including the quiet, grief-haunted woman with the hollow eyes, was secondary to that sacred duty.

With that firm resolution, Weston surrendered to exhaustion. His last conscious thought a prayer for Matthew's safety in the long journey ahead.

Chapter 3

As dawn broke over Independence the next morning, the camp was already stirring with purpose. Weston had been awake for an hour, checking final preparations, confirming the order of wagons, ensuring that those with the strongest teams would take the lead positions to set a steady pace.

"Hitch the teams!" he called, his voice carrying across the camp. "We move within the hour!"

The cry was taken up, repeated through the sprawling encampment as families hurried to complete final preparations. The disciplined chaos of departure unfolded—children being settled into wagons, livestock being hitched, last-minute adjustments to loads that often proved heavier than anticipated.

Weston oversaw it all with the sharp eye of experience, addressing problems before they threatened the day's progress. He stationed the Crofts' wagon second in line, knowing their steady team would help establish the rhythm for those behind. The Billings were in the tenth position, experienced enough to provide stability to the procession.

Ezekiel Vance attempted to position his wagon near the front, despite Weston's explicit instructions to maintain the order he had established.

"My animals are fresher than most," Vance insisted, his voice carrying that particular tone of a man accustomed to having his way through sheer persistence. "It makes more sense for us to set the pace."

"Position thirty, Mr. Vance, as assigned," Weston said firmly, not slowing his stride as he continued checking the other wagons. "Your team hasn't worked together enough to lead. They'd be bolting by noon and lame by Wednesday."

Vance's face reddened, but a pointed glance from Weston toward the watching pioneers, many of whom were clearly unsympathetic to his complaints, silenced further protest. Muttering, he directed his wagon to the assigned position.

Reverend Holloway's wagon held position twenty, solidly in the middle of the train, where his steady presence might help maintain cohesion. Weston had placed them there deliberately, despite some misgivings about the grief-stricken woman traveling with them. The Holloway's calm wisdom would be needed to steady those around them when hardships came, as they inevitably would.

"Reverend, Mrs. Holloway," Weston nodded as he approached their wagon. "All secure?"

"Ready as we'll ever be, Mr. Reynolds," James Holloway replied, his voice warm with the quiet confidence of a man who placed his trust in higher hands than his own. "The Lord has prepared the way."

Weston nodded, his eye-catching a potential issue with their wagon cover. "That seam needs reinforcing before we hit any weather," he said, pointing to a section where the canvas appeared stressed. "See Samson Early when we make camp tonight."

His gaze shifted briefly to Emily, who had not acknowledged his presence in any way, her attention fixed on some distant point beyond the camp's boundary. The stillness about her was almost unnerving, not the calm of peace, but the suspended animation of profound shock.

"Mrs. Wilson," he said, more out of courtesy than conversation. "First journey west?"

Her eyes shifted to him, focusing with visible effort, as if returning from a great distance. "Yes." The single word carried no inflection, neither interest nor anxiety.

Weston nodded, recognizing the boundaries of grief when he encountered them. "Stay close to the Holloway's. The first days are disorienting for most." He turned away, having fulfilled the minimum obligations of leadership, and continued his inspection.

By the time the sun had fully cleared the horizon, the wagon train was assembled in its prescribed order, a long, winding beast of wood, canvas, and human determination stretching behind Weston. He mounted his horse to take the lead position. Matthew was already settled in their wagon, placed first in line, and driven by Barnaby, who had agreed to manage it for different stages of the journey while Weston scouted ahead.

Weston raised his hand, and a hush fell over the company.

"The journey ahead is long and unforgiving," he called, his voice carrying the weight of experience. "Stay in formation. Keep to the pace I set. Watch for my signals. Help each other when needed." He paused, surveying the faces turned toward him—hopeful, anxious, and determined. "We leave civilization behind today. From here forward, we are our own community, depending on each other's strength, skills, and faith. May God grant us safe passage to Oregon."

A murmur of "Amen" rippled through the company.

With a final nod, Weston turned his horse westward and gave the signal. The lead wagon lurched forward, wheels cutting fresh tracks in the well-worn path that marked the beginning of the Oregon Trail. One by one, the wagons followed, creaking into motion, canvas billowing, a moving city embarking into the wilderness.

As Independence fell behind them, Weston felt the familiar sense of crossing a threshold between worlds. Ahead lay months of grueling travel, countless decisions with lives hanging in the balance, and hardships that would test each person's resolve and character. Lives would change irrevocably. Some would be lost. None would ever be as they were now at this moment.

His gaze swept back over the train, now strung out behind him like a great, lumbering serpent crawling across the vast prairie. Matthew was likely watching the town disappear out the back of their wagon, his young mind full of excitement and trepidation in equal measure. Somewhere, too, was Emily Wilson, carrying her unspoken burden of grief into the wilderness.

Weston faced forward again, his jaw set with determination. His duty was clear: lead them safely, make the hard decisions when necessary, protect his son above all else. The rest, individual struggles, personal dramas, and emotional entanglements, was not his concern, nor would he allow it to become so.

The Oregon Trail stretched before them, disappearing into the shimmering horizon where earth met the sky. They had begun.

Chapter 4

The constant, jarring rhythm of the wagon wheels bored into Emily's skull like a carpenter's drill, each rotation grinding against the rutted earth. Dust hung suspended in the air, invading her nose, coating her tongue, and settling into the creases of her clothing. The creaking wooden frame sang its monotonous song, punctuated by the occasional sharp jolt that threatened to throw her from the bench seat.

Emily gripped the edge of the wagon seat, knuckles white, refusing to cry out even as each violent lurch sent pain shooting through her spine. The vast expanse of prairie stretched endlessly before her, the wagon train a long, winding caterpillar inching its way across the seemingly infinite ocean of tall grass.

Two days out of Independence, and already the reality of the journey had stripped away any romantic notions anyone might have harbored about the Oregon Trail. It was simply this: dust, discomfort, and distance—endless, unrelenting distance.

"Would you care for some water, my dear?" Mercy Holloway's gentle voice interrupted Emily's thoughts. The older woman held out a tin cup, her face creased with genuine concern.

Emily accepted with a stiff nod. "Thank you." Two words, clipped and bare. The smallest possible acknowledgment without appearing utterly uncivilized.

Mercy seemed undeterred by her curtness. "The first days are always the hardest, they say. Our bodies must adjust to the rhythm of the trail." She paused, her kind eyes searching Emily's face for some crack in the wall of her reserve. "My sister traveled to California some years ago. She wrote that after a fortnight, the wagon began to feel almost like home."

Home.

The word landed like a stone in Emily's chest. Home was a ghost-filled house in Richmond, with dust sheets covering the furniture like shrouds waiting for the new owners to move in. Home was the place where she had watched her husband, her parents, and her sisters die one by one, helpless to save them despite all her medical training. Home was something Emily Wilson would never have again.

She returned the cup and fixed her gaze on the backs of the oxen ahead, solid and implacable as they plodded forward. "I'm quite certain I shall never grow accustomed to it." Her voice was flat, devoid of emotion. "But that is of no consequence."

Mercy opened her mouth as if to say more, then thought better of it. The older woman's hands returned to the small piece of mending in her lap, her thread moving in and out with patient precision.

Emily drew her shawl tighter around her shoulders, despite the growing heat of the day. The barrier between herself and the kind woman beside her was not physical, but it was impenetrable all the same. She had not come seeking friendship. She had not come seeking comfort. She had come seeking only the numbing exhaustion of hardship, and the merciful oblivion of a new life.

The wagon hit another deep rut, jolting them violently upward. Mercy quietly steadied her, her touch light but sure. Emily stiffened, but did not pull away.

"We shall stop midday to rest the animals," Mercy said after a long silence. "Reverend Holloway says we've made good progress thus far, despite the late spring mud. Mr. Reynolds keeps a steady pace."

Emily nodded, barely hearing. Mr. Reynolds. The wagon master. She had watched him from a distance during their preparations in Independence—tall, broad-shouldered, his face weathered by sun and wind, and his manner authoritative but not overbearing. He moved with the easy confidence of a man who knew his place in the world. A man untouched by the random cruelties of fate that could destroy a life in an instant.

The sound of hoofbeats approached from behind, and Emily turned slightly to see the man himself riding alongside the wagons, checking on everyone. His deep-set eyes, the color of a winter sky, scanned the horizon continuously, missing nothing. The boy, Matthew, was not with him this morning; perhaps he rode in one of the other wagons under someone's care. She had noticed the child often clung to his father's leg when not being tended by others, a quiet, watchful presence with his father's serious eyes.

"All well here, Mrs. Holloway?" Reynolds asked, his voice carrying over the creak of the wagon.

"Quite well, Mr. Reynolds," Mercy responded cheerfully. "Though I believe we're all looking forward to stretching our legs at the noon stop."

He nodded, his gaze briefly flickering to Emily. She felt it like a physical touch and looked away immediately, fixing her attention to a distant point on the horizon.

"The creek ahead has good water. We'll halt there for an hour." He delivered this information efficiently, then tipped his hat and moved on, his horse stepping easily through the tall grass alongside the trail.

Mercy sighed with evident relief. "That's welcome news. The dust is quite oppressive today."

Emily made no reply. The dust was oppressive. The heat was oppressive. The forced proximity to other human beings she did not know was oppressive. But it was precisely what she had sought, physical discomfort to distract from the deeper pain that threatened to hollow her out entirely.

As they continued their slow progress, Emily observed the other travelers moving alongside the wagons. Many chose to walk during the day, sparing the oxen and stretching their legs. Ahead, Martha Croft walked beside their team, her face weathered but resolute beneath her broad-brimmed bonnet. Her son Caleb, a boy of perhaps eight or nine, kicked at clumps of prairie grass, occasionally stooping to examine some treasure before his mother gently urged him to keep up.

Also ahead, the Billings family traveled with seemingly inexhaustible good humor. George Billings drove the wagon, and Liz, his wife, walked beside it smiling at her son, Luke, whose small figure darting in and out of the prairie grass like a sparrow, stopping to gather wildflowers for his mother.

Emily's heart constricted painfully at the sight. Little boys gathering flowers. Little girls playing with dolls. Simple, ordinary joys she would never experience. She closed her eyes briefly.

"Are you unwell, my dear?" Mercy's voice broke through the fog of memory. "The sun can be quite strong. Perhaps you should wear your bonnet."

"I am perfectly..." Emily started to reply, more sharply than she intended. "Thank you for your concern. You are probably right." She reached for her bonnet and placed it on her head, tying the ribbons.

The wagon train continued its laborious progress, the sun climbing higher in the vast blue dome of the sky. From somewhere ahead came the sound of a heated exchange, voices raised in argument.

"Oh dear," Mercy murmured. "That sounds like Mr. Vance again."

Emily followed her gaze to where a middle-aged man with a florid complexion was gesticulating wildly at another traveler, his voice carrying across the prairie.

"I paid good money for quality goods, not this second-rate trash!" Ezekiel Vance jabbed a finger at the other man's wagon. "The price we agreed upon was for prime merchandise!"

"And that's precisely what you got, Vance," the other man replied, his voice lower but equally tense. "Now get back to your wagon before you spook my team."

"I'll not be swindled, do you hear me?" Vance's voice grew louder. "I demand satisfaction!"

The commotion drew Weston Reynolds like a storm draws lightning. He appeared suddenly, guiding his horse between the two men.

"Gentlemen." Reynolds did not raise his voice, yet it carried with unmistakable authority. "Whatever the dispute, this is neither the time nor the place. We maintain order on this train."

"This is highway robbery, Reynolds!" Vance exclaimed, his face mottled with anger. "Buyers beware when dealing with the likes of Henderson here!"

Reynolds remained unmoved. "Your grievance is noted, Mr. Vance. Take it up at the evening camp when we're settled. For now, return to your position."

Emily watched the exchange with detached interest. Human conflict, so small and petty against the vast backdrop of the prairie. What did it matter who was right or wrong about some business dealing? What value did such trivial concerns have when measured against the precariousness of existence itself? When each breath could be your last, when those you loved could be torn from you without warning or reason?

"That man will be trouble before we reach Fort Kearny," Mercy observed quietly.

Emily shrugged slightly. "There is always someone of his nature in any group." Her voice was cool, indifferent. The trials of others were not her concern.

The wagon train finally reached the creek Reynolds had mentioned, a narrow ribbon of water cutting through the prairie. The cry went up to halt, and Emily felt a wave of relief as the constant motion and jarring finally ceased. Mercy immediately stepped into the back of the wagon and began gathering items for a simple cold meal, while Reverend James climbed stiffly down from his position at the front of the wagon.

"Ah, what a blessing this water is," James said, stretching his back with a slight grimace. He was a tall, spare man with kind eyes. "The Lord provides for our journey, just as He provided for the Israelites in the wilderness."

Emily stared at the creek, its surface glittering in the midday sun. The Israelites in the wilderness. Led by a pillar of fire and cloud. Fed with manna from heaven. Protected by divine intervention.

"Where was that protection when fever ravaged my family?" The bitter thought rose unbidden. *"Where was that divine guidance when I prayed until my voice gave out, begging for my husband's life? For my parents? For my sisters?"*

"Indeed," she said aloud, the word like ash on her tongue.

If James noticed her lack of enthusiasm, he gave no sign. He smiled gently and offered a hand to help her down from the wagon. "A short rest will do us all good."

Emily accepted his assistance out of necessity, though she withdrew her hand as soon as her feet touched the ground. Her legs felt strangely unsteady after hours of sitting on the hard bench seat. She straightened her skirts and moved away from the wagon, seeking a moment of solitude.

Emily found a spot a little apart from the others, beneath the sparse shade of a stunted tree. She sank down on a patch of grass, relishing the momentary escape from the confines of the wagon. From here, she could observe the activity of the camp while remaining apart from it.

The encampment was a flurry of activity. Women tended children and prepared simple meals, while men watered the oxen and checked wagons for any damage sustained during the morning's travel. The Calkins, a young couple just starting their marriage, struggled with their team, the animals resisting their inexperienced handling. Lavinia Calkins, barely out of girlhood herself, looked pale and uncomfortable in the heat, and her face already showing signs of sunburn.

She watched as the Reynolds boy, Matthew, appeared from one of the other wagons and ran to his father, who had dismounted and was consulting with Silas Croft about something. The child tugged at Weston's pant leg, his face animated as he held up what appeared to be a small carved wooden animal. Reynolds paused in his conversation, his stern features softening as he knelt to examine his son's treasure, his hand briefly resting atop the boy's head.

The simple tenderness of the gesture made Emily look away, her throat suddenly tight. She reached for her locket, her fingers closing around it like a drowning person clutching a flotsam.

"Miss Wilson?"

Emily's head jerked up. Reverend James stood before her, holding a tin plate with bread and dried apple slices.

"Mercy thought you might prefer to eat in the shade," he said, offering the plate. "The sun is quite strong today."

"Thank you." Emily accepted the food with as much grace as she could muster. "Please convey my appreciation to Mrs. Holloway."

Instead of leaving, he settled himself on the grass nearby, clearly intending to join her. Emily repressed a sigh. Apparently, solitude was to be denied her even in this small way.

"How are you finding the journey thus far?" he asked, breaking off a piece of bread from his own portion.

"It is as expected," Emily replied neutrally. "Challenging but manageable."

The reverend nodded thoughtfully. "The physical demands are considerable, but many find the spiritual journey equally significant. There is something about facing the vastness of God's creation that puts our human concerns into perspective."

Emily took a small bite of bread to avoid responding immediately. The last thing she wanted was a spiritual discussion. Her concerns were not trivial matters to be put into "perspective" by staring at an endless prairie.

"The Psalmist wrote, 'I lift up my eyes to the mountains, where does my help come from? My help comes from the Lord, the Maker of heaven and earth,'" Reverend Holloway continued, his voice gentle. "Many can find comfort in those words on this journey."

Emily set down her plate, her appetite suddenly gone. "I'm sure that is true for many," she said carefully, her voice tightly controlled. "I prefer to focus on the practical aspects of our travel."

"If the Lord is the maker of heaven and earth," she thought bitterly, *"then He also made the fever that took my family. He made the suffering I could not alleviate despite all my training. He made this emptiness that consumes me."*

Reverend James seemed to sense her resistance. He did not press further but shifted to more neutral topics: the weather, the condition of the trail ahead, and the estimation of their progress. Emily provided the minimum responses required for civility.

When the call finally came to prepare for departure, she felt a wave of relief. The rhythm of the trail, however uncomfortable, was preferable to well-meaning attempts at conversation and spiritual comfort.

As she climbed back into the wagon, she noticed Weston Reynolds organizing the train for the afternoon's journey. He moved with purpose, giving clear directions, his presence a steady anchor in the midst of the general chaos of the departing camp. She watched as he lifted Matthew onto his horse for a brief ride before the boy would return to whichever wagon was serving as his daytime perch.

There was something almost enviable in Reynolds' certainty, his clear understanding of his role and purpose. Emily turned away, settling herself on the hard bench seat. Purpose. Direction. These were luxuries she had forfeited when she buried her husband and family. All that remained was endurance.

Chapter 5

The afternoon passage was more difficult than the morning's travel. The sun beat down relentlessly, and the dust seemed to thicken with each mile. Emily's throat grew parched despite the water Mercy offered at regular intervals. Her mind drifted into a haze of discomfort and memory, the jarring of the wagon occasionally jolting her back to the present.

"Look there, Miss Wilson," Mercy said suddenly, touching her arm lightly. "Antelope, I believe."

Emily followed her gesture to where several graceful animals bounded across the prairie some distance from the wagon train. Their movement was fluid, effortless, and utterly free.

"Beautiful creatures," Mercy continued. "God's handiwork is evident in every part of this vast country."

Emily watched the antelope disappear into the distance. God's handiwork. The phrase echoed in her mind like a taunt. The same handiwork that created the typhoid bacillus? The same divine design that allowed illness to ravage the innocent? She turned away, fixing her gaze on her folded hands.

"Indeed," she said, the word barely audible above the creaking of the wagon.

The afternoon dragged on interminably. Emily's body ached from the constant jarring and the hard seat. The heat became oppressive. She found herself counting each rotation of the wagon wheels, focusing on the mechanical repetition rather than the thoughts that threatened to overwhelm her.

When they finally halted for the evening, the sun was beginning its descent, painting the western sky in shades of pink and lavender. Reverend and Mercy Holloway climbed down, moving stiffly after the long day's travel. She watched as the nightly ritual began, wagons circled for protection, animals tended, and fires kindled. The transition from traveling column to temporary settlement was remarkably efficient under Weston's direction.

Emily finally descended from the wagon, her legs protesting the sudden change. Women gathered at the central cook fires, and children were assigned simple tasks or played in the spaces between wagons under watchful eyes.

"Miss Wilson," Mercy called, "would you care to join us at the cook fire? Mrs. Croft has a remarkable recipe for trail biscuits."

Emily shook her head slightly. "Thank you, but I believe I'll walk a bit first. My legs need stretching after the day's journey."

It wasn't entirely a falsehood. Her body did need movement to ease the stiffness of travel. But more pressing was her need for space, for air, and for a moment away from the well-intentioned concern in Mercy's eyes.

She moved to the edge of the camp, careful to remain within the safe perimeter established by Weston but finding a spot relatively free of others. From here, she could see the entire circle of wagons, and the community forming among travelers with each passing day. Yet, she remained separate, an observer rather than a participant.

The Billings children, Luke, and his sister Abigail, chased each other between wagons, their laughter a counterpoint to the deeper voices of men discussing the day's progress. The Calkins struggled with their fire, Zach's inexperience evident as he attempted to coax a flame from kindling while Lavinia watched anxiously. Martha Croft intervened with quiet efficiency, demonstrating the proper technique with practiced hands.

These ordinary moments of human connection, help freely given, knowledge shared, and laughter rising into the evening air, had once been the fabric of Emily's life in Richmond. The dinner parties she had hosted, the patients she had tended to, the easy camaraderie with her sisters, and the profound understanding between herself and Thomas. All of it ash now, scattered by the merciless wind of circumstance.

A sharp cry drew her attention. Young Caleb Croft had fallen, his knee scraped bloody on the rocky ground near one of the wagons. His mother, Martha, hurried to him, soothing his tears and examining the injury.

Emily's hands twitched reflexively, her medical instincts rising to the surface. But she remained where she was, watching as Martha cleaned the wound with water from a canteen and applied a simple bandage. The boy's cries subsided to hiccuping sobs, then ceased entirely when his father produced a small piece of candy from his pocket, a rare treat on the trail.

"You're the midwife, aren't you?"

Emily started at the voice beside her. She turned to find Elara Jenkins, a woman traveling alone. Tall and self-possessed, with eyes that missed little, Elara had kept to herself much as Emily had, though for different reasons. Rumors in the camp suggested she was a widow seeking a fresh start, but Emily had paid little attention to the gossip.

"I am trained in midwifery, yes," Emily acknowledged.

Elara nodded toward the Croft family. "Thought so. Saw your hands when the boy fell. You wanted to help."

Emily shifted uncomfortably. "Old habits," she said shortly.

"Useful habits on a journey like this." Elara's tone was matter-of-fact. "Injuries and illnesses don't stop on the trail. Heard a train last year lost sixteen people to fever before Fort Laramie."

Emily stiffened, her fingers automatically seeking the locket around her neck. Fever. The word alone was enough to make her chest constrict.

"I'm sure Reverend Holloway would say we must trust in divine protection," she said, unable to keep the bitter edge from her voice.

Elara gave her a shrewd look. "Maybe. But I notice folks pray with one hand and keep their powder dry with the other. Practical skills like yours... that's as important as faith out here."

Before Emily could respond, Elara nodded briefly and moved away, returning to her solitary camp at the edge of the circle. Emily watched her go, unsettled by the encounter. She had not come to the Oregon Trail to be useful. She had not come to be needed. She had come to disappear, to lose herself in the vastness of the continent, to feel nothing but physical exhaustion until the pain in her heart was finally, mercifully, numbed beyond feeling.

Two hours passed, and the camp settled into its late evening routine. Meals had been consumed, children were tucked into wagon beds, and adults gathered in small groups to discuss the day's journey and tomorrow's prospects. Reverend Holloway held a brief prayer service for those who wished to attend, his voice floating across the camp, speaking of divine guidance and protection on the trail ahead.

Emily remained apart, accepting the plate Mercy brought her but eating little. As darkness fell, she finally returned to the Holloway wagon, climbing awkwardly inside to the small space allotted for her bedroll. The wagon was cramped, filled with the Holloway's' possessions and the essential supplies for the journey. Her own trunks took up precious space.

She brushed her hair, a small comfort in the strangeness of her surroundings, and wished for a bath of hot water. Through the canvas, she could hear the muted sounds of the camp settling for the night, the low murmur of voices, the occasional whinny of a horse, and the crackle of dying fires.

Mercy and Reverend Holloway would join her soon, taking their places in the crowded wagon. The thought of another night in such close proximity to others made Emily's skin crawl, but there was no alternative. Privacy was a luxury the trail did not afford.

She lay down on her bedroll, pulling the blanket up despite the lingering warmth of the evening. Outside, a man's voice rose in song, a slow, mournful tune about home and loved ones left behind. Others joined in, the melody drifting across the camp like a spirit.

Emily turned her face away, pressing it against the rough wood of the side of the wagon bed. She would not weep. She had done her weeping in Richmond, alone in the empty house with its echoes and memories. Now there was only the journey, the physical demands that would exhaust her body and perhaps, eventually, grant her mind some peace.

Sleep was a long time coming. When it finally claimed her, her dreams were filled with the relentless rhythm of wagon wheels, the vast emptiness of the prairie, and the faces of those she had lost, watching her from a distance she couldn't cross.

Chapter 6

Morning came too soon, heralded by the sounds of the camp stirring to life. Emily rose stiffly, her body protesting after another night on the hard floor of the wagon bed. She slipped out of the wagon before the Holloway's woke.

The air was cool and fresh, the light pearly and diffuse as the sun hovered just below the horizon. The camp was already active—fires being kindled, animals tended, and preparations made for the day's travel. Emily moved to the edge of the camp, her shawl pulled tightly around her shoulders against the morning chill.

"Good morning, Miss Wilson." The voice came from behind her, making her turn sharply.

Weston Reynolds stood a few paces away, holding the reins of his horse. In the early light, his features seemed less harsh and rugged.

"Mr. Reynolds." Emily acknowledged him with a slight nod.

"We'll be crossing a creek today," he said, his tone practical and impersonal. "Nothing like the river crossings ahead, but the banks are steep. The wagons will need to be double-teamed. Reverend Holloway mentioned you might prefer to walk that stretch rather than ride."

Emily blinked in surprise. She had expressed no such preference to the Holloway's, though the thought of being in the wagon during a potentially hazardous creek crossing was indeed unsettling.

"I... yes," she said finally. "I would prefer to walk, if that's permissible."

Reynolds nodded, his expression unreadable. "Many do. Safer on foot for that part. We leave in thirty minutes." He touched the brim of his hat briefly, then moved on, continuing his morning circuit of the camp.

Emily watched him go, puzzled by the exchange. Had the Holloway's truly discussed her with Reynolds, or had he simply noted her discomfort during travel? Either possibility was unsettling. She had no desire to be the subject of conversation or observation.

The camp quickly transitioned from morning preparations into departure readiness. Emily returned to the Holloway wagon to find Mercy already securing their belongings for travel.

"Good morning, my dear," she said warmly. "I trust you slept well? The nights can be difficult when one is unused to wagon travel."

"Well enough," Emily replied, helping to secure a loose bundle of bedding. It was not precisely a lie; she had slept, albeit fitfully and with disturbing dreams.

"James tells me we face a creek crossing today," she continued, adjusting her bonnet. "Nothing too daunting, I hope?"

"Mr. Reynolds indicated it would require double-teaming the wagons," Emily said, keeping her voice neutral. "He mentioned many prefer to walk that section."

Mercy nodded. "A wise precaution. James and I have crossed our share of creeks and rivers in our travels for the ministry. It's always best to be cautious."

The signal to depart came soon after, and the wagon train resumed its westward progression. The morning passed much as the previous day had—hot, dusty, and monotonous. Emily found herself almost grateful for the physical discomfort; it kept her mind occupied, and prevented it from wandering to darker places.

Around midday, the landscape began to change subtly. The terrain grew more uneven, and in the distance, Emily could make out the line of trees that generally indicated a water source. Reynolds rode up and down the column, giving instructions for the upcoming crossing.

When they finally reached the creek, Emily saw that his caution was warranted. Though the water itself was not particularly deep or wide, the banks on either side were indeed steep and treacherous. The lead wagons halted, and a flurry of activity ensued as extra oxen were hitched to the first wagon.

Emily climbed down, relieved to stretch her legs. Mercy opted to remain in the wagon, trusting her husband and the additional teams to manage the crossing safely. Emily moved a little apart from the others, watching the preparations with interest.

One by one, the wagons made the difficult descent to the creek bed, the extra oxen straining against the weight on the steep incline. The crossing itself was relatively simple, but the climb up the opposite bank required all the strength of the double teams, the animals laboring in their harnesses as men urged them on with calls and occasionally the snap of a whip.

It was not until several wagons had successfully crossed that Emily noticed a commotion at the creek's edge. The Calkins' wagon, driven by young Zach, had slipped sideways on the descent, one wheel precariously close to the edge where the bank had begun to crumble. Lavinia sat frozen on the wagon seat, her face pale with fear, while Zach struggled to control the nervous oxen.

Weston was there immediately. "Hold steady, Calkins! Don't pull them sideways!"

He dismounted in a fluid motion, handing the reins of his horse to the nearest person, who happened to be Martha Croft, and moved quickly to the troubled wagon. Several other men joined him, including Silas Croft and George Billings. Together, they positioned themselves alongside the wagon, ready to prevent it from tipping if the wheel slipped further.

"Now, Calkins," Weston directed, his voice calm but authoritative, "guide them straight down. Slow and steady."

Zach, visibly nervous, nodded and called to his team. The oxen moved forward reluctantly; the wagon inching down the steep incline. For a moment, it seemed the disaster had been averted.

Then the crumbling bank gave way entirely. The wagon lurched sharply to one side, threatening to overturn completely. Lavinia screamed, clutching the seat in terror. Zach lost his grip on the reins as he tried to brace himself and reach for his wife.

Weston and the others threw their weight against the wagon's side, straining to keep it upright. "Jump!" Weston shouted to Lavinia. "Jump clear now!"

Paralyzed with fear, the young woman remained frozen in the seat. The wagon tilted further; the contents shifting ominously. A trunk broke loose from its bindings and crashed to the ground, narrowly missing Silas.

Without conscious thought, Emily moved forward, her medical training overriding her desire to remain uninvolved. If the wagon overturned, there would be injuries—potentially serious ones.

She reached the edge of the bank as Weston made a decision. With a quick word to the others to hold the wagon, he climbed up the tilting side with remarkable agility and reached Lavinia. There was no time for persuasion. He simply lifted the slight young woman and half-passed, half-dropped her to George, who had positioned himself to receive her. Lavinia landed awkwardly but safely in Georges' arms, her scream cut short by relief.

The worst of the danger past, the men managed to stabilize the wagon enough for Zach to regain control of his team. With Weston's guidance, they carefully completed the descent to the creek bed, though the wagon, now listed to one side, clearly damaged.

Emily retreated, her momentary impulse to help faded now that the crisis had passed. She watched as the Calkins' wagon was assisted across the creek, the damaged wheel turning at an awkward angle. It would require repairs before they could continue.

As the remaining wagons made their crossings, more cautiously now, having witnessed the Calkins' misfortune, Emily watched Weston with a more critical eye. His handling of the situation had been impressive—decisive, calm, and effective. He had prioritized Lavinia's safety over the wagon and its contents, a choice that spoke to his character.

When it came time for the Holloway wagon to make the crossing, Emily walked alongside at a safe distance, ready to move quickly if needed. But Reverend Holloway, with years of experience and the benefit of having observed the earlier crossings, managed the descent without incident. The extra oxen strained against the weight, but the wagon passed safely through the shallow water and up the opposite bank.

By the time all the wagons had crossed, the sun was high overhead, and it was clear they would need to halt for repairs to the Calkins' wagon. Weston organized the stop efficiently, directing the wagons into a loose semicircle on the relatively flat ground beyond the creek.

The midday meal was a hurried affair, as many of the men gathered to assist with the wagon repairs under Silas's direction. Emily ate the cold lunch Mercy provided and then, seeking to escape the older woman's well-meaning but persistent attempts at conversation, walked to the edge of the encampment.

She found a spot in the shade of a lone tree, its gnarled branches offering modest protection from the sun. From here, she could observe the activity around the damaged wagon without being drawn into it. Zach Calkins hovered anxiously as Silas and the others assessed the damage, while Lavinia sat nearby, still pale and shaken from the ordeal. Emily felt a twinge of professional concern for the young woman. She was far too pale.

A small figure detached itself from the group near the wagons and moved in her direction. Matthew Reynolds, his small face serious beneath his too-large hat, approached with the deliberate purpose of a child on a mission.

He stopped a few feet from her, studying her with unabashed curiosity. "Papa says you're a doctor for ladies," he said finally, his voice clear and direct.

Emily blinked in surprise. "I... was a midwife in Virginia," she corrected carefully. "Not precisely a doctor."

Matthew nodded, accepting this distinction with a child's openness to new information. "Mrs. Calkins hurt her arm. She's crying but trying to hide it." He delivered this information matter-of-factly, as one professional to another.

Emily glanced toward the wagons, where Lavinia indeed sat on the ground near her wagon cradling her arm, her face turned away from the others, her shoulders shaking slightly.

"I'm sure someone will attend to her," Emily said, aware of the inadequacy of her response even as she spoke.

Matthew considered this, his small brow furrowed in thought. "Papa's helping fix the wagon. Mrs. Croft is making food. Nobody's helping Mrs. Calkins." He looked at Emily expectantly, with the simple, unshakable logic of a child who has clearly identified a problem and its solution.

Emily found herself caught in the directness of his gaze, so similar to his father's in color, but lacking the guardedness she had observed in the elder Reynolds. This was a child who had not yet learned to hide his thoughts or shield his heart.

"I see," she said finally. "And you think I should help her?"

Matthew nodded vigorously. "Papa says we all got to help each other on the trail. That's how we get to Oregon."

Oregon. The destination she had chosen not because she desired to arrive, but because the journey itself promised the physical hardship she sought. Yet here was this child, articulating a philosophy of mutual aid that was antithetical to her purpose of joining the wagon train. She had not come to help. She had not come to heal. She had come to endure in isolation.

But Matthew continued to look at her with absolute faith, and Emily found herself rising to her feet. "Very well. I'll speak with Mrs. Calkins."

Matthew's face broke into a sudden, brilliant smile that transformed his serious features. He turned and led the way back toward the wagons, glancing over his shoulder occasionally to ensure she followed.

Lavinia Calkins looked up in surprise as they approached, hastily wiping her tears with her good hand. "Oh! Miss Wilson, isn't it?" she said, attempting a smile. "Matthew, what have you been up to?"

"Miss Wilson's gonna help your arm," Matthew announced confidently. "She's a doctor for ladies."

Lavinia's face flushed. "Oh, I wouldn't wish to trouble—"

"It's no trouble," Emily said, the professional tone she had used countless times in Richmond emerging automatically. "May I examine your arm? Matthew seems to think you've injured it."

With Matthew watching in satisfaction, Emily knelt beside the young woman and gently took her arm, feeling for the source of pain. It was not broken, but there was significant swelling at the wrist, likely a sprain.

"You'll need to keep this immobilized for a few days," Emily said, her hands moving with efficiency as she fashioned a sling from a clean cloth she had retrieved from the back of the wagon. "It's a sprain, not a break, but it will be painful for some time."

"Thank you," Lavinia whispered, fresh tears welling in her eyes. "I was trying not to be a bother. Zach feels so terrible about the wagon already."

Emily completed the sling in silence, uncomfortable with the young woman's vulnerability and gratitude. "There," she said, stepping back. "Try to rest it as much as possible."

Matthew, who had been watching the procedure with intense interest, nodded solemnly. "Papa says you got to listen to people who know things," he informed Lavinia earnestly. "So you got to do what Miss Wilson says."

Emily felt a faint smile tug at the corner of her mouth. The child's earnest certainty was oddly endearing. "Your father is quite right," she said. "Though I suspect he meant you should listen to him."

Matthew considered this. "Him, and you, and Mr. Croft, and Reverend Holloway," he said finally, ticking off the authorities in his small world on his fingers. "And God," he added as an afterthought. "Papa says we always got to listen for God, even when He's real quiet."

The smile faded from Emily's lips.

"Listen for God."

"That's very wise," she said. "If you'll excuse me, Mrs. Calkins, I should return to the Holloway wagon."

She turned away, leaving Matthew looking after her, confused at her sudden shift in demeanor. She was halfway back to the Holloway wagon when a deep voice stopped her.

"Miss Wilson."

She turned to find Weston standing a few paces away, his expression unreadable.

"Mr. Reynolds." She acknowledged him stiffly.

"Thank you for tending to Mrs. Calkins," he said simply. "Matthew was right to seek your assistance."

So he had seen. Emily felt inexplicably defensive. "It was a simple sprain. Anyone could have diagnosed it."

"Perhaps. But not everyone would have taken the time." His gaze was direct, assessing. "Your skills are valuable on the trail, Miss Wilson. There is no doctor among us."

Emily looked away, uncomfortable with his scrutiny and the implied responsibility in his words. "I am not here in a professional capacity, Mr. Reynolds. I am not a doctor. I am merely a passenger to Oregon, like the others."

"We are all more than merely passengers, Miss Wilson," he replied, his voice quiet but firm. "Each brings something to the journey. Your medical knowledge may prove as essential as Silas Croft's skill with wagons or Samson Early's blacksmithing."

Before Emily could formulate a response, he continued, "The Calkins' wagon will be ready to travel within the hour. Please inform the Holloway's." With a brief nod, he turned and walked back to where the men were completing repairs on the damaged wheel.

Emily remained where she was for a moment, unsettled by the encounter. Reynolds had a directness that cut through her carefully constructed walls, an expectation of contribution that contradicted her desire for anonymity. He saw her skills not as a private matter, but as a resource for the community.

She returned to the Holloway wagon to find Mercy preparing to resume travel. "There you are, my dear," the older woman said warmly. "Reverend Holloway mentioned you were helping poor Lavinia. Such a blessing to have someone with medical training among us."

Emily made a noncommittal sound, busying herself with straightening her belongings. "Mr. Reynolds says we'll be leaving within the hour," she said, changing the subject. "The repairs are nearly complete."

Mercy nodded. "Wonderful news. We've lost some time today, but the good Lord willing, we'll make up for it in the days ahead."

"The good Lord willing."

The phrase echoed in Emily's mind as she climbed back into the wagon.

She settled onto the hard bench seat, her body already protesting the thought of more hours of travel. The unexpected interlude with Lavinia and Matthew had drained her more than she had anticipated.

Later, as the wagon train resumed its westward journey, Emily fixed her gaze on the horizon, vast and empty. Like her future. Like her heart. The sun beat down relentlessly and dust rose in choking clouds from the wheels.

She closed her eyes briefly, feeling the weight of the locket in her pocket, its metallic coolness a reminder of the loved ones she had lost. She had not come to the Oregon Trail to find purpose or community.

She had not come to heal or be healed. She had come to disappear into the vastness of the continent, to become as insignificant as a single grain of dust on an endless plain.

Yet within the first days of the journey, she had been drawn, however reluctantly, into the life of the wagon train. Matthew's direct appeal, Lavinia's need, and Weston's clear expectation that each member contribute to the common good. It was a complication she had not anticipated, a demand she had not sought.

As the wagon creaked and swayed beneath her, Emily tightened her grip on the seat and steeled her resolve. This momentary involvement changed nothing. She would maintain her distance. She would fulfill the minimum obligations required by civility but form no attachments. She would focus solely on enduring each day, each mile, and each moment of the journey.

The wagon train continued its slow, laborious progress across the prairie, a tiny, fragile line of humanity in the midst of a vast, indifferent wilderness. And Emily Wilson sat among them yet apart, her heart as closed as the Bible hidden in her trunk that she could not bear to open, her grief a wall between herself and the world. Her determination to remain isolated was the only certainty in a future otherwise empty of hope or purpose.

Chapter 7

Weston ran a hand through his dust-coated hair and surveyed the surrounding scene. The circle of wagons created a protective barrier against the night, an island of humanity in the vast sea of prairie grass. Inside this circle, life bloomed in the growing darkness. Small cooking fires dotted the space, figures moved in familiar patterns, and voices called out in greeting or instruction. This was the rhythm of the trail, the daily building and breaking of a temporary community bound together by shared purpose and necessity.

Matthew's small figure darted between two wagons, and Weston's eyes tracked him instantly, his heart quickening with the reflexive vigilance that never truly left him. But the boy was merely helping George Billings gather kindling, his small hands clutching twigs with serious determination.

A flutter of movement near the Holloway wagon caught Weston's attention. Emily stood slightly apart from Mercy, who was busying herself with their evening meal preparations. Even from this distance, Weston could see that Emily remained as she had been since joining the wagon train, present in body but dwelling somewhere far away, her slender frame wrapped in an invisible shroud of grief.

"That look in her eyes..." Weston thought. A look that spoke of a soul trapped between worlds, unable to fully leave the past, unwilling to step into the future.

He pulled his gaze away deliberately. *"Keep your focus where it belongs... on the trail ahead and on Matthew."*

As if summoned by his thoughts, Matthew appeared at his side, tugging at his dusty coat.

"Papa, I helped Mr. Billings gather wood for the fire," he announced, his small face smudged with dirt but alight with the simple pleasure of being useful.

Weston felt the familiar softening that only his son could summon. He crouched down, bringing himself to Matthew's level, and gently brushed a smudge of dirt from the boy's cheek.

"That was good of you, Matthew. Did you thank Mr. Billings for letting you help?"

Matthew nodded solemnly. "Yes, sir. He said I was the best helper he's had since leaving Independence."

"I don't doubt it." Weston smiled. "Are you hungry? Let's get our fire going."

Together, they walked to their wagon. Weston lifted his son onto the back, where the boy immediately began rummaging through their supplies. At six, Matthew had already developed a surprisingly practical understanding of their routine. He knew which crate held their cooking utensils, where the coffee was stored, and which crate or barrel held food supplies. Weston watched him with quiet pride, even as a familiar pang twisted in his chest.

"Susannah should be here to see this... to see him growing."

The thought arrived unbidden, as it often did in these quiet moments. Weston pushed it away with the practiced discipline of years. There was no use in dwelling on what couldn't be changed. His responsibility was to the living–to Matthew and to the people who had entrusted their lives to his guidance.

"Here, Papa." Matthew handed down their small cooking pot. "Can we have beans tonight? And maybe some of that jerky Mr. Hodge traded to us?"

"That sounds like a fine supper." Weston took the pot and set about building their fire, striking flint to steel, while Matthew arranged a circle of stones.

Across the camp, raised voices cut through the evening's murmur. Weston looked up instantly, attuned to the sounds of discord. Ezekiel Vance stood near the water barrels, gesturing emphatically at young Zach Calkins, whose face had reddened with either embarrassment or anger.

"Is everything all right, Papa?" Matthew asked, following his father's gaze.

"Stay here," Weston instructed, setting down the cooking implements. "Don't wander off. I'll be back shortly."

He crossed the camp with long, deliberate strides, arriving just as Ezekiel's complaints became clearly audible.

"...taking more than your rightful share! We all agreed on the water allowance, and I've been watching you, Calkins. That's the third time today you've—"

"My wife is unwell, Mr. Vance," Zach replied, his voice tight with restrained emotion. "The heat today was particularly—"

"We're all suffering from the heat," Ezekiel cut in, his voice carrying across the camp, drawing unwanted attention to the confrontation. "That doesn't entitle you to special—"

"Is there a problem here?" Weston interjected, his voice calm, but carrying a note of authority that silenced both men immediately.

Ezekiel turned, his thin face twisted with indignation. He was a narrow man in every sense of the word—lean to the point of gauntness, with eyes set close together beneath a prominent brow, and a disposition that seemed equally pinched and confined.

"Reynolds, glad you're here. Young Calkins here thinks the water rationing doesn't apply to his wagon. I've caught him taking extra twice before, and—"

"I took one additional dipper for my wife," Zach interrupted, his youthful face flushed. "Lavinia was feeling poorly in the heat. She barely touched her lunch."

Weston assessed the situation with a quick glance. Lavinia was indeed looking peaked, sitting listlessly by their wagon, a damp cloth pressed to her forehead. The young couple had been struggling with the rigors of the trail since leaving Independence, their enthusiasm for Oregon gradually wearing thin against the grinding reality of daily travel.

"Our water situation is secure," Weston stated calmly. "We'll reach a creek by tomorrow evening. An extra dipper for someone feeling ill isn't going to endanger anyone, Ezekiel."

Vance's face darkened. "It's the principle of the matter, Reynolds. We agreed on rations. If everyone starts taking just a little extra, we'll—"

"I'm well aware of how rationing works," Weston cut him off, his tone remaining level but carrying an unmistakable firmness. "And I'm also aware that we're a community, not just a collection of separate wagons. When someone is ill, we make accommodations."

He turned to Zach, softening his expression slightly. "Perhaps have Elara Jenkins or Mrs. Wilson take a look at your wife if she's not improving."

Zach nodded, relief evident in his posture. "Yes, sir. Thank you."

As the young man retreated toward his wagon, Vance stepped closer to Weston, lowering his voice, but not the intensity of his displeasure.

"You undermine the rules every time you make exceptions, Reynolds. The trail doesn't care about good intentions. If we run out of water before reaching that creek of yours—"

"We won't," Weston stated with quiet confidence. "And if anything changes, I'll adjust the rations accordingly. This isn't my first crossing, Ezekiel."

"No, but it might be your last if you keep prioritizing sentiment over sense," Vance muttered, just loud enough for Weston to hear.

Weston met the man's narrow gaze directly. "I prioritize the welfare of this company as a whole, which includes both physical necessities and maintaining the spirit that will get us to Oregon. Kindness isn't sentiment, Vance. Out here, it's as essential as water."

Without waiting for a response, Weston turned and walked away, his back straight despite the weariness settling into his bones. He understood the man's concerns on a practical level—resources were indeed precious, rules necessary. But the Ezekiel's inability to see beyond immediate self-interest to the broader needs of their community was becoming a frequent source of tension.

As he made his way back to his fire, where Matthew waited patiently, Weston noticed Emily again. She had settled on a small crate near the Holloway's wagon, a bowl of stew in her hands that she was eating mechanically, her gaze fixed on some point in the middle distance. Reverend Holloway sat nearby, speaking gently to her, but her responses, if any, were minimal. She seemed to have constructed an invisible barrier around herself, allowing only the most necessary interactions to penetrate.

"Something happened to her beyond just loss," Weston thought, the observation arriving unbidden. *"That's not just grief. That's something deeper... guilt, maybe."*

He recognized it because he had carried it himself—that particular weight that came not just from losing someone you loved, but from feeling somehow responsible for not preventing it. It had taken him nearly two years to begin shedding that particular burden after Susannah's death, to accept that some things lay beyond human control.

The fierce protectiveness he'd developed for Matthew had been his salvation in those darkest days – a purpose that demanded his full attention, pulling him back from the edge of despair day after day. But Emily Wilson appeared to have no such anchor, no immediate purpose beyond mere survival.

"Papa, the fire's ready," Matthew called, drawing Weston back to the present moment.

Returning to their wagon, he found that his son had arranged their simple supper ingredients neatly on a cloth. The sight of Matthew's earnest efforts brought a smile to Weston's tired face.

"You've done well," he praised, settling beside his son. "Let's get these beans cooking."

As they prepared their meal together, the simple routine of measuring water, adding beans and a precious pinch of salt, and setting the pot to heat, created a pocket of normalcy in the constantly shifting landscape of their journey. Matthew chatted about his day, about a jackrabbit he'd spotted darting through the tall grass, about Luke Billings showing him how to tie a special knot, and about the shapes of clouds he'd observed from the wagon seat.

Weston listened attentively, asking questions and offering comments, treasuring these moments when Matthew's natural childish enthusiasm broke through the sometimes grim reality of their journey. In these quiet exchanges, he could almost forget the weight of leadership that rested on his shoulders, the lives entrusted to his judgment and knowledge of the trail.

Their beans were just beginning to simmer when Barnaby approached their fire. The older man moved with the easy grace of someone who had spent a lifetime in the saddle, his leathery face deeply lined from years of sun and wind. At sixty-five, Barnaby was making his third crossing to Oregon, a fact that had initially caused Weston to wonder why the man hadn't simply stayed put after his first or second journey.

"Mind if I join you for a spell?"

"Please do," Weston gestured to a space beside the fire. "Coffee's just about ready."

Barnaby settled his frame onto a nearby crate with a soft grunt. "Obliged. Been watching that situation with Ezekiel. Man's got a talent for stirring trouble."

"That he does," Weston agreed, pouring a tin cup of the strong black coffee and handing it to the older man. "Though his concerns aren't entirely without merit."

"True enough," Barnaby acknowledged, accepting the cup with gnarled hands. "Resources matter. But so does how folk treat each other. You handled it right."

Weston appreciated Barnaby's assessment more than he let on. The older man's experience and wisdom had proven valuable on numerous occasions already, and his support helped counter the occasional doubts that crept in after particularly difficult decisions.

"Mr. Cobb," Matthew piped up, "are the stars in Oregon the same as these stars here? I can't remember!" He pointed upward at the increasingly visible night sky.

Barnaby chuckled, his eyes crinkling at the corners. "Well now, young Master Reynolds, that's a fine question. The stars themselves are the same, but they look different depending on where you're standing. When we get to Oregon, you'll see some of the same stars hanging in different parts of the sky."

Matthew considered this with solemn concentration. "So they move around?"

"In a manner of speaking." Barnaby nodded. "Though really, it's us that's moving under them. Stars are steady things, Matthew. Good for finding your way when other landmarks fail."

"Like Papa," Matthew said confidently. "He always knows which way to go."

The simple faith in his son's declaration tightened something in Weston's chest. If only such certainty were truly possible. Every decision he made carried consequences, some immediate, some that wouldn't be apparent for days or weeks. The responsibility weighed on him, especially in the quiet hours of the night, when doubts crept in like shadows.

"Your papa's a fine guide," Barnaby agreed, his knowing gaze meeting Weston's briefly over the rim of his coffee cup. "But even the best scouts check their bearings regular-like."

As they ate their simple meal, Barnaby shared stories of his previous crossings—tales carefully selected to be appropriate for Matthew's ears, focusing on natural wonders they would encounter rather than the hardships that undoubtedly lay ahead. The older man had a gift for storytelling, his deep voice painting vivid pictures of snow-capped mountains, vast forests, and the fertile valleys of Oregon.

"You've a fine boy there, Reynolds," he commented quietly when Matthew was distracted by a nearby moth. "I'm sure his mama is smiling down from heaven."

"She would have loved watching him grow up," he acknowledged, keeping his voice steady. "I wish she were still here with us. I miss her."

Barnaby nodded, understanding in his weathered features. "Loss leaves marks that time doesn't quite erase," he said simply. "Just changes their shape some."

The older man's gaze drifted briefly across the camp to where Emily sat, still separate, still wrapped in her private sorrow.

"That new widow's carrying a heavy load," he observed. "Seen that look before. The kind of grief that hollows a person from the inside."

Weston followed his gaze. "I've seen it too. But the trail demands everyone's full attention. Distraction can be deadly out here."

"True enough," Barnaby conceded. "But the trail has a way of making everyone's burdens overlap, sooner or later. No one travels this path truly alone, no matter how hard they might try." He set his empty cup down with finality. "Well, I'd best check the team before turning in. Thanks for the coffee and company."

After Barnaby departed, Weston helped Matthew prepare for sleep, their routine as familiar as the stars appearing overhead. He waited patiently while his son knelt beside their bedrolls and said his nightly prayers, Matthew's small voice lifting in simple, trusting faith.

"And God, please keep Papa safe, and me too, and all the people in the wagons," Matthew concluded. "And maybe help Miss Emily not be so sad all the time. Amen."

The mention of Emily caught Weston by surprise. "You've been thinking about Miss Emily?" he asked as Matthew climbed into his bedroll.

The boy nodded, his expression serious in the firelight. "She looks like you do sometimes when you're looking really hard up to heaven. Like you're looking for mama to peek out from behind a cloud. But worse, maybe. Doesn't she have anyone to help her not be sad, like I help you?"

Weston felt something twist in his chest at his son's perception. Children saw clearly sometimes, unclouded by adult complications.

"Miss Emily lost people she loved," he explained gently. "And everyone heals in their own time, Matthew. Some hurts take longer to mend than others."

"Maybe she needs friends," Matthew suggested, yawning. "Everyone needs friends, Papa."

"Perhaps. But right now, what we both need is sleep. Tomorrow will be another long day."

He tucked the blanket around his son's small form, smoothing back the sandy hair that so resembled Susannah's. "Sleep well, Matthew."

"You too, Papa," Matthew mumbled, already drifting toward sleep.

Weston remained beside him until the boy's breathing deepened and slowed. Only then did he leave the wagon to complete his nightly inspection of the camp.

The evening had settled fully now, most fires burning low, conversations subdued. He made his way around the wagon circle methodically, checking that the animals were secure, that the night watch was established, and that nothing seemed amiss. This final review was as much a part of his routine as breakfast would be come morning—a necessary precaution, but also a way to quiet his mind before seeking his own rest.

The vast prairie sky stretched overhead, an unimaginable expanse of stars that always reminded Weston of how small human concerns were in the greater scope of creation. Yet, he found comfort rather than insignificance in this perspective—the same God who hung those stars knew each member of this wagon train by name, knew their struggles, their fears, and their hopes.

"Be with us on this journey," he prayed silently. *"Guide our steps through whatever lies ahead."*

Near the eastern edge of the circle, he paused. Emily stood alone at the perimeter, just within the safe boundary of the wagons, her back to the camp as she gazed out at the vast darkness of the prairie. The light from the nearest fire caught her profile, illuminating the straight line of her spine and the tension in her shoulders.

Weston hesitated, but something about her stillness and her solitary figure against the night made him approach with care rather than just calling out a reminder of the rules.

"Mrs. Wilson," he said quietly as he drew closer, not wanting to startle her.

She didn't turn immediately, though the slight stiffening of her shoulders told him she'd heard. When she finally did face him, the hollow emptiness in her expression sent an unexpected chill through him. It was more than mere grief; it was the look of someone who had moved beyond pain into a dangerous numbness.

"Is it against the rules to stand here?" she asked, her voice carrying neither defiance nor particular interest in the answer.

"Not exactly," Weston replied. "But it's not safe to be too near the edge of camp after dark. Coyotes... sometimes worse. And it's easy to become disoriented in the dark prairie if you wander even a short distance."

A strange, bitter smile touched her lips. "Would it matter?"

Weston's chest tightened with concern. It was not merely the words, but the flat, hopeless way she spoke them.

"It would be to those who would have to search for you," he replied carefully. "And to those who depend on your skills should illness or injury arise."

Emily regarded him with those hollow eyes that seemed to look through him rather than at him. "No one here truly depends on me, Mr. Reynolds. I'm merely passing through, like all of us."

There was something in her tone, a deep, quiet certainty that troubled Weston more than any overt display of emotion would have. He'd seen grief take many forms on previous journeys, but there was something particularly disturbing about the absolute detachment in her gaze.

"We're all merely passing through in one sense or another," he said after a moment. "But while we travel this path together, each life here matters. Each person has a place and purpose within this community."

She looked away, back toward the darkness beyond the camp. "You sound like Reverend Holloway. He also speaks of purpose. I find it... difficult to share such certainty."

Weston studied her profile in the dim light. Her words weren't spoken with bitterness or challenge, but with a strange, hollow acceptance.

"Certainty isn't required," he said finally. "Just willingness to keep moving forward. One day at a time. One step after another."

"Is that what you did? After your wife?" The question came unexpectedly, catching Weston off guard.

He was silent for a moment, weighing his response. "Yes," he admitted finally. "And having Matthew to care for gave those steps direction when I had none of my own."

She nodded slightly, as if confirming something to herself. "A purpose, then. As you said."

"Mrs. Wilson..." He hesitated, uncertain of how to express the concern her words and manner had stirred in him. As wagon master, the physical and mental welfare of every member of the company fell within his responsibility. Yet, this felt like territory far beyond the parameters of his role.

"You needn't worry, Mr. Reynolds," she said, correctly interpreting his hesitation. "I won't wander off into the prairie. I'm not seeking that kind of end." A shadow of something, perhaps pain or perhaps simply weariness, crossed her face. "I merely find it... easier to breathe out here, away from the concerns and conversations of others."

Weston nodded, accepting her assurance while still feeling a lingering unease. "All the same, perhaps stay within clearer sight of the fires. The night watch changes every few hours, and not everyone would recognize you immediately in the darkness."

"As you wish," she conceded with quiet indifference. "Good night, Mr. Reynolds."

"Good night, Mrs. Wilson."

As he completed his circuit of the camp, Weston found his thoughts returning to the brief exchange. Emily Wilson's grief was her own to bear, her journey toward healing, if healing was what she sought, was not his to guide. Yet Matthew's innocent observation and Barnaby's words about overlapping burdens lingered in his mind.

"Lord, watch over her," he prayed. *"And help me know where my duty as wagon master ends and overstepping begins."*

Returning to his wagon, Weston checked once more on Matthew, who slept peacefully, one small hand curled against his cheek. The sight of his son eased some of the tension the encounter with Emily had stirred. This was his anchor, his purpose—this small life entrusted to his care. Whatever else happened on the long road to Oregon, whatever challenges arose within the company, Matthew remained his true north.

Weston settled onto his bedroll beside his son, his body aching with the day's exertions. Above them, the stars wheeled in their ancient patterns, indifferent to the small human concerns unfolding beneath their light.

As sleep finally began to claim him, Weston's last conscious thought was of Emily standing at the edge of camp, looking out into the darkness as though seeking something or perhaps nothing at all. The image troubled him in ways he couldn't quite define, stirring both professional concern and something more personal he was reluctant to examine too closely.

"Not my burden to carry," he reminded himself as consciousness slipped away. But even as he thought about it, some deeper part of him recognized its futility. On the Oregon Trail, all paths eventually converged, all burdens became shared, and all lives intertwined in ways both expected and surprising.

And there was still a very long way to go.

Chapter 8

The Kansas River stretched before them, a churning mass of muddy water swollen by spring rains. Emily clutched the side of the Holloway wagon, watching the first team of oxen struggle against the powerful current midstream. The animals' breaths puffed white in the cool air, their massive shoulders straining forward as men shouted and urged them on.

"The Lord tests us in many ways," Reverend Holloway murmured, his weathered face grim as he surveyed the crossing point. "This river's running higher than I've seen in years."

Emily remained silent, her throat tight. The men had chosen the shallowest point for crossing, but the recent rains had transformed the river into a treacherous barrier. She watched another wagon lurch into the murky water, wheels disappearing beneath the surface, the driver standing tall, calling commands that were half-swallowed by the river's constant voice.

"Mercy, you and Mrs. Wilson remain seated and hold tight," Reverend Holloway instructed his wife, climbing down to check the harnesses one final time.

Mercy nodded, her thin fingers intertwining with Emily's, squeezing gently. "The Lord sees us through all waters, deep or shallow," she said, though the tremor in her voice belied her composed words.

Emily managed a tight nod but didn't return the pressure. The river before them looked unstoppable, indifferent, and merciless. She fixed her gaze on the far bank, where people who had successfully crossed milled about, their faces reflecting relief and encouragement.

"Weston is having each wagon spaced well apart," Reverend Holloway commented, gesturing toward the tall figure directing traffic at the water's edge. "Smart precaution."

Emily's eyes found Weston, standing knee-deep in the shallows, the water darkening his trousers. He gestured with clear authority, his voice carrying across the commotion as he directed the order of the crossing. His young son waited behind him on the bank, clutching Martha Croft's hand, his small face solemn.

"Reverend!" Weston's voice cut through the din. "You're next. Stay right of that large branch caught midstream. The water's deeper than it looks, about twenty feet in."

The reverend acknowledged with a raised hand, then climbed up to the wagon seat, taking the reins from his wife. Emily felt the wagon shift as he settled beside them.

"Mrs. Wilson, secure your medical bag," he suggested, nodding at the leather satchel beside her feet. "Everything's likely to get jostled—or worse."

Emily pulled the satchel closer, her fingers curling protectively around its worn leather handle. Inside were her instruments, her remedies—the tools of her calling, now seemingly irrelevant to her empty life. Yet, she couldn't bear to part with them. They were the last remnants of the woman she had been, the healer, the one who fought against death instead of welcoming its shadow.

The wagon lurched forward, and Emily gripped the wooden seat, her knuckles white. The oxen stepped into the water reluctantly, their massive heads lowered as if sensing the danger. The wagon tilted slightly as the front wheels dipped into the river, and a coldness that had nothing to do with the water crept up Emily's spine.

At first, the crossing seemed manageable. The water rose around the wheels, splashing against the undercarriage, but the oxen moved steadily, following the path Weston had indicated. Emily's gaze fixed on the opposite bank, counting each foot of progress, each second that passed.

Halfway across, the current grew stronger. The wagon creaked ominously as it pushed against the water's force. Through the floorboards, Emily felt the vibration of the river's power, and saw the water rising higher around the oxen's legs. Mercy murmured prayers under her breath, a continuous stream of words Emily could barely discern over the rush of water.

Then came the sickening lurch. The right front wheel dropped suddenly into an unseen hole, and the wagon tilted sharply. Emily heard Reverend Holloway shout, saw him pull hard on the reins, trying to correct their course. The oxen bellowed in confusion, the water now high on their flanks.

"Hold on!" he yelled, reaching out to steady his wife as the wagon continued to tilt.

Emily braced herself against the seat, heart pounding. Water splashed over the side of the wagon bed, cold and shocking against her skirts. She heard shouts from the bank, saw figures wading toward them.

Another violent jerk. The wagon tilted further, caught in the current's grip. Emily heard the horrifying crack of wood giving way.

The world upended.

Cold. Shocking, consuming cold enveloped her as the river closed over her head. The water's roar filled her ears, mud, and silt blinding her. Her heavy skirts dragged her downward, the current tumbling her like a leaf. For a moment, Emily wondered if this was her end—if the river had come to claim. A strange peace washed over her at the thought.

Then her body betrayed her mind's surrender. Her lungs burned for air, her limbs fought against the weight of her clothes. She kicked hard, pushed against the muddy riverbed, and broke the surface with a desperate gasp. Water streamed from her face as she blinked rapidly, trying to orient herself in the chaos.

The wagon lay on its side, half-submerged, the canvas cover torn and sagging into the water. The oxen thrashed in their harnesses, eyes wild with panic. All around was shouting, splashing, and the sound of wood splintering further. Through the haze of water in her eyes, Emily saw Mercy's pale blue dress a few yards downstream, the woman's arms flailing.

Emily drove her body toward the struggling figure. Her waterlogged skirts hampered every movement, but she pushed through the current, reaching Mercy just as the older woman went under again. Emily's fingers caught the fabric of her dress, pulled upward with strength born of desperation.

"I've got you," she gasped as Mercy's head emerged, the woman coughing and sputtering. "Keep your head up. Don't fight the water."

Emily caught a glimpse of men wading toward them—Weston among them, his tall form cutting through the water with powerful strokes. Behind him, others were attending to the overturned wagon, to Reverend Holloway, who clung to the side, and to the panicked oxen.

"This way," Emily directed, guiding Mercy toward the closest bank, working with the current rather than against it. Her trained mind had taken over completely, the part of her that had spent years learning to stay calm in crises, to prioritize, and to act rather than hesitate. "Small steps. The bottom's uneven."

Mercy coughed violently but nodded, leaning heavily against Emily as they staggered toward the shallower water. Emily felt something solid strike her leg, a branch or piece of debris, and stumbled, nearly losing her grip on the older woman. Then strong hands were there, supporting them both.

"I've got her, Mrs. Wilson," Weston said, his voice steady despite the surrounding crisis. His eyes met Emily's for a brief second, sharp, assessing, and surprisingly warm, with something like approval or recognition. "Can you make it to shore?"

Emily nodded, releasing Mercy into his more capable strength. She struggled toward the bank, where willing hands reached to pull her up onto muddy ground. Her legs trembled violently, the sudden rush of energy already waning, leaving cold shock in its place.

"The reverend?" she asked, turning back toward the river.

"They're bringing him in," Silas replied, his face grim. "He's had a bad knock to the head, but he's conscious."

Emily's gaze swept the chaotic scene, her midwife's instincts cataloging needs, assessing priorities. "Who else is hurt?" she asked, pushing sodden hair from her face. Water streamed from her clothes, forming muddy puddles at her feet.

"Jacob Miller's got a gash on his arm from trying to cut the oxen loose," Martha reported, appearing at her side with a blanket that she wrapped around Emily's shoulders. "And Lavinia is in a state, though not injured. Terrified of the water, poor thing."

Emily nodded, her mind clearing as purpose overtook the shock. "My satchel," she said, scanning the riverbank, the debris being hauled to shore. "I need my medical bag."

"Is this it?" A young man held up the leather satchel, miraculously intact though dripping wet. "Was caught against the wagon wheel."

Emily took it with trembling hands, relief washing through her. "Thank you," she said, already moving toward where Reverend Holloway was being helped up the bank, blood streaming from a cut above his temple.

The next hour passed in a blur of activity. Emily moved from one patient to the next, her movements efficient despite her sodden clothing and the mud that caked her hem. She cleaned and bandaged the reverend's head wound, determining it wasn't as serious as the blood initially suggested. She stitched Jacob Miller's arm with neat, tight sutures from her satchel, using a thread that had somehow stayed dry in its oilcloth wrapping.

"Hold still," she instructed Jacob, as he winced. "Nearly finished."

"You've a steady hand, ma'am," he said, watching her work. "Better than the barber who stitched my brother after a fight in St. Louis."

Emily tied off the final suture, her focus unwavering. "Keep it clean. Change the bandage daily."

She moved to Lavinia next, giving her a few drops of valerian tincture to calm her near-hysteria, speaking in the low, soothing tones she'd used with frightened mothers in labor.

"Breathe slowly," she instructed, counting breaths with the young woman. "In... out... that's right."

Throughout it all, Emily remained keenly aware of Weston directing the larger recovery effort. His commanding voice cut through the confusion, organizing teams to salvage what they could from the overturned wagon, to secure the oxen, and to clear debris that might hamper the remaining wagons' crossing.

"Blankets," she directed a hovering young girl—one of the Billings children, she thought. "As many dry ones as can be spared. And hot water, if anyone has a fire going yet." The girl nodded eagerly and darted off.

Emily knelt beside Sarah Finch, who sat pale and trembling with her infant clutched to her chest. Both were soaked through, the baby whimpering softly. Sarah's husband had succumbed to fever just days before joining the wagon train, leaving her a young widow with a newborn. The sight of her, clutching her child with the raw desperation of recent grief, struck Emily like a physical blow.

"I should stay away from them," a voice whispered in the back of Emily's mind. *"My presence only brings death. I survived when they all died. What if I'm the curse?"*

She pushed the thought away, focusing instead on the immediate need.

"Let me see her," Emily said gently, holding out her hands for the child.

Sarah hesitated, her arms tightening around the bundle. "She's fine," she whispered. "Just cold. I kept her head above water."

Emily nodded, understanding the young mother's fierce protectiveness. "You did well," she assured her. "But we need to get you both dry and warm. May I help?"

After a moment, Sarah reluctantly loosened her grip, allowing Emily to examine the infant. The baby was indeed chilled but seemed otherwise unharmed, her cries healthy and strong. Emily wrapped her in a dry blanket that Martha provided, then helped Sarah change into dry clothes behind a hastily erected screen of blankets.

As she worked, Emily caught herself thinking of her younger sisters, Mary and Margaret. Emily had tended them both day and night, using every skill she possessed, every remedy she knew. It hadn't been enough. The memory of their graves, beside her parents', stabbed at her heart.

It was only as the immediate crisis began to subside that Emily felt the full impact of what had happened. Her legs suddenly weak, she sank onto a fallen log, her medical satchel clutched in her lap. Now that her hands weren't occupied with tasks, they began to shake violently. The cold of her wet clothing seeped into her bones, and she huddled into the blanket draped around her shoulders.

Around her, the camp was a scene of controlled chaos. Those who had crossed safely before the accident were setting up temporary shelters, building fires for warmth and drying. Those still on the far bank would have to wait until tomorrow, with the salvage effort and approaching dusk, making further crossings too dangerous.

Emily looked toward where the Holloway wagon lay, broken beyond repair in the shallows. Men were still working to drag it fully to shore, but even from here, she could see the extent of the damage—the shattered wheel, the broken axle, and the torn canvas. Most of the Holloway's‘ possessions that hadn't been swept downstream were ruined by water.

"Here, Mrs. Wilson." Mercy appeared beside her, holding out a steaming cup. Her hair hung in damp strands around her pale face, but her eyes were kind. "Mr. Hodge managed to get a fire going and made tea. It'll warm you some."

Emily accepted the cup with murmured thanks, wrapping her cold fingers around its welcome heat. "How is the reverend?" she asked.

"Resting." Mercy settled beside her on the log with a weary sigh. "That's a neat bit of stitching you did on his forehead."

"My midwife skills came in handy."

Mercy nodded, as if this confirmed something she'd suspected. "You have healing hands," she said simply. "The Lord blessed many through your skills today."

Emily looked away, unable to bear the warmth in the older woman's eyes. *The Lord did not bless my family despite my skills,* she thought bitterly. *"He took them one by one while I watched, helpless. What kind of blessing is that?"* Her hands, supposedly gifted for healing, had been useless against the typhoid that ravaged her home.

They sat in silence for a time, sipping hot tea. The sky was darkening, the day's drama giving way to the pressing practical concerns of the night and the journey ahead.

"Mrs. Wilson," Mercy finally said, her voice gentle but direct. "There's a matter we must discuss."

Emily turned to her, noting the distress in the woman's eyes.

"Our wagon..." Mercy gestured helplessly toward the river. "Everything we had was in it. The reverend and I... we've been offered shelter in the Finch's wagon for tonight, but..." She hesitated, clearly uncomfortable.

"But there's no room for me," Emily finished for her, the realization settling like a stone in her stomach. She had been a charity case for the Holloway's to begin with—a solitary woman paying a modest fee for passage in their wagon. Now, with their situation dire, that arrangement was impossible.

Mercy reached for her hand, squeezing it apologetically. "If there was any other way—"

"I understand." Emily withdrew her hand gently, not out of unkindness, but because she couldn't bear the woman's compassion. "You have nothing to apologize for."

"The reverend is speaking with Weston now," Mercy continued, "to see if—"

"Mrs. Holloway." Weston's deep voice interrupted her, and both women looked up. He stood before them, still damp from the river, and mud caking his boots. His face was composed, yet somehow troubled. Behind him, Emily could see Reverend Holloway sitting by a fire, his head bandaged, speaking with Silas.

"Ma'am," Weston said, nodding respectfully to Mercy. "The reverend asked me to let you know the Finch's have made space in their wagon." He hesitated, his eyes flicking to Emily. "He also mentioned your... situation."

Emily felt her spine stiffen, her chin lifting slightly. She had expected to be the subject of discussion, of course—a woman alone on the frontier was always a problem to be solved, a responsibility to be assigned—but the reality of it stung, nonetheless.

"If you'll excuse me," Mercy said, rising with surprising quickness. "I should see to my husband." She touched Emily's shoulder briefly, a silent communication of regret and concern, then moved away, leaving Emily alone with the wagon master.

Weston shifted his weight, clearly uncomfortable with the conversation ahead. "Mrs. Wilson," he began, his voice low and private, "the reverend explained—"

"That I'm without a wagon," Emily interrupted, her voice carefully controlled. "Yes. I'm aware."

"Yes," he said. "And as wagon master, it falls to me to—"

"To find a solution," she finished again, unable to bear being talked about like a piece of misplaced luggage. She rose from the log, clutching her medical satchel and the blanket around her shoulders. Though soaked and bedraggled, she managed a semblance of dignity. "I understand, Mr. Reynolds. Perhaps one of the families with children could use an extra pair of hands."

His expression shifted, and Emily realized belatedly how dismissive she had sounded. This man was responsible for the safety and progress of dozens of people; he didn't need her making his job more difficult with pride when she was in no position to afford it.

"I apologize," she said, more softly. "I'm... not at my best."

Weston studied her for a long moment, his blue eyes unreadable in the fading light. "Few of us are, after a day like this," he said. "The river took a toll on everyone." He glanced around the makeshift camp, where families huddled by fires, taking stock of what was saved and what was lost. "As for your situation... I have a proposition."

Emily tensed, waiting.

"There's room in my wagon," he said, the words coming reluctantly, as if dragged from some deep reserve. "It's not spacious, with Matthew and me and all our things, but it's dry, and there's room for your belongings."

Emily stared at him, caught completely off guard. Of all the solutions she had imagined, this was the last she expected. Weston Reynolds, the rugged, efficient wagon master, offering to share his private space? With her?

"I—I couldn't impose," she stammered.

"It's not an imposition," he replied, though his tone and the tightness around his mouth suggested it was exactly that. "It's a practical solution. You need a wagon. Mine has space." He paused, then added with unmistakable reluctance, "And Matthew... would likely appreciate the company."

The mention of his son shifted something in Emily's perception. She glanced toward where the boy sat near a fire, watching the adults with solemn eyes. Since joining the wagon train, she had kept herself separate from the children, unable to bear their innocent joy, and their reminder of the future she would never have. But Matthew had a quiet way about him that was different, less exuberant, and more watchful.

"This is a temporary arrangement," Weston continued, his voice dropping lower, almost warning. "Until we reach the next major settlement, where you might find other traveling companions, or until the Holloway's can acquire another wagon."

Emily understood what he was offering—not charity, but a practical, temporary solution to a logistical problem. Nothing more. It was precisely what she should want—a way forward without entanglement.

Yet, the thought of such close proximity, of sharing daily life with this man and his son, sent a jolt of fear through her. Her isolation had been her shield against further pain, her distance from others in a carefully constructed fortress. In the confined space of a wagon, there would be no such barriers. No place to hide when the nightmares came, or when the grief crushed her chest in the dark hours before dawn.

"Mrs. Wilson?" Weston prompted, his expression growing impatient. "I don't mean to rush you, but we've a camp to organize, and daylight's fading."

Emily glanced around the riverbank, at the fragments of lives scattered by the water's force. She had no choice, and they both knew it. Without a wagon, she was stranded—unable to continue the journey, and unable to return. Her path forward lay in accepting this uncomfortable arrangement.

"Thank you," she said quietly, the words difficult to form. "I accept your offer."

Weston nodded once, brisk and businesslike. "Good. We'll need to see what can be salvaged from your belongings." His gaze fell to the satchel she still clutched. "At least you've kept hold of your medical bag. Saw your work with the injured. Good, quick stitching on Miller's arm."

The unexpected comment caught Emily off guard. It wasn't effusive praise, but from the rugged wagon master, it felt significant.

"I..." She hesitated, then straightened her shoulders slightly. "I was trained by and worked hours beside a skilled physician."

He nodded, unsurprised. "That's valuable knowledge on the trail. Too valuable to lose if you'd been swept downstream."

It was a practical assessment, not a sentimental one, yet Emily felt an unexpected warmth at the acknowledgment of her skills.

"The salvage team pulled some trunks from the wagon," Weston continued. "They're laid out near the large oak. You should check if yours is among them while there's still light. I'll have Matthew help you carry what's yours to our wagon." He paused, his jaw tightening almost imperceptibly. "Which isn't much farther, just beyond that rise."

He pointed to a small hill where several wagons had already formed a rough circle for the night. Emily could just make out his wagon, slightly larger than most, its canvas cover a shade darker, its wooden sides sturdy and well-maintained.

"I'll see to my things," she said, forcing herself to focus on the practical task ahead rather than the implications of this new arrangement.

Weston nodded again and turned to go, then hesitated. "Mrs. Wilson," he said, his voice lower, for her ears alone. "I know this isn't what either of us would choose. But the trail doesn't often give us the luxury of choice."

The simple truth of his statement resonated deeply. The trail, like grief, forced paths upon you that you would never willingly take.

"No," she agreed softly. "It doesn't."

He held her gaze a moment longer, something unreadable passing through his eyes—a shadow of remembered pain, or perhaps recognition of her own—then turned and strode away toward where men were still working to secure the remaining wagons for the night.

Emily stood alone, the blanket clutched around her shoulders, her satchel heavy in her hands. The reality of what had just transpired washed over her—her near-drowning, the loss of the Holloway wagon, and her unexpected role in treating the injured, and now, this arrangement that would place her in daily, inescapable proximity with Weston Reynolds and his son.

"Mrs. Wilson?" A small voice startled her from her thoughts.

Matthew Reynolds stood a few feet away, watching her with solemn eyes that seemed too old for his young face. "Pa said I should help you find your things," he said, twisting his small hands in the fabric of his shirt, which was still damp from the river's spray though he hadn't been in it.

Emily stared at the child, feeling her chest tighten. He was so small, so vulnerable, and yet there was a quiet strength in his stance that reminded her forcibly of his father.

"Yes," she said, finding her voice. "Thank you, Matthew. That's very kind."

He nodded seriously, as if accepting an important mission. "Pa says we need to hurry 'fore it gets dark. Says you'll be staying in our wagon now." He tilted his head slightly. "Is that true?"

Emily swallowed against the lump in her throat. "Yes," she said. "It seems I will be."

Matthew considered this, his small face thoughtful. Then, unexpectedly, he offered his hand to her. "It's this way," he said, gesturing toward the oak tree Weston had mentioned. "I'll show you."

Emily hesitated, staring at the child's outstretched hand. Something about the simple gesture—so innocent, so trusting—threatened to crack the carefully constructed walls around her heart.

But refusing would hurt him, this small boy who offered kindness without reservation. And she had caused enough hurt in the world already, simply by surviving when others had not.

Slowly, her hand trembling slightly, Emily reached out and placed her fingers in Matthew's small grasp.

"Thank you," she said softly. "Lead the way."

Together, they walked across the muddy riverbank, toward the oak tree where salvaged trunks and belongings lay in haphazard rows. The sun was setting behind the distant hills, casting long shadows across the makeshift camp. All around them, people worked to create order from the day's chaos, setting up shelters, building fires, and tending to livestock.

Emily's two trunks had indeed been recovered, though one had been partially crushed in the accident. The other, which contained most of her clothing and personal items, was intact though sodden. Matthew insisted on dragging the larger one himself, his small face determined despite the trunk being nearly as big as he was.

"I can manage," he insisted when Emily tried to help. "Pa says I'm strong for my age."

Emily relented, carrying her medical satchel and the smaller, damaged trunk. They made slow progress toward Weston's wagon, the mud sucking at their feet, exhaustion weighing every step.

As they crested the small rise, Emily saw Weston standing beside his wagon, deep in conversation with Silas. He looked up as they approached, his expression shifting subtly at the sight of his son dragging the heavy trunk.

"That's too big for you, Matthew," he said, moving quickly to take it from the boy.

"I'm helping Mrs. Wilson," Matthew said proudly, reluctant to relinquish his burden.

A flicker of tenderness crossed Weston's face, so briefly Emily might have imagined it. "So I see," he said, his voice gentler than Emily had heard it before. "And doing a fine job of it. But let me take over now."

Matthew surrendered the trunk with obvious reluctance, and Weston lifted it easily, carrying it to the back of the wagon. Emily followed, feeling increasingly out of place, an intruder in this small family unit.

"We'll put your things here," Weston said, gesturing to a small space near the rear of the wagon bed. "It's not much room, but it should suffice."

Emily nodded, unable to find words.

"Thank you," she managed, as Weston took the damaged trunk from her arms and placed it alongside the other. "For... all of this."

He straightened, regarding her with those keen blue eyes. "You've had a difficult day," he said gruffly. "Get some rest. We'll sort out the arrangements more thoroughly tomorrow."

Emily nodded again, feeling the full weight of the day's events crashing down upon her. She was soaked, exhausted, and emotionally drained. Yet, the thought of climbing into this wagon, of laying her head down in this unfamiliar space, surrounded by these strangers who were suddenly thrust into her daily existence, was almost too much to bear.

"Pa," Matthew said, tugging at his father's sleeve. "Mrs. Wilson saved people in the river. I saw her. She pulled Mrs. Holloway out, and she fixed the reverend's head, and she made Baby Hope stop crying when she was all wet and cold."

Weston looked down at his son, then back at Emily, his expression softening almost imperceptibly. "Yes, she did good work today."

The simple acknowledgment, free from effusive praise or sentimentality, touched something in Emily that more florid compliments would have missed.

"There's a tent set up behind the wagon," Weston continued, gesturing to a small canvas shelter. "For changing. Martha brought over some dry clothes she thought might fit you until yours can be dried."

Emily glanced toward the tent, then back at Weston, struck by the unexpected consideration. "Thank you," she said again, the words seeming inadequate for all they were meant to convey.

He nodded once, then turned to his son. "Matthew, help me check on the oxen. Mrs. Wilson needs some peace."

The boy looked momentarily disappointed but obeyed, following his father toward where their oxen were tethered nearby. Emily watched them go—the tall, broad-shouldered man and the small boy who matched his stride despite his short legs—feeling a strange tightness in her chest.

Instead of dwelling on it, she turned toward the tent, her sodden skirts heavy around her ankles, her hair hanging in damp tendrils around her face. One step at a time, she told herself. Change into dry clothes. Find a moment's quiet. Face tomorrow when it came.

Yet as she ducked into the tent, seeing the simple dress laid out for her, a practical, serviceable garment, not unlike her own, Emily felt her carefully constructed facade begin to crack. The events of the day, the terror of the river, the loss of what little stability she had found with the Holloway's, the prospect of this new, unwanted intimacy with the Reynolds... it all converged in a wave of emotion too powerful to contain.

For the first time since locking her empty home in Richmond, Emily Grace Wilson allowed herself to weep. Silent, shuddering sobs wracked her body as she sank to her knees on the tent floor, her face buried in her hands. She wept for the family she had lost, for the life she could never reclaim, and for the barriers she had built that the river had so easily swept away. She wept for the terror of proximity to a small boy she already feared losing, for the awareness in Weston's eyes that seemed to see through her carefully maintained distance.

And beneath it all, barely acknowledged even to herself, was a tremor of the unsettling recognition that despite her best efforts to remain untouched, today had changed her. The river had pulled her back into the world of the living, where hands reached out to pull you to safety, where small boys offered to carry your burdens, and where gruff wagon masters made room in their carefully ordered lives.

It was terrifying. It was unwanted. It was, perhaps, inevitable. There was no turning back.

Chapter 9

The wagon lurched as a wheel dropped into an unseen hole, causing a shift in the trunks and barrels inside. The sudden movement sent Matthew toppling from his spot on the narrow bench. Weston reached for his son, but his hand connected instead with the thin arm of the woman who now shared their confined quarters.

Emily had caught Matthew with surprising quickness, her hands steadying the boy before he tumbled face-first onto the wooden floor.

"Careful there," she murmured, helping Matthew right himself before withdrawing her touch as if the contact had burned her.

"Thank you," Weston said, the words feeling stiff on his tongue. Four days since the river disaster that had claimed the Holloway wagon, and conversation still came in awkward bursts, each syllable like a pebble dropped into the vast silence that stretched between them.

The interior of the wagon had already been a cramped space, packed with the essentials of their journey—sacks of flour and beans, a barrel of water, tools and supplies, their bedrolls and personal items. But with Emily's two trunks added, it felt positively claustrophobic. What had once been Weston's private domain now carried the unsettling presence of a woman's belongings.

She seemed determined to become invisible, to fold herself into nothing, as if to apologize for the necessity of her existence. Yet despite her efforts, Weston found himself acutely aware of her, the rustle of her skirts when she shifted position, the rhythm of her breathing as she slept. The way she stared out at the passing landscape with eyes that seemed to look through it rather than at it.

Matthew, for his part, had adapted to Emily's presence with the easy resilience of a child. After an initial shyness, he'd begun to regard her with open curiosity, stealing glances at her when he thought no one was looking.

"Pa, how much further till we stop?" Matthew asked, brushing dust from his trousers. His sandy colored hair, so like his mother's, had grown too long, curling slightly at the nape of his neck. Weston made a mental note to trim it at the next extended rest.

"Another hour, maybe two," Weston replied, keeping a steady grip on the reins as the oxen plodded onward. "We'll make camp before sundown."

The landscape stretched before them, an endless ocean of prairie grass rippling in the wind. Behind them, the wagons created a meandering line across the vastness, white canvas tops like ships on a green sea. Spring had turned the plains vibrant, though Weston knew the lushness would fade as summer approached, and the relentless sun scorched the land.

He felt rather than saw Emily straighten behind him, adjusting her position on the hard bench. She'd refused his offer of an extra blanket for cushioning, accepting only the barest necessities with polite, distant thanks that made it clear she considered herself a temporary burden, nothing more.

"Miss Emily, look!" Matthew's voice broke through Weston's thoughts, the boy's excitement momentarily dissolving the thick atmosphere inside the wagon. "I found this yesterday when Pa let me walk. Isn't it nice?"

Weston glanced to see his son proudly extending his palm toward Emily. In it rested a smooth, oval stone, ordinary in every way except that it bore a faint pattern of lighter coloring that vaguely resembled a face.

Emily hesitated, tension visible in the set of her shoulders, before leaning slightly to inspect the boy's treasure.

"It does look rather like a face," she said. "A sleeping face, perhaps."

Matthew beamed, clearly pleased with her response. "I have more treasures! Want to see?"

Without waiting for an answer, he scrambled toward his small wooden box of belongings on the floorboard, nearly toppling again in his eagerness. Weston prepared to intervene, not wanting Matthew to overwhelm their reluctant guest, but something in Emily's face stopped him—a fleeting softness around her eyes, there and gone so quickly he might have imagined it.

"Careful, Matthew," was all he said instead. "Remember, Miss Wilson needs her space."

"It's alright. I don't mind."

The wagon hit another bump, and Weston returned his attention to the trail ahead. He silently asked for patience and wisdom—leading a wagon train was challenge enough without the complications of a grieving woman sharing their cramped quarters. He'd grown used to solitude with Matthew, their routine as familiar as breathing. Now every movement required careful consideration, every word weighed for its effect.

Behind him, Matthew continued his eager show-and-tell, his childish voice rising with excitement. "This feather came from a blue jay. And see this button? Pa says it belonged to a soldier."

Weston listened with half an ear as his son displayed his modest collection of trail treasures. Matthew had always been like this, finding wonder in ordinary objects, and seeing value where others saw nothing remarkable. It was a quality Weston treasured in his son, a reminder of innocence preserved despite their difficult circumstances.

"And this one's my favorite," Matthew was saying. "It's smooth because the river made it that way. Water can make rough things smooth, Pa says."

"Your father is very knowledgeable," Emily replied.

"Pa knows everything about the trail," Matthew declared with a child's absolute faith. "He can find north without seeing the sun, and he knows which plants we can eat and which one's make you sick."

Weston shook his head slightly, humbled by his son's unwavering confidence. Lord, help me live up to his trust, he prayed silently. The responsibility of being Matthew's sole parent weighed heavily at times, each decision carrying the burden of being both mother and father to this small, trusting soul.

"Do you know things too, Miss Emily?" Matthew asked, his natural curiosity undimmed by her reserve.

"I know some things. About medicine and helping people who are sick or hurt."

"Like when you helped Reverend Holloway after the river?"

"Yes, like that."

"Were you always a doctor?"

"I'm not exactly a doctor," she corrected gently. "I'm a midwife. I help when babies are born, and I know how to treat common ailments."

"What's a common ailment?"

Despite himself, Weston felt his mouth curve upward at his son's endless questions. Yet, Emily was answering each inquiry with surprising patience, her voice gradually losing some of its tight restraint.

He found himself trying to reconcile this Emily—the one who caught Matthew with quick reflexes, who patiently answered his questions, and whose voice softened when speaking to him—with the hollow-eyed woman he'd first observed in Independence. That woman had seemed barely present in her own body, moving through the world like a ghost. This woman, though still clearly wounded, showed brief flashes of something else—competence, patience, and a hint of warmth beneath the frost of grief.

The oxen lowed as they crested a small rise, and Weston noticed dark clouds gathering on the distant horizon. They'd need to make camp earlier than planned if those clouds continued their advance. Rain on the trail meant mud, difficult oxen, and the misery of damp clothing and bedding.

"Pa, Miss Emily says she can tell which plants help headaches," Matthew reported eagerly. "And she knows how to fix a broken arm!"

"Is that so?" Weston replied, echoing Emily's earlier response. "That's good knowledge to have on the trail."

"Yes, Mr. Reynolds, it is," Emily said. "Though I pray my skills won't be needed often."

"Amen to that," Weston agreed. He wondered about the state of Emily's faith, given the loss she'd suffered. His own had been severely tested after Susannah's death, anger, and resentment threatening to overwhelm his belief in God's goodness. Only time, prayer, and the immediate needs of a newborn son had gradually restored his trust, though it had emerged different—less certain, perhaps, but deeper, more reliant on God's presence even when His plan seemed incomprehensible.

The afternoon wore on, the wagon's rhythmic creaking a constant backdrop to Matthew's chatter, which gradually slowed as the day's excitement and the gentle rocking motion lulled him toward drowsiness. Weston felt a familiar surge of love as he watched his son's eyelids grow heavy, fighting sleep as any child does.

"Why don't you rest a while, son?" he suggested. "We've got some time before we make camp."

Matthew nodded sleepily but looked at Emily instead of settling into his usual spot. "Miss Emily, could you tell me a story? Pa sometimes tells me stories when I'm tired."

"I'm afraid I don't know many stories," she said, her voice tight again.

But Matthew wasn't easily deterred. His gaze had settled on Emily's medical satchel on the floorboard, specifically the ornate family Bible peeking out. While airing her clothes and wet belongings out, she had tucked the Bible in her satchel for safe keeping.

"You could read from your Bible," he suggested, his expression brightening. "Like Pa and Reverend Holloway do."

The silence that followed was so complete that even the creaking of the wagon seemed muffled. Weston turned slightly, catching sight of Emily's face. The color had drained from it, leaving her complexion ashen beneath her sun-flushed cheeks. Her eyes, fixed on the Bible, held a look so raw that Weston felt like an intruder witnessing something deeply private.

"Matthew," he began, ready to redirect his son's attention, but Emily spoke first.

"I haven't read from it in... some time," she said, her voice barely audible above the wagon's sounds.

Matthew simply nodded. "That's alright. My prayer book is small, but you can use it instead if you want."

Weston watched as Emily seemed to wage some internal battle, her gaze never leaving the Bible. Then she reached for the heavy book.

"No," she said quietly. "I can... I can read from this one."

Her hands trembled slightly as she lifted the Bible, its worn leather cover speaking of years of use before it had been closed and carried unused across half a continent. She balanced it on her lap, her fingers running over the embossed cover as if it held memories within its textured surface.

Matthew fell quiet. Even the oxen seemed to move with less jarring steps as Emily slowly opened the Bible, the pages rustling with a sound like dry leaves.

She stared down at the text for a long moment; her face was a mask of complicated emotions that Weston couldn't begin to fully comprehend.

"The Lord is my shepherd," she began, her voice unsteady. "I shall not want."

The familiar words of the Twenty-Third Psalm filled the small space of the wagon. Matthew leaned against the wooden slats, his eyes fixed on Emily, drinking in the ancient promises with the simple trust of childhood. But Weston found his gaze drawn not to the words but to the woman reading them and the visible effort each phrase cost her, the way her voice caught on certain lines as if they scraped against raw places in her soul.

"Yea, though I walk through the valley of the shadow of death, I will fear no evil..."

Emily faltered here, the words dying on her lips. For a terrible moment, Weston thought she might break down completely, but with a deep breath that seemed to draw on her last reserves of strength, she continued.

"For thou art with me; thy rod and thy staff, they comfort me."

The rest of the psalm came in a near whisper. The final words—"I will dwell in the house of the Lord forever"—spoken with such complexity of emotion that Weston felt like an intruder on a deeply personal confession.

When she finished, silence fell again, broken only by the constant sounds of the journey—the creak of wood, the jingle of the harnesses, and the distant lowing of cattle from further back in the train. Matthew's eyes had closed. The boy finally succumbing to sleep, his small chest rising and falling in the peaceful rhythm of childhood rest.

Emily closed the Bible and held it for a moment before placing it back among her belongings, her thin fingers lingering on its cover.

"Thank you," Weston said, not wanting to wake Matthew.

Emily glanced up, seemingly startled to find him watching her. Their eyes met across the small space, and Weston was struck by the depth of sorrow in her gaze.

"He's a good boy," she said, her voice steadier now as she nodded toward the sleeping Matthew. "You've raised him well."

"I've done my best," he replied. "It hasn't always been... easy, without his mother."

Her expression shifted, a flicker of pain crossing her features before she looked away.

"I'm sorry," she said simply.

"It was six years ago," Weston said. "Matthew was just born."

Emily nodded, her gaze fixed on something in the distance. "The Holloway's mentioned it. That you were widowed."

"They told me about your loss as well," he said carefully, watching her face. "I'm sorry for it."

Emily's expression closed like a door shutting. "Thank you," she said, the words clipped and final.

Weston didn't press further. He recognized the boundaries of pain, the territories of grief that no one could enter uninvited.

The wagon train continued its slow progress across the prairie, the miles marked by the rhythmic creak and sway that had become the soundtrack of their journey. Weston kept his attention on the trail, but his thoughts remained on the woman sharing his space, on the visible struggle she'd endured to read a simple psalm, and on the depth of pain glimpsed in that unguarded moment.

"Lord, she carries so much," he prayed silently. "Whatever You have in mind bringing her to our wagon, give me wisdom to handle it rightly."

Chapter 10

As the afternoon wore on, the clouds on the horizon darkened and expanded, promising rain before night. Weston assessed their position and the weather's approach, calculating whether they should push on or make an early camp.

"We'll set up camp at the next creek," he said. "Should reach it within the hour. Better to be settled before that rain hits."

When no response came, he glanced over to find Emily had dozed off, her features somewhat softened in sleep. Something about her vulnerability in that moment stirred an unexpected feeling of protectiveness in Weston's chest.

The emotion caught him off guard, its intensity surprising. He'd felt responsible for his passengers since the day they'd left Independence, but this was different—less the duty of a wagon master and more the concern of a man for a fellow traveler in pain. The distinction troubled him, its implications unwelcome. Emily Wilson was his passenger, a responsibility, nothing more. Once they reached Oregon, their paths would diverge, and the brief intersection of their lives would be nothing but a memory.

The wagon hit another rut, and Emily startled awake, her eyes darting around in momentary confusion before settling on Weston's back.

"I apologize," she said, smoothing her skirts with embarrassed haste. "I didn't mean to fall asleep."

"No need for apologies," Weston replied, keeping his voice low to avoid waking Matthew. "The trail takes a toll on everyone. Rest when you can."

Emily shifted on the bench, wincing slightly as she stretched her stiff limbs. "How much farther today?"

"Not far. There's a creek ahead where we'll make camp. Good water, decent protection from the wind." He gestured toward the gathering clouds. "Rain's coming."

Emily followed his gaze to the darkening sky. "The Holloway's mentioned you have an uncanny ability to read weather."

Weston shrugged. "Just experience. You spend enough time out here, you learn to read the signs."

A particularly strong gust of wind swept across the prairie, causing the canvas top behind them to flutter. Matthew stirred but didn't wake, his small body somehow finding comfortable rest despite the wagon's constant movement.

Weston reached for the canteen he kept ready. "Would you like some water?"

Emily hesitated, then nodded. "Thank you."

Their fingers brushed briefly during the exchange, and he noted how cool her hands were despite the warm afternoon.

"You should have a blanket for your shoulders when the rain comes," he said, more gruffly than he'd intended. "The temperature drops fast out here."

"I'll manage," she replied, but the stubborn independence in her tone was belied by the slight tremor in her hands as she sipped the water.

Weston reached under his seat and pulled out a worn wool blanket, passing it to her without meeting her gaze. "No sense in catching a chill. We're still weeks from Oregon."

"Thank you." After a moment's hesitation, she added, "You've been very kind. The Holloway's as well. I'm... grateful."

There was something in the way she said it, as if kindness were a language she'd once been fluent in but had forgotten how to speak, that struck Weston with unexpected force.

"We help each other out here," he said simply, trying to frame his actions as practical trail wisdom rather than individual consideration. "That's the only way to survive the trail."

The creek appeared ahead, a ribbon of silver cutting through the green prairie. Weston signaled to the wagons behind them, indicating they would make camp, and the message passed down the line like a ripple in a pond. The familiar routine of circling the wagons, unhitching the oxen, and setting up camp was the daily rhythm of life on the Oregon Trail.

As the wagon rolled to a stop, Weston turned to Emily. "It'll be busy for a while, getting everything set up before the rain. Matthew can stay with you in the wagon if you'd prefer not to be in the thick of things."

Emily glanced at the sleeping boy, then back to Weston. Something complicated passing across her features. "I can help," she offered hesitantly. "I'm not afraid of work. And I've imposed enough already."

"It's not an imposition," Weston replied, surprised by her offer. "But an extra pair of hands is always welcome."

As he climbed down from the wagon seat, Weston found himself reevaluating his initial assessment of Emily Wilson. He'd seen her as fragile, wrapped in grief so consuming it left little room for anything else. Yet, there had been moments today—her gentle responses to Matthew, her determined reading of the psalm despite the evident pain it caused her, her simple offer of help—that suggested a strength beneath the sorrow. A resilience that grief had dimmed but not extinguished.

The sky rumbled with distant thunder as Weston moved to unhitch the oxen. Around him, the wagon train transformed from a moving caravan to a temporary settlement, each family falling into their accustomed roles with the efficiency born of weeks on the trail.

He glanced back at his wagon to see Emily carefully waking Matthew, her hand hesitant but gentle on the boy's shoulder. His son blinked awake, his sleepy confusion giving way to a bright smile as he recognized who had woken him. The simple, unguarded interaction, a moment he wasn't meant to witness, caught Weston unexpectedly, like a hook somewhere beneath his ribs.

Emily was a passenger, a responsibility, nothing more. But as he watched her help Matthew from the wagon, steadying the boy with a carefulness that spoke of genuine concern, Weston felt something shift in his perception. Something that made his determination to maintain emotional distance suddenly feel less certain than it had that morning.

He turned away, focusing instead on the practicalities of making camp. There was water to fetch, a fire to build, and oxen to tend. Tasks that required no complex emotions, no wrestling with unexpected observations. The wilderness, unlike the human heart, was a territory he knew how to navigate.

The first heavy drops of rain began to fall as the camp settled into its evening routine. Weston secured a canvas tarp over their cooking fire, creating a small dry space where he, Matthew, and now Emily could eat their simple supper protected from the weather.

Matthew chattered happily about the treasures he'd shown Emily earlier, his natural buoyancy a contrast to the adults' more reserved demeanors. He seemed utterly unbothered by the rain pattering on the canvas overhead or the occasional rumble of thunder in the distance.

"Pa, can Miss Emily stay with us forever?" he asked suddenly, the innocent question landing like a stone in still water.

Weston nearly choked on his coffee. "Matthew," he began, searching for the right words, aware of Emily's sudden stillness across the small fire.

"Miss Wilson is traveling to Oregon, just like us," he explained carefully. "She'll have her own plans once we arrive."

"But I like having her with us," Matthew persisted. "She reads nice, and she doesn't mind my treasures."

Weston risked a glance at Emily, expecting embarrassment or discomfort at his son's directness. Instead, he found her gazing at Matthew with an expression so complex it defied simple description—sadness, yes, but mingled with a softness he hadn't seen before, a momentary lowering of the guard she kept so rigidly in place.

"That's very kind of you to say, Matthew," she said, her voice gentle. "But your father is right. Oregon is a big place, and we'll all have different paths to follow when we arrive."

Matthew's face fell slightly, but he nodded, accepting the explanation with the resilience of childhood. "Will you read to me again tomorrow? Pa likes Bible stories too, don't you, Pa?"

Weston cleared his throat. "Yes, I do." He paused, then added carefully, "But only if Miss Wilson feels up to reading."

"I don't mind," she said, though the slight tightening of her jaw suggested otherwise.

The rain intensified, drumming steadily on the canvas above them, creating a cocoon of sound that made their small shelter seem more intimate, more separate from the rest of the camp. Matthew's eyelids began to droop again, the excitement of the day and the rhythm of the rain overwhelming his determination to stay awake.

"Time for bed, son," Weston said, gathering their tin plates. "Say your prayers and then go into the wagon."

Matthew nodded sleepily, folding his small hands in the familiar gesture that never failed to tug at Weston's heart. "Dear God," the boy began, his high, clear voice solemn with the importance of the task, "thank you for this day and for the food and for Pa and Miss Emily and for all the people in our wagon train. Please keep us safe in the rain and help the sun come back tomorrow. And bless Mama in heaven. Amen."

Weston swallowed against the sudden tightness in his throat. Matthew always ended his prayers the same way, a ritual connection to the mother he had never known. Usually, it was a bittersweet moment shared between father and son. Tonight, with Emily's presence, it felt different, more exposed, somehow.

He glanced at Emily, expecting to find her uncomfortable or looking away to give them privacy. Instead, she was watching Matthew with a gentleness that transformed her features, making her look younger, less burdened. When she noticed Weston's gaze, however, her expression shuttering closed.

"That was a lovely prayer, Matthew," she said softly. "I'm sure God heard every word."

Matthew beamed at her approval, stifling a yawn. "Pa says God always listens, even when we don't say things out loud."

"Your father is right," Emily replied.

Weston helped Matthew up and into the wagon, settling the boy on his bedroll, tucking a blanket around his small frame. Within minutes, exhaustion claimed him, his breathing deepening into the peaceful rhythm of sleep.

When Weston returned to the fire, Emily was staring into the flames, her profile outlined in warm light that softened the angles of grief that had etched into her face. The rain continued its steady percussion on the canvas, creating a strange sense of isolation from the rest of the camp, as if they existed in a world of their own, defined by the boundaries of firelight and shelter.

"He's a remarkable child," Emily said without looking up. "So full of trust and joy."

"He is, though he has his difficult days, too. He's just a boy, after all."

"You've done well with him," she said, echoing her earlier compliment. "Especially... alone."

Weston busied himself banking the fire for the night, buying time before he needed to respond.

"I've had help," he finally said. "Friends. The community back home. Reverend Holloway on this journey." He paused, then added, "But yes, there are times when the weight of being both mother and father to him feels... impossible."

Emily nodded, her gaze still fixed on the flames. "I imagine it would."

Silence fell between them. The rain drummed on, and somewhere in the distance, an owl called, its mournful sound carrying through the damp night air.

"The sleeping arrangements..." Emily began, her voice uncertain. "I don't wish to intrude on your space more than necessary, but it would be difficult for either of us to sleep outside tonight without getting soaked."

"I've arranged things," Weston assured her. "Matthew and I will take one side of the wagon. You'll have the other. There's canvas for privacy." He'd spent part of the afternoon mentally reconfiguring their living space in his mind, determined to preserve what dignity and comfort he could for all of them in the confined quarters.

"Thank you," she said simply.

"We should get some rest. Tomorrow will be another long day."

Emily nodded, rising gracefully despite the obvious stiffness in her limbs. The rain had brought a chill to the air, and she drew the blanket he'd given her more tightly around her shoulders.

As they prepared to retire to the wagon, Weston found himself speaking again, the words coming unbidden. "The psalm you read today... it was Susannah's favorite. Matthew doesn't remember her, of course, but I've told him that. It's why he likes to hear it often."

Emily paused, her face half-turned away, making her expression unreadable. "I didn't know."

"No reason you should have," Weston replied. "I just wanted to explain...in case he asks you to read it to him."

"It was my father's favorite as well. He read it every Sunday morning before church, without fail. Even during his last days, when the fever had taken almost everything else from him, he would whisper those words."

The simple confession, the first personal detail she'd volunteered about her past loss, felt weightier than its few words would suggest. It was a small window, allowing Weston a brief glimpse of the person who existed before grief had reshaped her.

"I'm sorry," he said. "Truly I am."

Emily nodded once, a barely perceptible movement in the dim light. "As am I," she replied, and then turned toward the wagon, effectively ending the conversation.

Weston remained by the fire a moment longer, watching the play of flames against the darkness, listening to the steady rhythm of the rain. He thought of Susannah, of the psalm that had comforted her, of the strange twist of fate that had placed in his wagon a woman who carried a similar wound to his. Her father had found solace in the same ancient words.

It meant nothing; he told himself firmly. A coincidence, nothing more. Emily Wilson was a passenger, a responsibility. In Oregon, their paths would diverge, and this brief intersection of their lives would fade into memory, one small chapter in the long journey west.

Yet as he finally moved toward the wagon, Weston couldn't quite shake the feeling that something had shifted today, some subtle re-alignment that he couldn't yet name or understand. The certainty with which he'd begun the morning felt less solid now, undermined by the simple sight of Emily reading to his son. By the unexpected commonality of a shared psalm, by the glimpses of strength and gentleness beneath her profound sorrow.

Inside the wagon, Matthew slept peacefully, untroubled by the adult complexities that swirled around him. Emily had retired to her side of the space, the canvas partition providing the illusion of privacy in their shared confinement. Weston settled himself beside his son, listening to the rain on the wagon cover and the deep, even breathing of the two other occupants.

He closed his eyes, willing his mind to rest, yet finding his thoughts returning to the image of Emily's trembling hands on the Bible earlier that day. The complexity of emotion in her voice as she read the ancient words of comfort.

Chapter 11

A cry shattered the quiet of the dawn.

Emily jolted awake in the cramped confines of Weston's wagon, her heart hammering against her ribs. For a disorienting moment, she wasn't sure if the sound had been real or part of the nightmare that had pursued her through fitful sleep.

Then it came again—a woman's voice, high with panic.

"Help! Someone help, please!"

Emily threw off her blanket and scrambled to her feet, nearly bumping into Weston, who was already moving toward the wagon's opening, his face etched with concern in the dim light. Matthew stirred on his bedroll, blinking sleepily.

"Stay here, son," Weston said, his voice gentle but firm. He glanced at Emily, their eyes meeting briefly in a moment of shared alertness. "That's Martha Croft."

Emily's medical instinct surged forward. She reached for her satchel. "I'll go."

Outside, the camp was stirring in confused alarm. The eastern sky held just enough light to illuminate Martha's bent figure outside her family's wagon, her arms wrapped around young Caleb, who sagged against her.

"He's burning up," Martha cried as Emily approached. "He was fine yesterday, just a little tired, but now—"

Emily knelt beside them. Caleb's skin radiated heat, his nightshirt damp with sweat. His eyes were glazed, unfocused, his breathing rapid and shallow. The familiar signs sent a chill down Emily's spine.

"Let's get him back inside," she said, her voice adopting the steady, calm tone she'd used countless times before in sickrooms. "We'll need water. Cold water."

As Weston organized people to fetch supplies, Emily climbed into the Crofts' wagon. The confined space, the smell of sweat and fear, the close, stifling air, and the rustling of bedding struck Emily with such potent familiarity that her hands trembled briefly before she forced them still.

Not again. Please, not again.

The thought came, rising from her depths like a desperate plea, despite her fractured faith. She placed her palm against Caleb's forehead, feeling the dry, scorching heat of fever.

"How long has he been like this?" she asked, keeping her voice even as she opened her medical satchel.

"He complained of being tired last night," Martha said, hovering nearby. "But children get tired on the trail. We thought nothing of it. By morning, he was like this."

Emily's mind raced through possibilities, influenza, mountain fever, typhus, or typhoid. She pushed the last thought away forcefully, but it lingered, a specter at the edge of her consciousness. Too many illnesses presented with fever first. She couldn't jump to conclusions.

"Has anyone else been ill?" she asked, measuring Caleb's rapid pulse with her fingers. Too fast, too shallow.

"The Billings' youngest had a cough," Silas offered, his voice rough with worry. "And I heard Sarah Finch's baby was fussy yesterday."

Emily nodded, her movements mechanical and precise as she examined Caleb's throat for swelling and his skin for any telltale rash.

"I'll check on them as well," she said as she worked. "And anyone else showing symptoms, no matter how mild."

By midday, there were five confirmed cases of fever in the wagon train.

By evening, there were twelve.

***

The wagon train halted. There was no choice. Weston recognized the impossibility of continuing with a quarter of their company struck down by what Emily tentatively identified as a form of trail fever—a catch-all name for the various illnesses that plagued pioneer companies in the spring.

Emily helped establish a makeshift infirmary at the edge of camp—a collection of spare canvas tarps stretched between wagons, creating sheltered spaces for the sickest patients. The arrangement was crude but necessary; they needed to contain the illness as much as possible, though Emily privately feared it had already spread too far.

The isolation, the frantic pace, the desperate measures—all of it hurled her backward in time to the Richmond epidemic. Her hands moved with efficiency, but her mind was in two places at once: here in the dusty Nebraska territory and there in her family's elegant home, transformed into a house of death.

"Is this my fault?" The terrible thought crept in as she prepared a willow bark tea. "Did I bring this with me somehow? Am I cursed to witness death wherever I go?"

Kneeling beside Lavinia Calkins, whose fever had spiked dangerously high, Emily wrung out a cloth in cool water and placed it on the woman's forehead. The woman's skin burned against her fingers, her breath coming in shallow gasps.

"Is she...?" Zach Calkins hovered at Emily's shoulder, his young face haggard with worry.

"She's fighting," Emily said simply, avoiding empty reassurances. She'd heard too many of those herself.

"Can I stay with her?" Zach asked, his voice cracking.

Emily hesitated. Proximity meant risk. But the look in Zach's eyes, that desperate need to do something, anything, was one she understood too well.

"Yes," she said. "But you'll need to be careful. Wash your hands frequently. Don't touch your face."

As she moved to her next patient, Emily became aware of a presence behind her. Weston stood at the entrance to the makeshift tent, his eyes taking in the rows of pallets where the sick lay. Matthew was nowhere to be seen, safely with the Holloway's, she assumed.

"What do you need?" he asked.

The straightforward question, free of platitudes or panic, steadied her. Emily pushed a strand of hair from her face with the back of her wrist.

"More fresh water. Clean clothes. And..." she hesitated, then added practically, "... some of the women to help prepare willow bark tea. It won't cure the fever, but it might help reduce it."

"Consider it done." He started to turn, then paused. "When did you last eat or rest, Emily?"

The use of her first name, spoken with quiet concern rather than formality, caught her off guard. She couldn't actually remember her last meal. Time had blurred into a continuous stream of tending the sick, checking symptoms, and mixing remedies.

"I'm fine," she said automatically.

His expression told her he didn't believe her, but he didn't argue. "I'll have someone bring you food." He hesitated. "You're doing fine work here. These people are fortunate to have your skills."

Before she could respond, he was gone, his tall form moving purposefully through the camp. Emily stared after him for a moment, then turned back to her patients, that brief connection receding as she immersed herself again in the grueling work.

***

By nightfall, the mood in the camp had shifted from alarm to dread.

Two more had fallen ill. Reverend Holloway moved between the sick tents, offering prayers and comfort. Emily heard his sonorous voice as she worked, the familiar cadences of scripture and supplication floating through the air.

She was checking on Caleb, whose fever, thankfully, had broken slightly, when Martha approached with a steaming bowl.

"You need to eat," the older woman said firmly, her kind face lined with exhaustion. She'd been helping Emily for hours, displaying a practical competence that reminded Emily of her own mother's capable hands.

Emily started to protest, but her stomach betrayed her with a loud growl. She accepted the bowl, a simple stew, but at that moment, it smelled like the finest meal in Richmond.

"Thank you," she said, sinking onto a crate just outside the tent. The night air was cool against her face, a relief after the close heat of the sick tent. Stars spread above in a vast, indifferent canopy. She spooned the stew mechanically, barely tasting it, her mind still cataloging symptoms and calculating doses.

Martha sat beside her, her own bowl balanced on her knees. "Silas says Caleb's fever is lower."

Emily nodded. "It's a good sign. He's young, and strong."

"Thanks to you," Martha said, her eyes shining with unshed tears in the lantern light. "If you hadn't been here..."

"Anyone with basic medical knowledge would have done the same," Emily deflected.

Martha shook her head. "Not everyone has your skill. Or your dedication." She was silent for a moment, then added softly, "You lost someone close to you because of the fever, too."

Emily stiffened. "Who told you that?"

"No one had to tell me. I recognize the look," Martha said, her voice gentle. "I lost my first husband and two babes to cholera back in '47. The way you move about and hold yourself—I can see you've walked this path before."

Emily stared into her bowl, unable to meet the woman's eyes. The reminder of her loss, so casually mentioned, was like a physical blow. But there was something in Martha's tone, not pity, but understanding, that kept her from pulling away entirely.

"Yes," she said finally, her voice barely audible. "My entire family. Several months ago."

Martha's weathered hand found Emily's shoulder, a firm, warm weight. "The Lord doesn't waste our suffering, child. Sometimes it becomes our greatest gift to others."

Emily couldn't bring herself to respond. The idea that God had some purpose in her family's deaths, that her pain was somehow useful, stirred familiar anger. What kind of God would orchestrate such a tragedy just to make her a more effective healer? It was the kind of pious platitude she'd heard too often in Richmond; the words hollow against the depth of her loss.

Yet as she looked at Caleb's sleeping form, at Martha's lined face, at the flicker of lanterns where members of the wagon train lay sick on the ground, she couldn't deny that her experience had prepared her for this moment. She knew what to watch for. Her suffering had given her knowledge.

Martha seemed to sense her internal struggle and didn't press further. They finished their meal in silence; the night sounds of the prairie washing over them, crickets chirping, the distant lowing of cattle, and the soft murmur of voices from the camp.

After Martha left, Emily sat alone, too exhausted to move, yet unable to rest. The weight of responsibility pressed on her shoulders. These people were relying on her, their trust a burden she wasn't sure she deserved.

"Am I bringing this with me?" The thought that had haunted her since the first cry this morning surfaced again. "Is death following me?"

It was irrational. She knew disease on the trail was common. It had nothing to do with her presence. Yet, the timing, the echoes of Richmond, felt too coincidental to ignore completely.

A soft cry drew her attention. From one of the smaller tents came the distinctive wail of an infant. Emily rose, her body protesting after hours of constant movement, and made her way toward the sound.

Sarah Finch sat on a bedroll, baby Hope fussing in her arms. The young widow looked up as Emily entered, her face a mask of exhaustion and fear.

"She won't settle," Sarah whispered, bouncing the infant gently. "And she feels warm. I'm afraid..." Her voice broke.

Emily moved forward, kneeling beside the pair. Hope was indeed warmer than she should be. Her tiny face flushed. Not dangerously so, but concerning.

"Let me check her," Emily said, gently taking the baby. She examined Hope with careful hands, noting the slightly elevated temperature, the restlessness, but also the strong pulse and clear eyes. "I think she's just feverish from the heat and disruption. Not the illness that's affecting the others."

"Are you sure?" Sarah's voice trembled. "I can't lose her too, not after my Josiah..." She couldn't finish the sentence.

Emily looked at the young mother, so recently widowed by the fever that had taken her husband just weeks before. The raw grief in Sarah's eyes was like looking into a mirror of her own pain.

"I know," she said softly, the words coming from somewhere deep and wounded within her. "I know this pain, Sarah. You are not alone in it." She hesitated, then added, "And I will do everything in my power to keep Hope safe."

"You've lost someone too."

"Everyone," Emily said simply.

The single word hung between them, heavy with meaning. Sarah reached out, her hand finding Emily's in a gesture that required no further explanation. They sat together in the dim tent, connected by a shared understanding.

Emily showed Sarah how to bathe Hope with cool water to bring down her mild fever, and how to recognize signs of more serious illness. As she worked, she found herself sharing quiet, practical advice, the kind her mother had once given her about caring for infants. It felt strange to access those memories, to speak them aloud, but also strangely healing.

When Hope finally settled into sleep, Emily rose to leave, her patients elsewhere needing attention.

"Mrs. Wilson," Sarah called softly.

Emily turned.

"Thank you. For understanding. For not saying it was God's will or that it happened for a reason."

Emily nodded, a lump forming in her throat. "Rest while she sleeps. Call if you need me."

As she stepped back into the night air, Emily felt subtly but undeniably lighter by the encounter.

Chapter 12

Weston stood before Emily, holding a steaming cup of coffee. Dark circles shadowed his eyes; he'd clearly been up through the night as well.

"You need rest," he said without preamble, handing her the cup.

Emily accepted it gratefully, the bitter warmth a shock to her system. "There's no time. Lavinia's fever is worse."

"And you'll be no use to any of them sick if you collapse," Weston countered. His tone was firm, but not unkind. "At least eat something."

Before Emily could protest, a commotion erupted from one of the nearby tents. A man's voice raised in alarm, followed by Reverend Holloway's calmer tones, trying to soothe him.

Emily was on her feet immediately, coffee forgotten, as she rushed toward the sound. Weston followed close behind.

Inside the tent, Samson Early stood over the pallet where his young assistant Phillip Clark lay ill, gesticulating wildly. The boy—barely eighteen, Emily recalled—tossed restlessly, his face flushed with fever.

"This is unacceptable!" Samson was saying, his normally carefully groomed appearance disheveled from worry. "The boy needs proper care, not these folk remedies! Why, back east, physicians would apply cupping glasses and administer calomel for such ailments!"

"Mr. Early," Reverend Holloway said placatingly, "Mrs. Wilson is doing everything possible with the resources we have. Your assistant is receiving the same care as everyone—"

"That's precisely the problem!" Samson cut in. "I didn't invest in this journey to have my employee treated like a common—"

"That's enough." Weston's voice, though quiet, carried an unmistakable authority that silenced the tent immediately. "Every person in this camp receives equal care. If you have a specific concern about the boy's treatment, you can address it respectfully to Mrs. Wilson."

Samson turned, noticing Emily for the first time. His expression shifted, a veneer of charm replacing his outrage. "Mrs. Wilson, I was simply expressing my concern for the boy. Perhaps if I could suggest some additional treatments? I've read extensively about the medical sciences."

Emily moved past him without acknowledging the condescending offer, kneeling instead beside the sick youth. She checked his pulse, his temperature, and the state of his breathing.

"He's no worse than yesterday," she reported, speaking to the boy directly rather than to his employer. "Phillip, can you hear me? I'm going to give you some medicine for the fever."

"He needs more than herb teas," Samson persisted, hovering at her shoulder. "Have you considered bloodletting? The humors must be balanced."

Emily turned, fixing him with a level gaze. "Bloodletting would weaken him further. What he needs is rest, fluids, and to be spared additional stress." The last words carried a pointed meaning that even Samson couldn't miss.

His face flushed. "I merely thought—"

"Your concern is noted," Weston interrupted, placing a hand on the man's shoulder and firmly steering him toward the tent entrance. "Now let Mrs. Wilson work. I'm sure you have other matters requiring your attention."

As Samson was led away, still protesting, Emily caught Weston's eye and gave him a small nod of thanks. He returned it with the barest hint of a smile before following Samson outside, presumably to ensure the man didn't return to disrupt her work.

The interaction left Emily with an unexpected feeling of being protected, not in a way that undermined her ability, but that respected and supported it. It was a novel sensation.

***

The crisis stretched into its second day, then its third. The rhythm of caring for the sick became Emily's entire world, checking temperatures, administering willow bark tea, bathing fevered bodies with cool water, changing linens soaked with sweat, and offering sips of broth to those strong enough to take it.

Throughout it all, the surrounding community responded in ways that continually surprised her. Mercy organized a group of women to prepare meals, ensuring that both the sick and those caring for them were fed. Martha, despite her own exhaustion from tending Caleb and assisting with the others that were ill, helped wash soiled linens in the nearby stream. Silas and other men set up additional shelters as more patients needed isolation.

And Weston was everywhere, coordinating efforts, ensuring supplies reached where they were needed, maintaining order in the restless camp, and somehow, impossibly, appearing at Emily's side at critical moments with exactly what she required. Water when her throat was parched. Food when she'd forgotten to eat. A clean apron when hers was soiled beyond use. A quiet word of encouragement when a patient took a turn for the worse.

He kept Matthew away from the sick tents, entrusting him to Elara Jenkins' care during the day. Emily glimpsed the boy occasionally, playing with Luke Billings under the watchful eyes of his mother.

On the fourth evening, as Emily knelt beside Phillip, Samson's assistant—whose fever had finally broken that afternoon—she became aware of the silence that had fallen over the camp. The normal sounds of preparation for the night had ceased, replaced by a somber hush.

She looked up to find Samson standing in the tent entrance, his massive frame silhouetted against the fading light. The blacksmith's expression was grave.

"Mrs. Wilson," he said, his deep voice unusually soft. "They need you at the Abbott's wagon."

Emily's heart sank. Joseph Abbott, an elderly man traveling west with his daughter- and son-in-law, had become ill as well and his daughter insisted on keeping him in their wagon. His fever had been dangerously high from the start.

She gathered her satchel and followed Samson across the camp. A small crowd had gathered around the Abbott's wagon. Reverend Holloway stood with his arm around Joseph's daughter, Wilma, whose quiet sobs broke the stillness.

Weston was there too, his face solemn as he spoke in low tones with Abbott's son-in-law, Mark. He looked up as Emily approached, meeting her gaze with a silent acknowledgment of what they both knew: they had lost their first patient to the fever.

Emily moved through the group to the wagon, where Joseph Abbott lay still on his pallet. His weathered face, lined with years of hardship and joy, was at peace now, the fever finally yielding to death's cooler touch.

She checked for a pulse out of medical habit, though she knew she would find none. Then she gently closed the man's eyes, her throat tight with emotion. Death was an old adversary, one she'd faced too many times.

She turned to Wilma, who stood trembling in Reverend Holloway's supportive embrace. "I'm so sorry."

Wilma nodded tearfully. "He knew," she whispered. "This morning, he said he was going home soon to be with Momma and God." She glanced skyward. "He said to thank you for your kindness."

Emily swallowed hard, unable to respond. She had done so little, really. Just offered what care her training allowed, a cool hand on a fevered brow, and a gentle voice in moments of confusion. Yet to this family, it had clearly meant something.

"We'll need to bury him at first light," Weston said, his voice gentle but practical. "I'll organize men to dig the grave."

"I'll prepare a service," Reverend Holloway added, squeezing Wilma's shoulders. "A proper farewell."

As plans were made around her, Emily stood silent, struck by the simple dignity of how this community—barely formed, composed of strangers thrown together by circumstance—handled death among them. There was grief, yes, but also purpose, support, and shared responsibility. No one was left to bear the burden alone.

She recalled the hollow, echoing rooms of her Richmond home after the epidemic. The crushing isolation, the empty chairs, and the silence broken only by her own ragged breathing. How different this experience was—death acknowledged, mourned communally, and the bereaved surrounded by care rather than emptiness. When the initial arrangements were complete, the small crowd dispersed to give the family privacy with their grief. Emily turned to go as well, intending to return to the other patients, but Weston's hand on her arm stopped her.

"You've done all you can today," he said quietly. "You need rest."

She started to protest, but the words died on her lips as exhaustion swept over her like a physical force. For days, she had pushed herself past normal endurance, functioning on brief naps and iron will. Now, with Joseph's death breaking the feverish rhythm of constant care, her body was demanding its due.

Weston seemed to read her surrender in her expression. "Silas and Martha can watch the others for a few hours," he said. "Come. At least sit by the fire and have something hot to eat."

Too tired to argue, Emily allowed him to lead her away from the sick tents, toward the main campfire. The simple act of walking beside someone, of being guided when her own strength was failing, felt foreign but necessary. She couldn't recall the last time she'd permitted herself to lean on another, even slightly.

At the fire, Mercy pressed a bowl of stew into her hands. Emily sank onto a log, suddenly aware of every ache in her body, every strain in her muscles from days of bending, lifting, and working. The stew was simple but nourishing, and she ate mechanically, barely aware of her surroundings until Matthew's small form appeared beside her.

"Miss Emily," he said, his voice small and serious. "Papa says you've been making people better."

Emily glanced at Weston, who stood nearby, watching his son with a mixture of love and concern. He gave a small nod, permitting the interaction despite his obvious desire to keep Matthew away from anyone who had been among the sick.

"I'm trying," she said honestly, setting her empty bowl aside. "Some people are getting better."

Matthew nodded, his face solemn. "But Mr. Abbott died, Luke Billings said so. He went to heaven like my mama did."

Emily glanced again at Weston, whose expression had tightened at the mention of his late wife, but he made no move to intervene.

"Yes," Emily said after a moment, unsure of what else to say. "I believe he did."

"Papa says heaven is nice," Matthew continued, settling beside her on the log. "No more being sick or scared or hurt. Do you think it's nice, Miss Emily?"

The question pierced straight through Emily's exhaustion to the core of her fractured faith. Did she still believe heaven was real? That her family was there now, free from suffering?

"I think... I think heaven is beautiful, Matthew."

"I'm glad you're helping people not go to heaven yet," he said, patting her hand with his small one. "Papa says you're really brave."

"Your papa is brave too," she said.

"I know. Papa's the bravest. But he looks sad sometimes, like you do." He tilted his head, studying her with a child's uncanny perception. "Are you sad 'cause people get sick?"

Emily felt something flutter in her chest. This child, with his innocent questions and his ready acceptance of pain as part of life, somehow bypassed all her defenses.

"Yes," she admitted softly. "That's part of it."

Matthew nodded. "Papa gets sad, too, sometimes. When he thinks I'm sleeping. He talks to Mama up in heaven." He looked at Emily earnestly. "Do you talk to people in heaven, too?"

The question blindsided her completely. Did she? Once, in those first raw days after the epidemic took her family, she had talked constantly to them—raging, pleading, and bargaining with them as if they could somehow respond. But as the silence stretched on, as God remained mute to her suffering, she had stopped. It hurt too much to speak into that void.

"I used to," she said.

"Maybe you should again," Matthew suggested with a child's simple logic. "Papa says it helps sometimes, even if they can't talk back."

Weston returned, crouching before his son. "Time for bed, Matthew," he said gently. "Mrs. Wilson needs her rest, and so do you."

Matthew yawned and nodded, then surprised Emily by leaning forward and hugging her.

"G'night, Miss Emily," he murmured. "I hope the sick people get better tomorrow."

"Goodnight, Matthew," she managed, touched beyond measure by the simple gesture of affection.

As Weston led his son away toward their wagon, Emily remained by the fire, turning Matthew's words over in her mind. Maybe you should again. As if reconnecting with those she'd lost was as simple as choosing to speak to them across the divide of death.

Yet as she stared into the dancing flames, something in the boy's suggestion resonated with a place deep within her. Not because she believed her family could hear her, but because perhaps, in acknowledging them, in speaking to the memory of them, she might find some form of connection that her silence had severed.

Around her, the camp was settling for the night. In the sick tents, the patients slept or endured, fighting their private battles against the fever. Among the wagons, families drew together, sharing the day's worries and small triumphs. And somewhere in that vast, star-strewn sky above, perhaps there was something more, something that even her grief and anger couldn't entirely extinguish.

Emily closed her eyes, too exhausted to move and too restless to sleep. For the first time since Richmond, she allowed herself to silently form the names of her lost loved ones in her mind—not with rage or despair, but with a quiet acknowledgment of their absence and the hole it had left in her life.

"I'm still here," she thought to them, her heart aching with the admission. "I don't know why, but I'm still here."

It wasn't a prayer, not exactly. But it was the closest she had come since boarding the stagecoach in Richmond, fleeing the ghosts that now, somehow, felt marginally less terrifying to face.

Chapter 13

The dawn broke clear and crisp, a beautiful day that seemed obscenely at odds with its purpose. Joseph Abbott was laid to rest in a simple grave at the edge of a small copse of trees. He was the first member of their company to find his final rest along the trail rather than in the promised land of Oregon.

Reverend Holloway conducted the service with dignity and compassion, his resonant voice carrying across the gathered pioneers. Emily stood at the back, unwilling to intrude too closely on the family's grief, yet compelled to attend out of respect for a man who had, however briefly, been under her care.

"The Lord is my shepherd; I shall not want," Holloway intoned, the familiar words of the 23rd Psalm floating over the assembled mourners. "He maketh me to lie down in green pastures: he leadeth me beside the still waters."

Emily's lips moving silently with the verses ingrained from childhood. Her family had been buried with these same words. She'd stood numb and silent then, the scripture washing over her without penetrating the shell of her shock. Now, months later and hundreds of miles away, the words seemed to carry a different weight.

"Yea, though I walk through the valley of the shadow of death, I will fear no evil: for thou art with me; thy rod and thy staff, they comfort me."

Was God with them in this wilderness? With her in the valley of grief she still traversed? She couldn't feel His presence, couldn't sense the comfort these words promised. Yet looking at the surrounding faces, weary, lined with hardship, but standing together in shared humanity, she could witness something that, if not divine, was at least profound: connection, endurance, and the choice to continue forward despite loss.

After the burial, as the community slowly dispersed, Emily returned to the sick tents, her brief respite over. The patients needed her, and in caring for them, she found a strange solace, a purpose that, while not erasing her pain, gave it a context beyond mere suffering.

Throughout the day, she moved between cases, noting with cautious relief that the crisis seemed to be abating. Caleb was recovering well, sitting up and taking broth. Phillip was weak, but alert. Six more patients' fevers had broken during the night. Only Lavinia Calkins remained seriously ill, her condition precarious.

Emily was preparing a fresh poultice for another patient when Weston appeared at her side, his presence now so familiar that she barely startled at his approach.

"How many are still critical?" he asked quietly, his eyes scanning the tent.

"Just Mrs. Calkins," Emily replied, her hands continuing their work. "The others are improving. I think the worst has passed."

Weston nodded, relief evident in the slight relaxation of his shoulders. "How long before we can move on?"

The question was practical, and necessary. They couldn't remain camped indefinitely, not with supplies dwindling and the season advancing. Yet Emily felt a stab of concern for the recovering patients.

"Those who are improving will need at least another two days of rest before they can withstand the jolting of the wagons," she said. "Mrs. Calkins... I can't say yet."

Weston absorbed this with a thoughtful nod. "We'll give it two days, then reassess. The animals could use the rest as well."

He seemed about to say something more when a commotion outside drew their attention. Raised voices, angry in tone. Weston's expression darkened as he recognized the sound.

"Ezekiel," he muttered, already moving toward the tent entrance.

Emily followed, curious and concerned. Outside, a small group had gathered around Ezekiel Vance, whose face was flushed with indignation as he gestured expansively.

"Five days we've sat here!" he was saying as Emily and Weston approached. "Five days of using supplies, going nowhere, all because a few people caught a fever that most survive, anyway!"

"My father didn't survive," Wilma said quietly, her face tight with anger.

"And I'm sorry for your loss," Ezekiel said, not sounding sorry at all. "But we all knew the risks when we started this journey. People die on the trail. It's a fact. What's not a fact is that we agreed to risk everyone's lives by sitting like ducks while resources dwindle and valuable travel time is wasted."

"No one is being asked to risk their lives," Weston said evenly, stepping into the circle. "We stopped because continuing would have endangered those who were ill and risked spreading the disease further."

Ezekiel turned, his eyes narrowing at Weston's approach. "And who made that decision? You? Or was it our resident grieving widow, playing at doctor?" He glanced dismissively at Emily. "For all we know, she brought this illness with her."

The accusation, so close to Emily's own irrational fears, landed like a physical blow. She stiffened, unable to respond.

"That's enough, Vance." Weston's voice was dangerously quiet. "Mrs. Wilson has worked tirelessly to care for people who otherwise might have died. You will show her the respect she deserves, or you will keep your opinions to yourself."

"I'll speak my mind," Ezekiel retorted, though he took a step back from Weston's imposing presence. "And my mind says we've lost valuable time because of an overreaction. Joseph Abbott was old. He might have died anyway. The rest are recovering. We could have continued."

"And risked losing more? Including your own hide, Ezekiel, since disease doesn't care how loud you complain." This came from Silas, who had joined the group, his weathered face stern. "My boy is alive because Mrs. Wilson knew what to do. We all owe her a debt."

Murmurs of agreement rose from several others. Emily glanced around, surprised to see nods from Martha, Mercy and from Sarah Finch, who stood at the edge of the group with baby Hope in her arms.

"You have the right to your opinion," Weston said firmly to Ezekiel. "What you don't have is the right to endanger others with selfish demands. We move when the sick are stable enough to travel safely. Two days, by Mrs. Wilson's assessment. That's final."

Ezekiel scowled, clearly unhappy, but recognizing he was outnumbered. "Fine," he spat. "But when we're short on supplies because we wasted time, don't expect me to share mine." He stalked off, a few others—those who had been nodding at his complaints—following after.

As the group dispersed, Emily stood motionless, still processing Ezekiel's accusation and the unexpected defense she'd received. She was accustomed to bearing blame, to shouldering the weight of guilt. The idea that others would stand up for her, would value her contribution enough to speak against this man's criticism, was almost incomprehensible.

"Don't mind him," Silas said, pausing beside her. "He'd complain about the quality of gold if you handed him a nugget."

Emily managed a small, tight smile. "He's not entirely wrong. We have lost time."

"Time well spent," Silas countered firmly. "My boy is alive. Others too. Some things matter more than miles covered." He glanced toward the sick tents. "I should get back to Caleb. Martha's been with him all morning."

As he walked away, Weston turned to Emily, studying her face with an intensity that made her want to look away.

"Ezekiel is a cold-hearted fool," he said quietly. "You know that, don't you?"

Emily hesitated. "He speaks what others might think, but don't say."

"Some, perhaps," Weston acknowledged. "But not most. Not those who matter." He gestured toward the camp, where life was slowly returning to normal after the crisis. "These people have seen what you did, Emily. How you fought for every patient. They won't forget that."

"I didn't save Joseph Abbott," she said.

"No," Weston agreed simply. "No one could have. God needed him. But you gave him dignity during his illness, and comfort to his family. That matters. Just as it matters that you've barely slept or eaten for days while caring for others."

Emily opened her mouth to deflect the observation, then closed it, suddenly too tired to maintain the pretense that she didn't need care for herself. "I should check on Mrs. Calkins," she said instead.

Weston nodded, recognizing her need to return to work rather than dwell on Ezekiel's accusations. "I'll have food sent over," he said, not making it a question this time. "And Emily—" His use of her first name still caught her attention every time. "—when this is over, when we're moving again, you will take time to rest. The wagon train needs you whole."

He turned and walked away, his tall figure moving purposefully through the camp. Emily watched him go, struck by his words. *The wagon train needs you.* Not just as a medical practitioner, but as a person.

It was a novel thought—that she might have value beyond her skills, that her presence might matter to these people not just for what she could do but for who she was. That Weston might see her as more than a convenient source of medical care for his charges.

With that unsettling idea, she turned back toward the sick tents, where Lavinia Calkins waited and where duty called her to focus on tasks rather than emotions. Yet as she resumed her work, checking temperatures and changing compresses, Emily was aware of a fragile recognition that she was beginning to heal from her grief. She was beginning to feel alive again.

Chapter 14

Emily slipped away from the bustle of the camp, seeking the solitude that had become her refuge. The wagon train had settled for the night, fires burning low, voices quieting as exhaustion claimed the weary travelers. She found a spot at the edge of Weston's wagon, far enough from the main gathering to feel alone, yet close enough that she could still hear if anyone called for her.

Over three weeks on the trail, and the past days had tested them all beyond measure. The illness that swept through the camp had finally loosened its grip.

Emily drew her shawl tighter around her shoulders. The night air carried a chill that reached past wool and cotton to settle in her bones. Or perhaps that chill came from within—from the memories stirred by watching another Joseph Abbott's grave being dug, another life cut short.

Ezekiel Vance's accusatory words from yesterday still scraped against her consciousness.

The words had found their mark, piercing the careful armor she'd constructed. They gave voice to her deepest, most irrational fear—that somehow she carried destruction with her, that her survival was a cruel twist of fate that condemned others to death in her stead.

Emily tilted her head back, feeling both crushed and freed by the sheer enormity of the night. The vast canopy of stars spread overhead, countless pinpricks of light in the darkness. The prairie stretched around her, empty and boundless, making her feel small and fragile.

The sound of footsteps approached, steady and deliberate. She recognized them immediately and tensed, caught between the desire to flee and the lack of anywhere to go.

"Thought you might want this," Weston's voice was low as he extended a tin cup of coffee toward her.

"Thank you."

The coffee was bitter and strong, but the warmth seeping through the metal into her palms was welcome. Weston lowered himself onto a fallen log a respectful distance away, his own cup cradled in his hands. His profile was sharp against the darkness, his features half-illuminated by moonlight.

"Matthew's finally asleep," he said. "Took three stories tonight."

"I believe Mr. Abbott's death is bothering him," Emily replied softly.

Weston nodded. "I believe you may be right."

The silence stretched between them. Emily could feel him wrestling with something, his usual composed presence disturbed by an inner turmoil. She waited, allowing the quiet to settle, unwilling to breach the careful distance they maintained.

"Mrs. Wilson," a different voice called, breaking the moment. "A fine evening, isn't it?"

Emily turned to see Clarence Hodge approaching, his manner as meticulously arranged as his appearance. Even after weeks on the trail, he managed to maintain an air of genteel propriety that seemed absurdly out of place amidst the dust and hardship.

"Mr. Hodge," she acknowledged with a slight nod, unable to summon even the pretense of welcome.

"I couldn't help but notice you sitting here beneath this magnificent sky," he continued, gesturing upward with a flourish that made Emily wince internally. "It puts one in mind of the divine handiwork, doesn't it? As the Good Book says, 'The heavens declare the glory of God.'"

"Indeed," she replied.

"I wonder if you might permit me to join your contemplation of the firmament? I've been composing some thoughts on our journey that I believe you might find illuminating."

Before Emily could respond, Weston shifted, his movement subtle but somehow commanding attention. "Hodge," he said, his tone neutral but carrying an undercurrent of authority, "Silas was looking for someone to help with the perimeter checks. Thought you might be interested."

Clarence straightened, clearly torn between the desire to stay and the implicit directive from the wagon master. "Ah. Well. Duty calls, I suppose. Another time, perhaps, Miss Wilson?"

"Perhaps," Emily murmured, relief washing through her as Clarence reluctantly retreated.

When he was safely out of earshot, she noticed the slight tug at the corner of Weston's mouth—not quite a smile, but something close.

"You didn't have to do that," she said.

"Silas really does need help," Weston replied, though they both knew the timing was more than coincidental.

Emily sensed that whatever Weston had been on the verge of saying before Clarence arrived was still there, waiting. She should excuse herself, retreat into the wagon, and maintain a careful distance. Instead, she stayed.

"It's Matthew's birthday in two weeks," Weston said finally. "He'll be seven. Susannah would have known what to do, how to make it special, even out here." He stared into his cup. "There's so much she should be here for."

Emily felt a tightening in her chest at the raw emotion in his voice. She'd heard him speak of Susannah before, but never like this, never with this exposed undercurrent of pain.

"How long were you married?" she asked.

"Almost two years. Not long enough. Not nearly long enough." He set his cup down, clasping his hands between his knees. "We met in St. Louis. I was guiding settlers west, coming back between trips. She worked at a boarding house where I stayed."

He paused, and Emily saw his throat work as he swallowed hard. When he continued, his voice had softened.

"She had this laugh... It would start quiet, then just take over her whole body. Couldn't help but laugh along with her." He shook his head slightly, as if trying to clear the memory.

Emily remained perfectly still, afraid any movement might break the spell, might cause him to retreat behind the composed, capable mask he always wore. This glimpse of the man beneath the wagon master's authority was fragile and unexpected.

"We had rented a small house outside the city. It wasn't much, but it was ours. When she told me about the baby, I took a job that kept me closer to home. Planned to build a house of our own." His voice faltered momentarily. "I was out cutting timber on the property we had just bought when it happened. The neighbor woman sent her boy running for me. By the time I got back..."

The pain in his voice was so familiar it seemed to echo inside her own chest, stirring memories she fought daily to contain.

"The midwife said it was bad from the start. Breech birth, then bleeding they couldn't stop." His fingers curled into fists. "Susannah held on long enough to name him. Matthew Clay Reynolds. Made me promise to tell him about her every day."

Weston looked up then, his eyes finding Emily's in the moonlight. "I've kept that promise. Every day, I tell him something about her. But the boy's never known a mother's touch, not really. And I..." He faltered. "I've never known how to fill that space for him."

The rawness of his confession struck Emily with physical force. This man, so capable, so controlled, carried a wound that mirrored her own—not identical, but similar in its depth and permanence. She recognized in his words the same questions that haunted her: How do you continue when part of your heart has been torn away? How do you bear the weight of survival when those you love have not?

"I'm telling you this because..." Weston paused, seeming to search for words. "Because I've seen how Matthew is with you. How he seeks you out. How he lights up when you tell him stories. I haven't seen him like that with anyone. And it terrifies me."

Emily's breath caught. "Terrifies you?"

"Losing Susannah nearly broke me," he said, his voice steady now, though the effort it cost him was visible in the tension of his shoulders. "If not for Matthew, for having to be strong for him, I don't know if I would have survived it. The thought of him getting attached, of him losing someone..." He shook his head. "The trail is dangerous. Life is dangerous. And opening yourself up to caring for someone... it's inviting pain in."

Emily felt the truth of his words resonate through her, articulating the very fear that had driven her to seek the punishing isolation of the Oregon Trail. The irony wasn't lost on her—that here, in the place she'd sought to escape all human connections, she was being confronted with the possibility of it in its most raw form.

"I understand," she whispered, the words inadequate against the magnitude of what he'd shared, what she felt stirring within her.

"I know you do," Weston replied, his gaze holding hers. "I've seen it in your eyes since that first day in Independence. The same thing I see in the mirror." He hesitated. "Loss."

Emily looked away, unable to bear the intensity of his gaze, the uncomfortable sensation of being seen so clearly. Her fingers found the locket at her throat, clutching it like a talisman.

In the distance, a coyote called, its lonely cry echoing across the emptiness of the prairie. Another answered, farther away. The sounds penetrated Emily's thoughts, reminding her of the vastness beyond her, beyond the tight confines of her grief.

"I don't mean to burden you," Weston continued after a moment. "And I'm not asking you to share your story. I just wanted you to understand... about Matthew. About why I've been..."

"Wary?" Emily supplied.

A ghost of a smile touched his lips. "That's a kind way to put it."

The night enfolded them in its quiet embrace as they sat in silence, the weight of shared understanding settling between them. Emily felt strangely suspended, caught between the instinctive urge to flee this unexpected intimacy and an equally powerful pull toward the recognition she saw in his eyes, the acknowledgment of a pain that matched her own.

This shared understanding created a kind of bridge across the solitude she'd so carefully cultivated. It was terrifying and compelling in equal measure, a connection formed not through happiness or ordinary circumstance, but through the dark terrain of grief they both had walked.

"Susannah loved the spring," Weston said suddenly, his voice softer now, almost reflective. "Used to gather wildflowers by the handful. She filled every jar and cup in the house. Said it was God's way of reminding us that even the hardest winter gives way, eventually. I'm not sure I believed that for a long time after she died."

Emily wanted to ask if he believed it now, if he'd found his way back to that hope, but the question felt too intrusive, too personal. Instead, she remained silent, letting him speak.

"I didn't intend to tell you all this," he admitted, running a hand through his hair. "But seeing you sitting here alone, the way you looked after the burial yesterday…" He paused. "I recognized something in your face. Something I've carried too. I just felt drawn to speak with you."

Emily sat with her head bowed, feeling the weight of his confession.

"It's getting late," Weston said finally, rising to his feet. "We'll probably head back out on the trail the day after tomorrow."

Emily nodded, still unable to meet his eyes, afraid of what he might see in hers—the turmoil, the fear, the unexpected and unwelcome tug of connection.

"Thanks," she said, the words barely audible. "For the coffee."

What she didn't say, couldn't say, was thank you for trusting me with your pain, for showing me I'm not alone in this wilderness of grief. The thought itself was terrifying.

He hesitated, as if there was more he wanted to say. Then, with a slight nod, he turned and walked away, his footsteps fading into the sounds of the sleeping camp.

Emily remained seated. The vastness of the night pressed in around her, but for the first time, she didn't feel its isolation as a comfort. Instead, she felt exposed, vulnerable, as if the careful walls she'd built had been breached—not violently, but through the gentle persistence of shared understanding.

Her fingers traced the outline of the locket against her chest. Inside were the faces of everything she had lost—husband, parents, sisters. Their absence was a physical ache, a void that could never be filled.

And yet, here in this desolate place, miles from everything familiar, she'd found yet another person who carried a similar void, and understood the shape of such emptiness.

She rose finally, wrapping her shawl tighter around her shoulders against the chill of the night. As she turned toward the wagon, her gaze caught on the vast field of stars overhead, countless and brilliant in the clear prairie sky. For a brief moment, she remembered her father, a knowledgeable man who'd loved the natural world, pointing out constellations to her as a child, his voice full of wonder at the order and beauty of creation.

"You see, Emmy," he'd say, "even in the darkest night, there's light to guide us home, if we just know how to look."

The memory came unbidden, sharp, and clear, the first time she'd recalled her father's voice without the immediate, crushing weight of loss accompanying it. It was gone in an instant, leaving her breathless.

In its wake came a realization that disturbed her deeply: the vast silence of the night sky, which should have emphasized her insignificance, and her isolation, instead reminded her of connection—to her father's memory, to the earth beneath her feet, and now to Weston Reynolds and his quiet grief.

His words replayed in her mind: "It terrifies me." She understood that fear all too well. The dread of caring and connecting, only to lose again.

She closed her eyes as more of his words echoed in her mind: "Even the hardest winter gives way, eventually."

Chapter 15

Weston sat beside the campfire near the wagon, his broad shoulders silhouetted against the infinite darkness.

Emily drew a breath that trembled slightly as she walked toward him and sat down across from him. The words she'd kept locked inside for so long pressed against her chest, demanding release.

"The fever came with little warning," she said. "My husband, Thomas, complained of a headache, nothing more. I made him breakfast and sent him on his way to work. I asked him to take it easy that day."

Weston remained utterly still, his eyes reflecting the faint glow of embers.

"By evening, he couldn't keep water down. His skin burned beneath my hands." Emily's fingers twisted together in her lap. "I knew then it was typhoid. I'd seen it before. But knowing didn't help. Nothing helped."

"Emily—" Weston began.

"They all fell ill within days of each other," she continued, her voice low, the words gaining momentum. "First Thomas, then my mother. Then my father. Then my sisters, Margaret and Mary."

"I cooled foreheads, changing linens, and tried to get them to take water. I made poultices, brewed teas, prayed…" Her voice caught. "I prayed so hard my knees bore bruises. I bargained with God. I begged Him."

Emily stared into the darkness, seeing not the prairie night but the sickroom of her Richmond home, smelling not the clean, cold air but the cloying scent of sweat and disease. The sharp tang of camphor and chloride of lime did nothing to mask the smell of impending death. She heard again the labored breathing, the muttered deliriums, and the terrible silence that followed final breaths.

"Thomas died first. Four days from the first fever. He…" She swallowed hard. "He was delirious at the end. Didn't know me. Didn't know himself. Just stared through me with glassy eyes while I held his hand. Then he simply… stopped breathing."

"My father followed the two days later. Then Margaret, she was only eighteen. Then my mother." Emily's voice had taken on a flat, detached quality, as if she were reciting facts about strangers. "Mary lasted longest. Almost a week. I thought perhaps…I allowed myself to hope…" She shook her head sharply. "I buried them all in the church cemetery, days apart from each other. Five graves in a row. The minister spoke words I couldn't hear over the roaring in my ears."

She fell silent, the weight of memory pressing down upon her.

"And you never fell ill?" Weston asked.

"No." The word came out bitter, twisted. "I never even coughed. I who moved between them, touched them, and breathed the same air. I who should have—" She cut herself off, hands clenching, so tightly her knuckles showed white in the dim light.

"Should have what, Emily?" Weston's voice was steady, gentle.

"Should have died with them!" The words tore from her throat, ragged with conviction. "What sense does it make? Why was I spared? To what purpose?"

She lifted her face to the vast, uncaring sky. "I keep thinking there must have been a reason. Something important I'm meant to do. Some grand design that justified their suffering, their loss. But there's nothing. Just emptiness. Just an endless horizon of days without them."

Weston shifted slightly, a log cracking in the fire, sending a brief flare of light across his features. His eyes held no pity, only profound understanding.

"Did anyone tell you it was God's will?" he asked, his voice low. "That He had a plan?"

Emily let out a sound that might have been a laugh if it hadn't been so raw with pain. "Everyone. The minister, the neighbors, and even the undertaker. 'The Lord gives, and the Lord takes away.' As if that explained it. As if that made it right."

She reached for the locket around her neck, finding the familiar contours. "There was a moment, after they lowered Mary into the ground, when I stood alone by those five mounds of fresh earth. The church bells rang, and I realized I would never step inside those doors again."

A tear spilled down her cheek, catching the faint ember-light. "I couldn't. Not when every prayer had gone unanswered. Not when He had abandoned us so completely."

"You think God abandoned you?" Weston asked, not challenging, merely seeking to understand.

"What else am I to think?" Emily's voice rose slightly, the first hint of animation breaking through her flat recitation. "I was faithful my entire life. My family too. We attended services, gave to the poor, and lived by His word. And in return? He took everything." She drew a shuddering breath. "Everything I loved, everything I was, gone in the space of two weeks."

"And left you alone to bear it," Weston added.

"Yes." Her shoulders bent forward as if under an unbearable weight. "That's the cruelest part. Not just that they died, but that I remain. Every morning I wake up still breathing, still living, when they cannot."

Her next words came as a whisper, a confession. "Sometimes I wonder if I'm being punished. If I'm...tainted somehow. If death follows me."

"That's why...when the fever broke out here..." She gestured vaguely to the surrounding encampment. "I kept thinking, what if it's my fault? What if I brought this? What if everyone I touch is cursed?"

"Emily." Weston spoke her name firmly. "Disease isn't a curse. It isn't punishment. You know that."

"Do I?" Her eyes, hollow in the fading firelight, searched his face. "My mind knows. But my heart..."

"Your heart is wounded," he finished for her, his voice gentle. "Deeply wounded."

They sat in silence for several breaths, the enormity of her confession hanging between them.

"After Susannah died," Weston said, his voice thoughtful, "I was so angry. At the midwife, who couldn't save her. At myself for not doing...something. I don't know what." He rubbed a hand across his face. "At God, most of all."

Emily looked up, surprised by his admission. "You were angry with God?"

"Furious," he confirmed. "I had a newborn son who needed his mother, and she was gone. I demanded answers. Why Susannah? Why leave Matthew motherless? What possible good could come from such pain? I stopped praying for a time. Couldn't bring myself to speak to Him. The silence from heaven was deafening."

"What changed?" Emily asked. "How did you...find your way back?"

Weston was quiet for a moment, choosing his words carefully. "It wasn't a sudden revelation. More a slow surrender. I took work as a trail scout soon after. Spent weeks in the wilderness, just me and Matthew."

He lifted his eyes to the lightening sky. "Out here, with just the land and sky and a child who needed me...I began to sense God's presence again—not in answers, but in the way the prairie grasses bent and rose with the wind, resilient and enduring. In the stark beauty of a mesa silhouetted against the sky at dusk. In the unexpected strength I found to rise each morning and care for Matthew."

"That feels...too simple," Emily said, a trace of the old bitterness returning.

"It wasn't simple," Weston corrected gently. "It was the hardest thing I've ever done. To accept that, I might never understand why Susannah was taken. To acknowledge that God's ways are beyond my comprehension. To choose faith in spite of that."

He leaned forward, his eyes intent on her face. "I still wrestle with God sometimes, Emily. I still ask why. The difference is, I've stopped demanding an answer before, I'll believe."

Emily absorbed his words, feeling them settle into the raw, wounded places within her. "I don't know if I can do that. Accept without understanding."

"I'm not saying you should," Weston replied. "I'm just telling you what helped me. That and..." he hesitated, "finding God in the pain, not just beyond it."

"In it?" She frowned.

"When I finally started praying again, it wasn't pretty. It was raw—angry, confused, and desperate. But in those moments of honesty…" He paused, struggling to articulate something deeply felt. "That's when I felt Him closest. Not removing the pain, but sitting with me in it. Like someone who doesn't offer empty words, but simply stays beside you in your darkest hour."

"I don't think I know how to pray like that," she admitted. "Honest prayers. Everything I was taught about faith feels…insufficient now. Like children's stories shattered by adult truths."

"Maybe that's not a bad thing," Weston suggested. "Perhaps real faith begins when the easy answers end." He lifted a hand, then let it fall, as if unsure whether to reach out to her. "Your doubt, your anger—I think God can bear it. Might even welcome it. It's at least a conversation, not silence."

Emily considered this, turning the notion over in her mind. The idea of a God who could hear her rage, her questions, and her rawest pain without condemnation or platitudes felt both terrifying and strangely comforting.

"I don't know if I'm ready. To really try again. To risk believing."

"Just…consider that God might be with you, even in your doubt. That He hasn't abandoned you, even if it feels that way."

From inside the wagon, Matthew's small voice called out sleepily, "Papa?"

"I'm here, son," Weston responded, his voice immediately gentler. He glanced at Emily, hesitant to end their conversation. "We should—"

"Yes," she agreed, wiping hastily at her cheeks.

But as she moved to rise, Weston's hand touched her arm lightly, stopping her. "Emily." His voice was low, earnest. "Thank you for trusting me with your story. With your pain."

She nodded, unable to form words past the sudden knot in her throat.

"I want you to know," he continued, his blue eyes holding hers with quiet intensity, "I don't believe you're cursed or tainted. I believe you're incredibly strong... to have endured such loss and still be capable of kindness and healing others." He paused. "I believe God brought you to this wagon train for a reason, though perhaps not the one you first thought."

Chapter 16

The wagon lurched violently as it struck a deep rut, sending Emily's medical satchel sliding across the rough wooden floor. She caught it before it tumbled into Matthew, who sat cross-legged in the narrow space between their belongings, carefully arranging small treasures on a square of cloth. A smooth stone with a streak of white running through it, a jay's feather, and the dried husk of a beetle.

The constant, rhythmic creaking of the wagon had become the backdrop of her days, as familiar now as the sound of her own breathing. Outside, beyond the canvas walls that defined their shared world, the prairie stretched endlessly; the wind stirring the grass. Inside, the space was cramped and close, every inch occupied by necessity. Their trunks and supplies were methodically arranged and secured to prevent shifting. The scent of canvas, woolen blankets, and leather permeated everything.

Emily tucked the satchel securely between two crates and settled back against her trunk, allowing her gaze to drift to the slice of landscape visible through the gap in the canvas covering. They had been traveling for days now, since the illness had passed and the previously sick members of the wagon train were able to travel, putting mile after mile of prairie behind them. The monotony was broken only by river crossings and changes in terrain.

Here, in the confines of Weston's wagon, something unexpected had happened. The bitter solitude she had wrapped around herself in Richmond had eased. She couldn't retreat completely into herself, not with Matthew's constant, innocent presence. Not with Weston's quiet, steady competence always nearby, driving the oxen, guiding the wagon, his deep voice occasionally carrying back to them when he called instructions to the team.

"Miss Emily?" Matthew's voice pulled her back to the present. He held up his jay's feather, twirling it between his small fingers. "Do you think birds get sad when they lose their feathers?"

"I don't believe so," she answered. "They lose old feathers so new ones can grow. It's part of how birds live."

Matthew considered this seriously, his brow furrowed in concentration. "So losing things isn't always bad?"

A tightness formed in Emily's throat. "Some losses are part of life," she said carefully. "Like feathers or leaves in autumn. But other losses..." She faltered. "Other losses are harder to understand."

He nodded solemnly, as if she had confirmed something he had long suspected. "Papa says Mama is with Jesus in heaven. That's why she can't be with us." He arranged the feather carefully beside his other treasures. "But sometimes I get sad about that."

She reached out, hesitating just a moment before smoothing his unruly hair. "That's all right, Matthew. It's all right to be sad sometimes."

The wagon creaked and swayed, rocking them gently in its steady, forward rhythm. Outside, someone called to a straying ox, the voice thinned by distance and wind.

"What about you, Miss Emily?" Matthew looked up at her with innocent curiosity. "Why are you sad?"

Emily drew a careful breath. "I lost people I loved very much," she said simply. "My husband, my parents, and my sisters."

"All of them?" Matthew's eyes widened, the enormity of such loss clearly beyond his comprehension.

"Yes. All of them."

"But you have us now," Matthew stated with a child's straightforward logic, not understanding the vast complexity of grief and connection. He gestured to the cramped wagon space with a sweep of his small hand. "Me and Papa and everybody."

The wagon slowed, then stopped. Weston's voice carried through the canvas. "Short rest. We need to water the oxen."

The sudden stillness after hours of movement felt strange. Outside, people called to one another as they stretched cramped limbs and moved about, performing necessary tasks with the efficient haste of those who knew time was precious.

Matthew gathered his treasures carefully, wrapping them in the cloth. "Papa lets me help with the oxen sometimes," he explained, tucking the bundle safely away. "They're nice when you get to know them."

"Be careful," Emily cautioned automatically, as he scrambled toward the back of the wagon.

He paused, looking back at her with that sudden, bright smile that transformed his entire face. "I will. I'm coming right back. I want to show you something special after."

She watched him climb carefully down from the wagon, where Weston waited, his hand extended to help his son. Through the opening, she caught a glimpse of their interaction—Weston's strong hand engulfing Matthew's small one. The careful, protective way he guided the boy, the subtle softening of his expression when he looked at his son. There was such tenderness there, beneath the rugged exterior. She looked away quickly, feeling as though she had intruded on something private.

Left alone in the wagon, Emily let out a slow breath. The sudden silence was both welcome and unsettling. She closed her eyes, feeling the weight of Matthew's innocent question pressing upon her. But you have us now. As if people could be replaced, as if hearts could simply transfer affection from the dead to the living without the terrible ripping pain of it.

And yet, wasn't that what had happened, in some small measure? The boy had worked his way into her heart with his treasures and questions and unguarded smiles. And Weston, steady, capable Weston, who carried his own grief with such quiet dignity, had become more than just the wagon master, more than just a reluctant host in this cramped, shared space.

A shadow fell across her, and she opened her eyes to find Matthew clambering back into the wagon, his face flushed with excitement and exertion. In his hands he held a small, simple book bound in worn leather.

"Look, Miss Emily," he said, settling beside her. "This is mine. It's my prayer book. Papa reads it to me every night." He looked up at her with earnest eyes. "It has nice stories in it, about Jesus and people who needed help, and how God takes care of everybody."

Emily's throat tightened as she looked at the small volume, clearly cherished, its corners rounded from handling, its spine cracked from frequent opening. A child's book of faith, filled with simple truths and certainties.

"That's very nice, Matthew."

"Papa says the stories help me remember that God loves me, even when sad things happen." He flipped through the pages with careful reverence. "Like this one, about the lost sheep. The shepherd goes and finds it and brings it home even when it got all lost and scared."

Emily looked at the simple illustration, a bearded shepherd carrying a lamb over his shoulders. She remembered this story from her own childhood, remembered the comfort it had once brought, the assurance that no one was ever truly lost to God's sight.

Matthew leafed through the small book, showing her his favorite stories, explaining them with the earnest authority of a child who has heard them many times and accepted their truths without question. There was trust in his voice, security in his understanding of a world watched over by a loving God. Emily found herself envying his simple faith even as she marveled at its resilience.

When he came to the end of his book, he looked up at her with sudden inspiration. "Miss Emily, will you read me a story from your Bible again?" His eyes were bright with innocent expectation. "Papa reads me the one about the shepherd and the sheep, but from his big Bible. He says it's called a... a sam."

"A psalm," Emily corrected automatically, her mouth suddenly dry. "Psalm 23."

"Yes! That's it." Matthew nodded eagerly. "Will you read it, Miss Emily? Please?"

Outside, people were beginning to return to their places, voices calling back and forth as the brief rest came to an end. Soon Weston would return, would guide the oxen forward, and this moment would pass.

"Please?" Matthew repeated, his voice soft but persistent, his small face earnest.

Emily looked at him—this child who had lost his mother, yet still found joy in feathers and colored stones, who believed with complete conviction that God loved him and found lost sheep.

She reached for her satchel and retrieved her Bible. For a long moment, she simply stared at the closed cover, feeling the weight of it against her knees. With trembling fingers, she opened it. The familiar scent of the pages rose to meet her—paper and leather and memories. The first pages contained her family record, names and dates inscribed in careful handwriting. She turned quickly past them, unable to bear the sight of those lost names.

The pages whispered as she turned them, searching for the familiar passage. Matthew leaned against her, a warm, solid presence at her side. And then she found it, Psalm 23, the words her father had read countless times, words that had once been a comfort and then became a mockery in the face of such devastating loss.

"The Lord is my shepherd; I shall not want," she began, her voice barely audible, catching on the words. She cleared her throat and continued, forcing steadiness into her tone. "He maketh me to lie down in green pastures: he leadeth me beside the still waters."

The wagon creaked as someone climbed up—Weston, returning to his position. She glanced up briefly, meeting his eyes for just a moment before looking back at the page, heat rising in her cheeks. What did he see, watching her like this, vulnerable and exposed in this moment of connection with his son? Did he notice the tremble in her hands, the hesitation in her voice?

"He restoreth my soul," she continued, the familiar words flowing now despite the ache in her throat. "He leadeth me in the paths of righteousness for his name's sake."

Outside, the wagons were moving again. But within their canvas walls, a fragile, quiet moment held.

"Yea, though I walk through the valley of the shadow of death, I will fear no evil: for thou art with me; thy rod and thy staff, they comfort me."

Emily's voice faltered at these words. She had walked through that valley, had seen death claim everyone she loved, one by one. The sickroom in Richmond, the smell of disinfectant, her husband's labored breathing, her mother's hand growing cold in hers—there had been no comfort, no divine presence, only silence and the relentless progress of disease.

Matthew pressed closer against her side, his eyes fixed on the page as though he could read the words himself. She felt Weston's attention, knew he was listening, and witnessing this moment of her deepest vulnerability.

Emily took a steadying breath and continued. "Thou preparest a table before me in the presence of mine enemies: thou anointest my head with oil; my cup runneth over."

"Surely goodness and mercy shall follow me all the days of my life: and I will dwell in the house of the Lord forever."

Emily closed the Bible slowly, her heart beating too fast, her emotions a tangled knot that she couldn't begin to unravel.

"That's a good story," Matthew said, lifting his face to hers with a smile. "I like the part about the green grass and the water. And how God keeps us safe." He said it with absolute certainty.

Emily managed a small nod, unable to speak past the tightness in her throat. She had expected pain in reading these words, had anticipated the bitter memory of unanswered prayers and silent heavens. What she hadn't expected was the strange, painful longing that now welled up within her—a yearning for the faith she had lost, the certainty she had once known. She missed it, she realized with a start, like a limb suddenly gone.

"Did reading make you sad?" Matthew asked, noticing her silence, his eyes suddenly concerned.

"No," she said softly, surprised to find it wasn't entirely a lie. "Just... reminded of things."

"Papa says remembering can hurt, but it's important." He touched the Bible's leather cover gently. "Can we read another one tomorrow?"

"Perhaps," she said, unable to either promise or refuse.

The wagon rolled steadily onward, the creaks and groans of wood and canvas surrounding them. Outside, the prairie stretched toward the horizon. Emily carefully returned the Bible to her satchel, her mind filled with echoes of the ancient words—green pastures, still waters, the valley of the shadow.

The afternoon wore on, the wagon's steady progress marked by the changing angle of light filtering through the canvas. Matthew eventually grew drowsy, the gentle rocking motion of the wagon lulling him toward sleep. Without thinking, Emily guided his head to rest against her lap, her hand smoothing his hair in a gesture that felt both foreign and achingly wonderful.

His breathing deepened into the easy rhythm of childish slumber.

Emily looked down at the sleeping child, this boy who had lost his mother yet retained the capacity for joy and trust. Matthew's simple acceptance of both sorrow and hope put her own bitterness into sharp relief. Children understood loss in their own way—not less deeply, but perhaps more honestly, without the complications adults layered over their grief.

The wagon slowed as they navigated a small incline. Through the opening at the back, Emily caught glimpses of the landscape they traversed—the prairie grass stretching to the horizon, the occasional stand of trees marking a water source, the endless expanse above. So different from the familiar streets of Richmond, from the world she had fled.

Had she been wrong to reject faith in her grief? Faith hadn't protected her from loss. Nothing could have. But perhaps it might have provided a path through the devastating wilderness of grief, a direction when all sense of purpose had been stripped away.

She remembered Weston's words from their conversation by the fire—how he had found God not in answers or understanding, but in the quiet presence within his pain, the stubborn trust that persisted even when the path was dark.

Could she find her way back to such faith? Did she even want to?

The wagon jolted slightly as it crested the rise, and Matthew stirred in his sleep, his small hand clutching unconsciously at her skirt. Emily steadied him, her touch gentle. The simple action of caring for this child, of offering comfort and stability, felt healing in some indefinable way.

Later, as the light began to fade and the wagon train prepared to make camp for the night, Weston looked back through the opening after he pulled to a stop. His eyes moved from Matthew, still sleeping against Emily, to her face, a question in his expression.

"He's been asleep for some time," she said softly, answering the unspoken inquiry.

Weston nodded, his gaze lingering on his son with tender concern. Then his eyes met hers, and she saw understanding there before he climbed down to help organize the camp, leaving Emily with her thoughts.

Chapter 17

A sickening crack rent the air, followed by a splintering groan.

"Whoa! Hold there!" Weston called, already turning his horse toward the sound, dust kicking up beneath the animal's hooves. The steep incline they'd been navigating had claimed its victim. The second wagon in the line, belonging to the Croft family, listed dangerously to one side, its rear axle shattered under the strain of the rocky ascent.

"Halt the train!" Weston's command carried across the line of wagons, stretching back along the unforgiving terrain. Men scrambled to secure their teams, while women clutched children close, faces tight with worry.

Weston dismounted in one fluid motion, his boots hitting the hard ground with a thud that sent a jolt up his spine. He ducked beneath the tilted wagon, fingers probing the splintered wood of the axle. The break was clean and catastrophic. No simple patch would suffice. His stomach knotted with the realization of what this meant: a full-day lost at minimum, precious supplies consumed while stationary, and many souls halted in vulnerable terrain.

Barnaby's weathered face appeared beside him, lined with quiet distress. "Bad?"

"Worse," Weston replied, keeping his voice steady despite the gravity of the situation. "Clean break. We'll need a complete replacement."

In the trail's calculus, a broken axle could spell abandonment for a wagon and sometimes for the family who owned it.

A crowd gathered, faces pinched with the collective understanding of what this meant. Every hour delayed was water and food consumed, miles not traveled, and dangers not outrun.

"Can't be fixed? We've got to move on," came Ezekiel Vance's voice, cutting through the murmurs. The man pushed his way forward, his face a mask of impatience. "We're burning daylight on this godforsaken stretch."

Weston ignored him, turning instead to the blacksmith. "Samson, what do you think? Can you forge a replacement?"

Samson knelt beside the broken axle, his substantial frame casting a shadow over the damage. His calloused hands ran over the splintered wood with the sensitivity of a physician examining a patient. The sharp scent of broken oak and wagon grease filled the air between them.

"Got enough iron for bindings," Samson said thoughtfully, his deep voice rumbling like distant thunder. "We need good hardwood, though. Osage orange would be best, but oak might do."

"There's a stand of trees about half-a-mile back," Weston said, already calculating the time, manpower, and risk involved. "Not sure what type, but worth checking."

"This is madness," Vance interjected, louder this time. "One wagon holds back the rest? The Crofts can redistribute their belongings and join other wagons. We agreed to make Oregon before winter—this delay risks all of us."

Martha clutched her husband's arm, her knuckles white against his sun-browned skin. Their son Caleb, looking impossibly small beside the broken wagon, stared up at Weston with wide, trusting eyes that pierced straight through to his conscience.

Weston straightened, meeting Vance's gaze directly. "We leave no one behind, Vance. That was clear from the start. Everyone here agreed to travel as a company, not just when convenient."

"Poor leadership, that's what this is," Vance spat, his voice carrying to ensure everyone heard. "Risking the many for the few. That's not wisdom, that's foolishness."

Weston felt a flare of anger rise in his chest, but tamped it down. Getting drawn into Vance's provocations would only waste precious time and energy they couldn't afford to lose.

"Silas, I'll need your expertise on selecting the right wood," he said, deliberately turning away from Vance. "Samson, get your forge ready. George, you've got experience with wagon work?"

George nodded, stepping forward. "Built three before coming west."

"Good. You'll help with the refitting, Barnaby as well." Weston turned to the gathering crowd, raising his voice. "We've got work to do. We'll need men to help fell and transport suitable timber. Women can set up a cooking station—we'll need hot food to keep strength up. The rest of you help secure wagons and tend to the animals. We'll be here until this is fixed. That's how we'll continue... together."

The crowd dispersed with purpose, the mutual understanding of shared survival overriding individual complaints. All except Ezekiel, who stood with arms crossed, his mouth twisted in displeasure.

"You're making a mistake, Reynolds," he said, quiet enough now that only Weston could hear. "One day, your bleeding heart will get people killed."

"Better than abandoning folks to certain hardship," Weston replied evenly. "Move your wagon to level ground and make yourself useful, Vance. Or stay out of the way."

He watched the man slink away, then returned his attention to the task at hand. The incline where they'd stopped was treacherous—a steep, rocky grade. The wagons would need to be repositioned on flatter ground above or below, the animals unhitched and led to water, a proper camp established for what would likely be at least a full day's delay.

As he issued instructions and watched the train reconfigure itself, Weston caught sight of Emily. She'd climbed down from his wagon and was speaking quietly with Martha, one hand resting gently on the older woman's arm in obvious comfort. Matthew hovered nearby, clutching the small wooden toy horse Weston had carved for him during an evening watch.

Emily glanced up, her gaze meeting his briefly across the bustling camp. The reserve that typically had shadowed her features had softened into something Weston found himself increasingly drawn to, a quiet steadiness that spoke of deeper strength than her slender frame suggested. She gave a small nod before returning her attention to Martha, and Weston found himself staring a moment too long before forcing his attention back to the crisis at hand.

"Wagon master!" called Zach Calkins. "There appears to be a good level stretch just up ahead for the night camp."

Weston nodded approval. "Get the Carson brothers to help you scout a defensive circle. We'll need solid protection... we're exposed here."

The work of establishing camp proceeded with the grim efficiency born of necessity, while Weston led a small party back to the stand of trees he'd noted earlier.

"I need to make sure this is done right," Silas said, his weathered face resolute. "That wagon carried my father before me. My boy Caleb's meant to drive it someday after I'm gone. Can't let it be lost on my watch."

The meaning of the wagon to Silas settled deeper into Weston's determination. This wasn't just about conveyance or supplies, it was about legacy, family connections stretching back and forward through time.

They found a suitable oak, and the rhythmic swing of axes soon filled the air. Weston worked alongside the other men, his muscles burning with the effort, sweat coursing down his back in rivulets. The oak's heartwood was dense and unyielding, requiring careful cuts to ensure the right grain for an axle that must bear tremendous weight over punishing terrain.

He sent up silent prayers as he worked, for strength, for wisdom, and for the safety of the train left behind with only half its usual guard. Lord, guide our hands. Make this timber strong. Keep us all safe while we're vulnerable. The silent communion steadied him as he worked, the familiar conversation with his Creator as much a part of his daily existence as breathing.

When they returned with the timber strapped behind horses, the camp had transformed. Wagons formed a protective circle on a relatively level area just beyond the incline. Campfires burned, tended by the women who'd already organized cooking duties. Martha directed the food preparation with calm efficiency despite her own wagon's precarious position at the site of the breakdown, where Samson had already set up his portable forge.

The hard work of repair began in earnest. Samson's forge glowed orange against the deepening afternoon, the rhythmic clang of his hammer on metal creating a strangely comforting backdrop to the crisis. The acrid scent of hot iron mixed with the sharp smell of wood shavings as Silas and George worked on the timber, carefully shaping it to match the specifications of the broken axle.

Each man brought his particular gift to the task, Samson's powerful, precise hammer strokes forming the metal bands that would reinforce the wood; Silas's knowing eye guiding the shaping of the timber; George's careful measurements ensuring proper fit. Others, including young Zach Calkins, assisted wherever needed, fetching tools, holding pieces steady, learning the craft through necessity. Weston moved among them, coordinating efforts, lending his strength where required, and supervising the delicate balance between speed and quality.

"The Lord provides what we need," Weston thought as he watched the diverse skills at work. "Different gifts, but one purpose. Even in this wilderness, we're not without resources when we work as He intended us to... together."

"Water for the workers!"

Weston looked up to see Emily approaching, carrying a wooden bucket and ladle. Matthew trailed behind her, carefully balancing a smaller bucket with both hands, his face a study in concentration.

"Thought you might need this," she said, offering the ladle to Weston first. Her expression remained composed, but he noticed something new in her eyes, a quiet purpose and engagement that contrasted with the distant, grief-shrouded woman who had first joined their company. Her sleeves were rolled up, her hands reddened from work, a smudge of flour on her cheek suggesting she'd been helping with the cooking as well.

"Much obliged," he replied, taking a long drink. The water was cool and sweet, a mercy in the heat of labor. He wiped his mouth with the back of his hand, suddenly acutely aware of his sweat-soaked shirt and dirt-streaked face. "How's Martha holding up?"

"Perfectly fine," Emily said, a hint of admiration in her voice. "She's keeping busy with the cooking. Says idle hands only lead to worry."

"Wise woman." Weston watched as Matthew carefully offered water to Silas, the boy's small face serious with the importance of his task. Pride swelled in his chest at his son's eagerness to help, to be part of something larger than himself. "And you? I see you've found plenty to keep your hands busy as well."

Emily glanced down at her reddened hands, a slight flush coloring her cheeks. "There's always work that needs doing. Martha needed help with the biscuits, and then Sarah needed someone to hold the baby while she helped gather more food for the fire..." she trailed off, seeming almost embarrassed by the recounting of her contributions.

Weston wanted to tell her how much he appreciated her quiet integration into the work of the train. Instead, he simply nodded, not trusting himself to find the right words without revealing too much of the growing warmth he felt for her.

"Papa?" Matthew called, breaking the moment. "Is the wagon going to be better after it's fixed? Caleb's worried about his special rock collection."

Weston smiled despite the strain of the day. "That's the plan, son. Might even roll smoother than before if Samson and Silas have their way."

"Can I help?" the boy asked, his eager expression a mirror of Weston's own childhood enthusiasm for any task involving tools.

"You already are," Weston assured him, gesturing to the water bucket. "A workforce needs water to keep going. That's an important job."

Matthew beamed with pride, his slender shoulders straightening as he continued his rounds with renewed purpose.

"He wants to be useful," Emily remarked quietly as they watched the boy. "Like his father."

A commotion from the main camp drew their attention. Vance's voice carried clearly. "—wasting precious time! At this rate, all the good land in Oregon will be claimed!"

Weston handed the ladle back to Emily. "Duty calls," he said with a grimace.

"He seems determined to make everything harder," she observed.

"That's his special talent," Weston agreed, then hesitated a moment. "Thank you for the water, and for helping Martha. For all of it."

Emily nodded, a ghost of a smile touching her lips. "We all do what we can."

Weston headed toward the main camp, steel gathering in his spine. He found Ezekiel holding court among a small cluster of pioneers, his hands gesturing expansively as he spoke. "The Crofts should leave that heap of a wagon behind. It's the sensible approach."

"The sensible approach," Weston interrupted, his voice carrying across the gathering, "is keeping this train together as agreed when we left Independence and remaining calm. The Crofts' wagon will be repaired by tomorrow noon, with all of us pulling together."

Vance turned, his expression souring at Weston's arrival. "A full day lost, and for what? Sentiment over an old wagon?"

"For community," Reverend Holloway interjected, stepping forward from the crowd. "For the principle that we face hardships together, not just when convenient."

Murmurs of agreement rippled through the gathered pioneers. Weston noted with satisfaction that Vance's audience seemed unpersuaded by his arguments.

"Fine sentiments," Vance countered, "but sentiments don't get us to Oregon before winter. Sentiments don't claim land or build homes. Sentiments won't keep us alive if we're stuck in mountain snow because we wasted time on broken wagons."

"Neither does abandoning folks who've trusted their lives to this company," Weston responded evenly. "The wagon will be fixed, and we'll move on together. Anyone who can't abide by that is free to leave on their own." He let the challenge hang in the air, his gaze steady on Ezekiel.

The man's face flushed an angry red, but he made no move to accept the implicit invitation to depart. Instead, he scoffed and pushed his way through the crowd, muttering about foolishness and wasted time.

As the gathering dispersed, Reverend Holloway approached Weston, his kind face creased with concern.

"That man sows discord wherever he goes," the reverend observed quietly.

"Like it's his calling," Weston agreed.

"Perhaps it is, in a way," Holloway mused. "Every community needs its tests. Ezekiel is ours." He paused, watching the activity around the broken wagon, where Samson's hammer continued its steady rhythm. "I've been praying for patience... for all of us, but especially for you, Weston. Leadership is a burden God understands well."

Weston nodded, touched by the man's insight. "Appreciate those prayers, Reverend. We'll need more before we reach Oregon."

"Indeed." Holloway smiled gently.

The work continued as afternoon stretched toward evening. Women continued to cook, while children were sent to gather buffalo chips and what wood could be found for more fuel. The livestock had been led to a small stream Zach had discovered nearby, and grazed under watchful eyes.

Weston divided his attention between overseeing the wagon repair and ensuring the camp's security. This exposed position left them vulnerable, and he doubled the usual watch, positioning men at strategic points around the perimeter.

As twilight descended, Emily appeared at his side again, this time with a tin plate of beans and salt pork.

"Martha insisted," she explained, handing him the plate. "Said you'd work through the night without food if someone didn't remind you."

Weston accepted the meal gratefully. "She's not wrong," he admitted, sinking onto a nearby rock. "Thank you."

Emily hesitated, then sat beside him, smoothing her skirts with careful hands. Weston found her presence comforting after hours of crisis management.

"How's the repair coming?" she asked, watching Samson and Silas conferring over a piece of shaped timber in the fading light.

"Slow but steady," Weston replied between bites. "Samson's forged the metal supports. The wood's nearly ready. We'll assemble at first light when we can see properly."

They sat in companionable silence for a moment, the sounds of the camp—clinking cookware, murmured conversations, and children's occasional laughter—creating a pocket of normalcy amid the crisis.

"Does this happen often?" Emily asked. "Major breakdowns like this?"

"Often enough," Weston nodded. "The trail's hard on equipment. We've been fortunate so far... mostly minor repairs until now."

"The Crofts seem well-liked," she observed. "People rallied quickly."

"They are good people. Silas knows wagons better than most, and Martha's got a good hand with medicine plants—not your level of knowledge, but useful. They've helped plenty of folks out during our journey west. Community remembers those things." He paused, considering his next words carefully. "I've noticed you doing the same today, helping wherever needed."

Emily's hands twisted slightly in her lap. "It felt... right. To help. It made me feel useful." She looked up, meeting his gaze directly.

"I believe you're finding your purpose in life again," Weston supplied quietly.

She nodded as Matthew came running up, his face smudged with dirt and something sticky that looked suspiciously like preserves.

"Papa! Mrs. Croft made blackberry jam biscuits for the helpers!" he announced, clearly counting himself among this important group. "She said I should bring you one."

He thrust a slightly squashed biscuit toward Weston, his expression earnest. Weston accepted it, recognizing the offering for the treasure it was.

"That was mighty thoughtful of you to bring it all this way without eating it yourself," he said, breaking the biscuit in half. "Should we share it? Seems to me Miss Emily might appreciate Mrs. Croft's jam, too."

Matthew considered this suggestion, then nodded seriously. "Miss Emily helped a lot today. She showed me how to fold bandages for Mr. Samson's burned hand and helped Mrs. Croft with the cooking. And she helped me with my water bucket when it got too heavy."

Emily accepted her half of the biscuit. Weston watched as her expression softened, while looking at Matthew, her face transforming with an inner light that caught at something deep in his chest.

The brief moment of peace was shattered by a shout from the perimeter of the camp.

"Riders approaching! Three of 'em, coming fast from the east!"

Weston was on his feet instantly, a hand going to the pistol at his hip. "Get to the wagon," he told Emily, already moving toward the eastern edge of the circle. "Keep Matthew inside."

She didn't argue, gathering the boy with a swift, protective gesture that sent a flash of grateful warmth through Weston even as he focused on the potential threat.

The riders turned out to be a small scouting party from a train two days behind them, bearing news of increased Pawnee activity in the region. No direct threats, but enough to warrant extra vigilance. Weston thanked them for the warning and shared information about the trail ahead, along with the location of the small water seep they'd found.

By the time he had organized additional night watches and ensured the warning was properly communicated throughout the camp, twilight had deepened into true darkness. The repair site was quiet, tools carefully stowed for the night, and the timber securely positioned for morning work.

Weary to his bones, Weston made his way back to his wagon. He found Matthew sound asleep on his bedroll, one small hand clutching the wooden horse, his face peaceful in slumber.

Emily sat near the wagon's open back, a blanket wrapped around her shoulders against the evening chill. She looked up as he approached, her face half-illuminated by the distant glow of campfires.

"I thought you might sleep at the repair site," she said quietly.

"Considered it," Weston admitted, lowering himself to sit on the wagon's edge, muscles aching from the day's labor. "

Emily drew her blanket closer. "Matthew wanted to wait up for you, but sleep won that battle."

Weston glanced at his son's peaceful form. "Did he continue to help you today?" he asked.

"More than I expected," she admitted. "He's quite capable for his age. Organized the younger children to gather fuel, and helped carry water."

Pride warmed Weston's chest. "That pleases me," he said. "I worry about what kind of man he'll become without his mama here to show him gentleness alongside strength."

"Whatever guidance he missed, you've made up for it in your own way. He has your strength, but there's a tenderness in him too."

The simple validation eased something tight in Weston's chest. The quiet fear that had haunted him for six years—that he wasn't enough, that Matthew would somehow be less without a mother's love—felt suddenly less oppressive under Emily's calm, observant gaze.

"Thank you," he managed, the words inadequate for the gift she'd given him. "That means more than you know."

She nodded. "You should rest, as you often say... tomorrow will come early."

"That it will," he agreed, stretching his sore shoulders before retreating to his bedroll on the opposite side of the wagon. Bone-weary but mind still racing with the day's events, tomorrow's challenges, and the complicated tangle of feelings stirred by the woman sitting watch in the darkness. Her quiet strength had become a comfort he found himself increasingly relying on, a realization that both soothed and terrified him.

Chapter 18

Weston was up before first light the next morning, checking the camp's perimeter before heading to the repair site. He found Samson waiting to begin the day's work, the metal pieces he had made laid out in precise order.

Silas joined them soon after, followed by George and a handful of other men eager to help. They began the delicate process of fitting the new axle. The replacement timber, shaped through hours of careful work, needed to be precisely aligned and reinforced with the metal bands Samson had forged.

"Hold it steady now," Silas directed as four men lifted the wagon's rear corner while others positioned the axle. "Easy... easy..."

The work required strength, precision, and patience.

Before long, the camp was fully awake and active. Women prepared a hearty breakfast, children were set to simple tasks, and a constant stream of water bearers kept the work crew hydrated. Emily had organized a rotation of helpers, ensuring no one person bore too much of the burden, a system Weston noted with approval and a deepening appreciation for her practical mind.

"She's got a good head for organization," Silas commented, noticing Weston's gaze following Emily as she directed a group of children filling water buckets from the barrels. "Reminds me of my Martha when she was younger. Quiet-like, but sees what needs doing and does it."

Weston nodded, turning his attention back to the wagon. "Let's get this wheel mounted. The sooner we're moving again, the better."

The final stages of repair proceeded smoothly until a commotion from the main camp caught their attention. Vance's voice, raised in anger, carried clearly to the repair site.

"—absolute lunacy! We've lost an entire day now! The water supply won't—"

Weston sighed heavily, wiping sweat from his brow. "Keep working," he instructed the men. "I'll handle this."

He strode toward the camp, irritation building with each step. As he approached, he saw Vance gesturing wildly, his face flushed with anger as he addressed a group of people gathered around the main cooking fire.

"—and when we're rationing water because we wasted time here, remember who insisted on this delay!"

Reverend Holloway stood opposite Vance, his expression calm but firm. "Mr. Vance, your concerns have been noted, but this constant agitation serves no one."

"I'm speaking sense in a wilderness of foolishness," Vance retorted. "Someone must!"

"That's enough, Vance," Weston interrupted, stepping into the circle. "The wagon's nearly repaired. We'll be moving within the hour."

Vance rounded on him, jabbing a finger toward his chest. "Convenient timing, Reynolds. Just as people are beginning to question your leadership."

Weston arched an eyebrow, glancing around at the gathered faces. He saw concern, weariness, but no evidence of the rebellion Vance claimed to represent.

"Seems to me you're the only one questioning anything," he observed mildly. "The rest are pitching in where needed."

"Because they fear being left behind if they speak up!" Vance insisted. "You've made it clear... fall in line or face abandonment."

"That's a curious accusation," Weston replied, keeping his tone level despite his rising anger. "Coming from the man who suggested we abandon the Crofts yesterday."

A murmur ran through the gathered pioneers. Martha, standing nearby with a cooking ladle in hand, fixed Ezekiel with a steely glare that belied her usual gentle demeanor.

"Is that so, Mr. Vance?" she asked, her voice carrying clearly. "You thought we should be left behind?"

Vance faltered momentarily, clearly not expecting direct confrontation from the soft-spoken woman. "I merely suggested practical solutions to avoid unnecessary delay," he blustered. "Any sensible party would consider all options."

"The only option this train considers," Weston stated firmly, "is moving forward together. That was agreed upon before we left Independence, and that's how we'll continue. As I stated before, anyone who can't abide by that understanding is free to depart on their own recognizance."

He met Vance's gaze steadily, the challenge plain. Once again, the man made no move to accept the invitation to leave, revealing the hollow nature of his complaints. He wanted the protection and advantages of the group while rejecting its shared responsibilities.

"Fine words," Vance muttered, breaking eye contact first. "We'll see how they hold up when tougher choices come—and they will."

He pushed past Weston roughly, shouldering his way through the crowd. Several people stepped deliberately aside, their expressions making clear which side of the dispute held their sympathy.

"He's afraid," came a quiet voice beside him. Weston turned to find Emily standing there. "Fear makes men like him dangerous."

"Fear makes most folks dangerous in some fashion," Weston replied, watching Vance stalk back to his wagon. "But he's right about one thing... tougher choices will come before we reach Oregon."

Emily studied his face for a moment. "You've made them before."

"Comes with the territory," he acknowledged. "Trail doesn't leave much room for indecision."

A call from the repair site drew his attention. "Wagon master! We're ready to test it!"

Weston excused himself and headed back to where Samson, Silas, and the others waited beside the repaired wagon. The new axle gleamed with a coat of tallow, the wheel remounted and secured.

"She's ready," Samson announced, his usual taciturn manner giving way to quiet pride. "Need to take her slow for the first few miles. Let the wood and metal settle together, but she'll hold."

Silas ran a hand along the new timber, his weathered face creased with emotion. "Fine work, Mr. Early. My father would have approved."

The two men, so different in background and circumstance, exchanged a look of mutual respect, born of shared labor and skill. Weston was struck again by the unlikely bonds forged on the trail, connections that transcended the divisions of the world they'd left behind.

"Let's hitch her up," he directed. "Get your team ready, Silas. We'll test her on level ground before tackling that incline again."

The oxen were brought forward and hitched to the repaired wagon.

A small crowd gathered to watch the test. Martha stood with Emily and Sarah, the women's hands clasped in shared anticipation.

"Easy now," Weston cautioned as Silas took up the reins. "Just a gentle pull to start."

Silas clicked his tongue, urging the oxen forward. The team strained against the yoke, muscles bunching under their hides. For one heart-stopping moment, the wagon didn't move—then, with a slight creak of protest, it rolled forward smoothly.

A cheer went up from the gathered crowd. Martha pressed her apron to her mouth, eyes bright with unshed tears of relief. Caleb darted forward, running alongside the slowly moving wagon with childish exuberance.

"Steady pace," Weston called, walking beside the wagon, watching carefully for any signs of stress on the new axle. "Circle back, and we'll check the fittings."

Silas guided the team in a wide arc, bringing the wagon back to its starting point. Samson immediately ducked beneath, examining his handiwork with critical eyes.

"Holding true," he announced after a thorough inspection. "No signs of strain."

Weston nodded with satisfaction. "Good work, all of you. Silas, get your belongings packed and secured. We move out within the hour."

The camp burst into activity. The delay had cost them a full day, but Weston felt a deep satisfaction in the successful repair and the unified effort it had required.

As he supervised the preparation for departure, he noticed Emily helping Martha reorganize her wagon's contents. Matthew hovered nearby, handing up items as directed, his small face serious with the responsibility.

When the time came to depart, Weston positioned his wagon at the head of the wagon train, surveying the line behind him with critical eyes. The Croft wagon climbed the incline and took its place behind his wagon.

"Move out!" he called and nodded to Barnaby, who was riding Weston's horse now.

As the wagon train stretched out behind him across the vast landscape, he smiled. This particular group of pioneers, despite Vance's divisive efforts and the natural challenges of the trail, possessed something special. A resilience born not just from individual determination, but from their willingness to function as a community, to recognize that their individual strengths, when combined, created something far more powerful than the sum of its parts.

Beside him, Emily and Matthew rode on the wagon seat. The boy's chatter carried forward on the breeze.

He touched the brim of his hat in a small gesture of acknowledgment to the sky above, a habit formed through years of silent communication with the Almighty. "Thank you, Lord, for the strength of these people, for the skills You've given them, and for guiding our hands in this work. Keep us safe on this long road."

Chapter 19

The fiddle's distinct sound drifted through the evening air, wavering at first like a tentative question before finding its strength. Emily paused beside the creek where she'd been washing her face, water dripping from her fingertips, as the unexpected melody reached her. The simple tune, hopeful and sweet, rose above the usual camp sounds, transforming the very air around her.

The wagon train had found camp in a small valley tucked between rolling hills, with a creek winding through stands of cottonwood trees, whose leaves whispered in the light breeze. After endless days of relentless travel through dust and exposure, this pocket of beauty felt like a gift. The livestock grazed contentedly on thick grass, drinking from the clear water. The cottonwoods offered generous shade, and wildflowers dotted the meadow in unexpected bursts of color.

As Emily walked back to the camp, a lantern in her hand, she heard voices carrying a note she hadn't heard in days—pleasure. The usual grim efficiency of the camp had softened. Faces that had been drawn with exhaustion now turned toward one another in conversation.

Children darted between wagons, their tired faces brightened with renewed energy.

It was as though everyone had simultaneously exhaled after holding their breath for far too long.

Another fiddle joined the first—a higher, sweeter voice in harmony. Then came the simple notes of a harmonica. Emily was drawn toward the music.

As she approached the center of the camp, she saw people gathering around a large fire. Silas sat on an overturned bucket, his hands moving with surprising grace over the fiddle strings, his foot tapping steadily in the dust. Beside him, young Zach Calkins mirrored the tune on a smaller fiddle, his face alight with concentration. George Billings played his harmonica, the tiny notes weaving through the deeper tones of the fiddles. His wife Liz moved among the group with a wooden dipper and bucket of clean water. Reverend Holloway stood with his arm around Mercy, her head resting on his shoulder, both wearing expressions of peaceful contentment. Martha swayed gently as she stirred a pot over their fire, occasionally casting fond glances at her husband.

The music had drawn nearly everyone now. Even Sarah had joined the group, sitting on a blanket with baby Hope cradled against her chest. The young widow's face still carried the hollow look of grief, but tonight her eyes were lifted to the gathering rather than fixed on the ground.

"I believe you're smiling."

The quiet voice beside her made Emily turn. Weston stood there, his tall frame half in shadow, half in firelight. She hadn't heard him approach, which was unusual. Typically, Weston moved with purpose through camp, his presence announced by his steady footfalls and the natural deference of others.

Tonight, he looked different. The constant vigilance that tightened his features had eased. His shoulders, usually rigid with responsibility, had relaxed. Without his wide-brimmed hat, his face was fully visible, his deep blue eyes catching the firelight in a way that revealed flecks of lighter blue she'd never noticed before.

"Was I?" Emily touched her face, surprised.

Weston nodded, his gaze moving across the gathered travelers. "Been a long while since I've seen everyone like this. Reminds us there's more to living than just surviving."

Emily followed his gaze to where Caleb tugged his mother into an impromptu dance. The boy's face split with a wide grin. Martha laughed—actually laughed—allowing herself to be pulled into a dance by her son, her usual serious efficiency nowhere to be seen.

"They forget so quickly. Last week, so many were ill, and we buried Mr. Abbott."

"They're not forgetting," Weston said quietly, meeting her eyes. "They're remembering why it matters to keep going. Why we bear the hardships."

His words settled into her, resonating with the unexpected truth. She studied the faces around the fire—tired, weathered, and marked by weeks of grueling travel and fear—yet tonight, reclaiming something essentially human that had been buried beneath exhaustion and worry.

"Perhaps you're right," she conceded. "Perhaps these moments of joy make the burden of sorrow all the more bearable... though they also make its return more painful."

Weston nodded slowly, understanding in his eyes. "Like rain after drought. The earth appreciates the water more for having known the thirst."

His simple eloquence caught her off guard. He seemed about to say more when Matthew burst from the crowd and ran toward them, his small boots kicking up puffs of dust.

"Papa! Miss Emily!" he called, breathless with excitement. "They're dancing now! Real dancing, like you told me about Papa!"

Indeed, the music had quickened, and several couples had formed a loose circle, stepping and turning in time with the fiddles' lively tune. George had abandoned his harmonica and swung Liz in a wide arc that made her skirts billow, both of them laughing. Nearby, Reverend James danced with Mercy.

"You should join them, Matthew," Emily suggested, smiling at his excitement.

Matthew shook his head, his eyes bright with determination. "You! Papa used to dance with Mama. He told me so."

"That was a long time ago, Matthew," Weston said gently.

"But you remember how, don't 'cha?" Matthew persisted.

Weston's gaze moved from his son to Emily, then back again. "I reckon I do."

He turned back toward Emily, and the look on his face made her heart quicken. Gone was the efficient wagon master, the vigilant scout, and the careful single father. In their place stood simply a man, hesitant and vulnerable, his usual certainty replaced by something far more human.

"Emily?" His voice was rough at the edges, like well-worn cotton. "Would you... would you like to dance?"

Dance? The very idea seemed to belong to another life, another world—to the Emily who had been happy once, who had laughed and loved without the shadow of death hovering over every moment.

Memories rushed through her with painful clarity—her wedding day, Thomas leading her in a graceful waltz while family and friends clapped in time; her sisters twirling in the parlor while their father played the piano; family gatherings where even her reserved mother would eventually be coaxed into the dancing.

The memories carried the bitter sting of loss, yet beneath that familiar pain ran something else as well. A current of longing so powerful it frightened her. Not just longing for what was gone, but for what might still be. For warmth, for connection, and for the simple human comfort of being touched with kindness after so many months of feeling alone.

She looked at Weston's outstretched hand, strong and calloused from handling reins and ropes.

"I don't—" she began, uncertain what she was even refusing—the dance itself, or the doorway it might open.

"Just one dance," Weston said, his voice steady, but his eyes revealing a vulnerability that matched her own. "Like you said to Matthew that day about reading from your Bible—sometimes we need to remember how."

Emily's throat tightened at the gentle reminder. Matthew looked up at her, his small face hopeful and innocent of the complex currents swirling between the adults.

"Please, Miss Emily?" he asked.

Emily drew a trembling breath. She extended her hand toward Weston's. His fingers closed gently around hers, warm and solid.

"Yes," she said. "One dance."

Weston's expression softened, relief flickering across his features. He led her toward the circle around the fire, Matthew trailing behind with barely contained excitement.

The couples moved in simple patterns to the lively fiddle tune. Emily felt exposed under the gazes that turned their way, conscious of the quiet stir their appearance together created. Dancing with the wagon master—it would feed camp whispers for days.

But as Weston turned to face her, resting one hand lightly on her waist while maintaining his gentle hold on her other hand, those concerns faded. The music seemed to swell around them, Silas's fiddle singing a melody both melancholy and hopeful.

They moved, awkwardly at first. Emily couldn't remember the last time she'd been touched with such deliberate gentleness. Her body felt stiff and hesitant, like a language she'd forgotten how to speak. Weston's movements were similarly uncertain, a man relearning forgotten steps.

"I'm afraid I'm terribly out of practice," she murmured, eyes fixed on the space between them.

"We both are," Weston replied, his voice low. "But we're managing."

They were finding a rhythm together, their steps becoming smoother as they moved in gradual circles. The initial awkwardness began to dissolve into something else, something both frightening and exhilarating.

Physical awareness blossomed between them. The warmth of his palm against hers. The careful distance he maintained between their bodies, respectful yet undeniably intimate. The simple touch of his hand against her waist sent waves of sensation through her body, awakening nerves she'd thought long deadened by grief.

Emily was suddenly, intensely aware of her breathing, of the fabric of her dress moving against her skin as they turned, and of the soft ground beneath her feet. It was as though her body, numb for so long, was remembering what it meant to be alive, to be present in the world.

"Matthew seems pleased with himself," Weston observed, nodding toward where his son stood watching them, beaming with satisfaction.

Emily glanced at the boy, feeling a rush of tender affection. "He seems determined to bring people together."

"It's his nature," Weston said, guiding her in a gentle turn. "He worries about you, you know. About your sadness."

"He told you that?"

Weston nodded, his eyes meeting hers. "Children see more than we give them credit for. Especially ones who know the shape of sorrow themselves."

The realization that Matthew had spoken of it to his father sent a complicated wave of emotion through her. Shame that her pain was so visible, even to a child. Tenderness that he cared enough to worry. Fear of the attachment growing between them.

"I never meant to burden him with my troubles."

"It's not a burden to him," Weston replied, his voice dropping to nearly a whisper. "It's simply love."

Love. Emily's step faltered slightly, but Weston's steady hand kept her from stumbling.

"He has a generous heart," she managed.

"Like his mother," Weston said quietly. Then, after a pause: "I think she would be glad to know he's found someone who reads to him, and who listens to his stories. Someone who cares."

Emily knew what it cost him to speak of his wife, how carefully he guarded those memories.

"I'm sure she would be proud of how you've raised him," she offered, her voice barely audible above the music. "He's a remarkable child."

Weston's eyes softened, his gaze drifting to where Matthew stood. "He's the best of her. Her kindness, her way of seeing good in everything." His voice held a note of wonder. "Sometimes I think the Lord knew I'd need that reminder, after she was gone."

Around them, the music and dancing continued, and Emily found herself increasingly aware of only Weston. The steady rhythm of his breathing, the surprising grace of his movement, the careful way he held her, as though she were something precious that might break or flee if handled too roughly.

For so long, she had been adrift in her grief, anchored only to the memory of what she had lost. But here, now, her body was responding to another living presence, awakening to the simple human comfort of being held, and of moving in harmony with another person. It was terrifying. It was exquisite.

Weston's gaze met hers and held it. In the flickering firelight, she could see the understanding in his eyes, the shared knowledge of loss that bound them together, even as something new and unnamed sprouted in the space between them.

"Mrs. Wilson!"

The booming voice cut through their moment. Emily turned her head to see Clarence Hodge approaching with his characteristic swagger. The well-dressed widower from Kentucky had made his interest in her clear over the past weeks, despite her consistent coolness.

"Might I cut in for the next dance?" he asked, his tone suggesting he expected an affirmative answer. "I was quite renowned for my waltzing back in Louisville society."

Emily felt Weston's hand tighten almost imperceptibly at her waist. She looked up, meeting his eyes, and found a carefully composed neutrality that nevertheless failed to hide a flare of something possessive.

"I believe Miss Wilson may be tired after this dance, Mr. Hodge," Weston said evenly, his tone courteous but firm. "The day has been long for us all."

Clarence glanced between them, his expression sharpening with sudden understanding. "Of course, of course. Perhaps another time, then. When you're... less occupied."

He backed away, bowing slightly, his smile not quite reaching his eyes. Emily watched him go, relieved yet unsettled by the exchange. It had marked a public acknowledgment of whatever was growing between her and Weston.

"I apologize for answering for you," Weston said quietly. "If you wished to dance with him—"

"I didn't," Emily interrupted. "I don't."

The music was slowing now, the fiddle's notes becoming more drawn out, more contemplative. Silas seemed to be tiring, and the evening was deepening toward true night. Around them, some dancers had already stopped, returning to their fires or gathering in conversational groups.

But Weston still held her, their movements gentler now, barely more than swaying. The space between them had somehow diminished, their bodies closer than they had been. Emily could feel the warmth radiating from him, could detect the faint scent of leather and wood smoke that clung to his clothes.

"We should probably stop," she said, even as her body continued to move with his, unwilling to break the fragile connection between them.

"Probably," he agreed, making no move to release her.

For a suspended moment, they simply stood there, barely moving, caught in a strange limbo between dance and embrace. Emily felt dizzy with conflicting emotions—grief and hope, fear and longing battling within her like opposing currents.

The music finally faded into silence. The spell broke. Weston stepped back, slowly releasing her hand.

"Thank you for the dance," he said, his voice carrying the rough quality she had noticed earlier.

Emily nodded, not trusting her voice. Around them, the camp was settling, the brief celebration winding down as fatigue reclaimed its hold. The practical realities of the trail reasserted itself.

Matthew appeared at Weston's side, yawning widely despite his excitement. "That was nice," he said sleepily. "You both looked happy."

Happy. Such a simple word, yet it struck Emily like a physical blow. Had she looked happy? Had she, perhaps, for a brief moment, actually been happy?

The possibility was almost too much to bear. Happiness felt like betrayal—of Thomas, and of her family. Yet there it was, a fragile spark of happiness she couldn't deny.

"Time for bed, son," Weston said, placing a gentle hand on Matthew's shoulder. "We've got an early start tomorrow."

"Can Miss Emily tell me a story first?" the boy asked, looking up at her with hopeful eyes.

"A very short one," Weston compromised, glancing at Emily. "If Miss Emily is willing."

"Of course," she replied automatically, though her mind was still tangled in the aftermath of their dance.

They walked together toward Weston's wagon, Matthew between them, chattering sleepily about the music and dancing.

Near the wagon, Emily paused, looking up at the vast expanse of stars overhead. They seemed closer tonight, more brilliant, as if the thin mountain air brought the heavens nearer to earth.

Looking at them now, she felt a strange, fleeting connection to the faith of her childhood. The belief that God watched over the world and that nothing happened outside His notice or care. That sense had abandoned her after the typhoid epidemic, replaced by bitter doubt and the conviction that if God existed, He had turned His face away from her suffering.

Tonight, though, beneath the canopy of stars, having just experienced an unexpected moment of beauty and connection, she found herself wondering—was this, too, part of some greater pattern? Could even this small, precious moment of warmth be a sign of grace working in the most unexpected ways?

"Penny for your thoughts?" Weston asked.

Emily glanced at him, finding his expression open, attentive. "I was thinking about the stars," she said. "How they remain unchanging while everything beneath them shifts and transforms."

He followed her gaze upward. "My father used to say they're God's campfires, lit to guide travelers home."

"That's a comforting thought."

"He was a man of simple faith," Weston replied. "Believed the Lord's hand was in everything—the good and the difficult alike."

"Miss Emily! I'm ready!" Matthew called from the wagon, already in his nightshirt.

The child's voice pulled her back to the present moment. "Coming, Matthew," she replied, moving toward the wagon.

Weston caught her hand lightly, stopping her. "Emily," he said.

She turned, finding him closer than she'd expected, his expression intent in the starlight.

"Yes?"

He seemed to struggle for words, unusual for a man typically so direct. "Thank you for the dance. For... being here."

Simple words, yet Emily heard the depth behind them. Being here—not just physically present in the wagon or on the journey, but emotionally present, gradually emerging from the fortress of her grief into something uncertain but alive.

"And I thank you for asking me," she replied.

His eyes held hers for a moment longer, then he released her hand with a nod. "I'll check on the oxen," he said.

Emily climbed into the wagon, where Matthew waited with eager eyes despite his obvious fatigue. "Which story tonight?" she asked, settling beside his small bedroll.

"The one about the shepherd finding his lost sheep," Matthew decided. "I like that one."

As Emily began the parable, her voice soft in the confined space of the wagon, she was acutely aware of her surroundings. The canvas walls glowing faintly with reflected firelight, Matthew's small form curled trustingly beside her, and the sounds of Weston moving around the wagon, checking on the animals and security for the night.

It felt, with a suddenness, that stole her breath, like home. Not the home she had lost, but something new and fragile, taking shape around her.

Matthew fell asleep before she finished the story, his breathing deepening into the perfect rhythm of childhood slumber. Emily sat beside him for a moment longer, studying his peaceful face, so like his father's, in the calm lines of his brow and chin.

She heard Weston approach. He paused outside the wagon, his shadow visible against the canvas.

"He's asleep," she called softly.

"Good," Weston replied, his voice equally low. "You should rest too. It's been a long day."

Emily rose quietly, careful not to disturb the sleeping boy. She moved to the wagon's opening, where Weston stood looking up at her, his face half-illuminated by distant firelight.

"I will," she assured him. "Though I find myself less tired than I should be."

"The dancing," he suggested with the hint of a smile. "Brings its own kind of energy."

"Perhaps."

A comfortable silence settled between them. Emily studied his face, noting the lines at the corners of his eyes, the stubble darkening his jaw, and the quiet strength in his features. She had begun to read his expressions, to understand the subtle shifts that revealed his thoughts.

Right now, he was looking at her with a tenderness that made her heart beat faster, a look that held no expectation, only appreciation.

"Good night, Emily. Sleep well. If you wouldn't mind listening for Matthew throughout the night, I feel the need to sleep outside tonight."

"I understand. Good night, Weston," she replied.

He nodded once, then turned away, moving toward his sleeping roll laid out beside the wagon. Emily retreated into the wagon's interior, settling onto her bedding.

In the darkness, she raised her fingers to her face, surprised to find her cheeks damp with tears. Not tears of grief, for once, but something more complex—release, perhaps. Fear, certainly. But also a trembling possibility that terrified and beckoned her in equal measure.

She had danced tonight. She had moved in rhythm with another person, and had allowed herself to be held, and to be seen. She had allowed her frozen heart to thaw, just enough to remember what warmth felt like.

And for the first time since the fever had stolen everything she loved, Emily found herself wanting to be part a part of ordinary life again.

The possibility was as terrifying as it was alluring—opening herself to connection meant opening herself to loss. Loving meant risking devastation.

"Lord," she whispered, "I don't understand. I don't know if I can bear this."

As she drifted toward sleep, the memory of Weston's hand holding hers, steady and warm, followed her into dreams. And those dreams were not haunted by what she had lost, but tentatively shaped by what might, against all odds, still be possible.

Chapter 20

The flat prairie vanished, replaced by a world of stone. Weston's shoulders tensed as his horse picked its way up the rugged incline. The trail—if it could still be called that—had narrowed to a path barely wide enough for a single wagon, bordered on one side by a sheer rock face and on the other by a steep drop. Behind him stretched the wagon train, a fragile line of canvas-topped vehicles straining against the growing incline.

He pulled his mount to a halt, tasting dust as he surveyed what lay ahead. The Rocky Mountains loomed against the sky, their jagged peaks cutting into the clouds like knives. What had appeared distant and almost beautiful from the prairie now seemed an impenetrable wall of stone, indifferent to human ambition.

"Easy, girl," he murmured as his horse shifted nervously beneath him. The animal sensed his unease.

The air felt different here—thinner and cooler, carrying scents of pine and damp stone instead of prairie grass. Each breath required more effort, a reminder of their increasing altitude. The sounds had changed too. Gone was the rhythmic creak and sway of wagons rolling over open land. Now he heard the strain of wood under pressure, the labored breathing of oxen, the sharp crack of whips, and the occasional shouts as drivers urged their teams forward.

Weston's eyes narrowed, calculating. The pass they needed lay higher still. Three more days' of hard travel if the weather held. The supplies were running lower with each passing day. Several families were already on reduced rations. The animals showed signs of wear despite careful management. Even the strongest oxen moved with less vigor.

A shout from below pulled his attention back to the immediate trail. He turned to see one of the wagons—the Calkins'—listing dangerously as its wheel caught on a jutting stone. Zach was frantically trying to steady the team, while Lavinia clutched the wagon seat, her face pale with terror.

Weston spurred his horse down the slope. "Hold them steady!" he called. "Don't let them back up!"

He dismounted in a fluid motion, tethering his horse to a scrubby pine before moving to the struggling wagon. The right rear wheel had lodged against a jagged outcropping, tilting the entire wagon toward the drop-off. The oxen strained in their yokes, confused by the uneven pull.

"Ease off on the brake," Weston instructed, his voice calm despite the danger. He positioned himself at the high side of the wagon, pressing his shoulder against the wooden frame. "When I say so, give them a gentle command forward."

Zach nodded, his young face streaked with sweat and dust. Lavinia remained frozen on the seat, her knuckles white where she gripped the wooden edge.

Weston dug his boots into the rocky soil, muscles tensing. "Now, Calkins."

Zach clicked his tongue, urging the team forward. For a moment, the wagon resisted, creaking ominously. Weston pushed harder, feeling splinters dig through his shirt into his shoulder. The wheel suddenly freed itself from the stone with a jolt that nearly sent the wagon tipping in the opposite direction. The oxen lurched forward, finding level ground.

"Praise God," Lavinia breathed, one hand pressed against her chest. "I thought we were going over for certain."

Weston nodded, slapping dust from his clothes. "Take it slower from here. Watch for those outcroppings." He glanced meaningfully at Zach. "Might be better to walk beside the team for a stretch."

The young man ducked his head in acknowledgment, chagrined. "Yes, sir."

Returning to his horse, Weston mounted again and continued up the trail. Each wagon would face similar challenges on this stretch.

His gaze traveled to his wagon, carrying what mattered most. Matthew and Emily. His chest tightened.

"Lord," he whispered, the word carried away by the mountain wind, "keep them safe."

***

By midday, the caravan had made frustratingly little progress. Weston rode back and forth along the line, helping where needed, offering encouragement, making instant decisions when challenges arose. The physical toll was considerable, but the mental strain pressed heavier.

Emily sat on the driving bench of his wagon, handling the reins with more confidence than she'd shown weeks earlier. Matthew's face appeared in the gap of the canvas covering, his eyes wide with a mixture of fear and excitement at the dramatic landscape.

"Papa!" he called. "The mountains... I had forgotten how big they are!"

Despite his exhaustion, Weston managed a small smile. "They get much bigger, son."

Emily's gaze met his, and in that brief exchange, he read concern.

"How much farther today?" she asked.

Weston glanced at the sky, judging by the remaining daylight. "There's a wider spot about two miles ahead. Not ideal, but the best we'll find. We'll camp there."

She nodded, her hands steady on the reins. The sight of her competent grip, her calm in the face of such demanding conditions, stirred something in him. Emily had transformed from the grief-paralyzed woman he'd first met in Independence. The trail had not broken her as she might have once wished; instead, it had revealed a core of strength that matched the demands placed upon it.

"You've been riding all morning," she observed. "Have you eaten?"

When had he last thought of food? "I'll eat when we make camp."

Emily frowned slightly, then reached behind the seat and produced a small bundle wrapped in cloth. "Biscuit and dried beef. Not much, but better than nothing."

Their fingers brushed as he took the offering, sending a rush of awareness through his dust-numbed senses.

"Thank you."

Matthew peered out again. "Papa, are there bears in these mountains?"

"There are," Weston admitted, seeing no point in concealing the truth. "But they usually stay away from large groups like ours."

"Usually?" Emily raised an eyebrow.

Weston gave her a look that was half apology, half amusement. "We'll post extra guards at night."

"Be careful," she said softly, her eyes holding his. "The wagons need you... we all need you."

He nodded once, throat suddenly tight, and spurred his horse forward.

****

The campsite was barely adequate—a slightly wider stretch of the trail where it curved around a protruding shoulder of rock. Wagons were positioned tightly, forming a rough circle more oval than round due to the constraints of the terrain. Unlike the prairie camps where livestock could graze freely, here the animals had to be kept close, fed from the dwindling supplies of grain carried in the wagons.

Weston completed his final check of the perimeter as dusk settled over the mountains. The guards were posted. Fires kindled in the center of the circle, where they posed the least danger of spreading. The usual hum of conversation was subdued tonight. Everyone felt the strain of the day's journey.

He found Emily sitting near his wagon, Matthew leaning against her as she ran a comb gently through his dusty hair. The boy's eyelids drooped with exhaustion, and he was fighting sleep.

"There you are," Emily said softly as Weston approached. "I saved your supper."

The simple domestic moment struck Weston with unexpected force. In the midst of this harsh, dangerous place, here was this small pocket of warmth and care. It felt like a gift he had done nothing to deserve, one that could be snatched away at any moment.

He accepted the plate—beans, a small portion of salt pork, and a piece of hardtack softened in the bean liquid. Nothing special, barely enough, but prepared with attention.

"You should eat too," he said, noting she had no plate of her own.

"I did earlier, with Matthew." She continued combing the boy's hair, speaking quietly. "He wanted to wait up for you. Said he has important mountain questions."

"What questions, Matthew?"

The boy blinked owlishly, then rallied. "How high are the mountains, Papa? Higher than the church steeple in Independence?"

The innocent comparison made Weston smile despite his fatigue. "Much higher. Higher than you can imagine."

"Higher than the clouds?" Matthew persisted.

"Some of them reach right up into the clouds," Weston confirmed.

Matthew's brow furrowed in concentration. "Did God make them that high, so we'd be closer to Him when we cross them?"

Weston glanced at Emily, who had stilled her combing, waiting for his answer.

"I think," Weston said carefully, "God made them to remind us how small we are, and how much we need Him when the path gets steep."

Matthew nodded, satisfied with this explanation. "That's why you pray more up here, isn't it?"

Weston felt a flush of self-consciousness, unaware his son had noticed his increased reliance on prayer. "Yes," he admitted. "That's why."

"Good," Matthew murmured, leaning heavier against Emily, his eyes finally closing. "Because I'm scared sometimes, but you're not scared when you pray."

The comment landed hard on Weston's chest. How wrong his son was—he was terrified, prayer or not. But perhaps that was a father's burden: to convert fear into faith in the eyes of his child, regardless of his own inner turmoil.

"Time for bed," Emily whispered, gathering the now-sleeping boy into her arms. Weston moved to help, but she shook her head. "Finish your supper. I'll settle him."

He watched as she carried Matthew to their wagon, his son's complete trust in her evident in the way he nestled against her shoulder. The sight stirred complex emotions—gratitude, tenderness, and fear.

When Emily returned, she sat beside him on the ground, close enough that he could feel the whisper of her skirts against his leg.

"You're exhausted," she observed.

"It was a difficult day," he allowed, finishing the last of his meal. "Tomorrow will be harder."

"Matthew prays for you every day while we are in the wagon, and you are on horseback," Emily said.

"Does he?"

She nodded, her profile softened by firelight. "He asks God to keep you safe when you ride ahead, and to help you find the best path for us all." She hesitated. "I've found myself joining him in those prayers."

The simple admission touched Weston deeply. The thought of Emily and Matthew together, asking God's protection over him, created a warmth no fire could match.

"I need those prayers more than either of you know."

Emily turned to look at him directly. "You carry too much alone, Weston." Her voice held no accusation, only concern.

"It's my responsibility."

"Yes," she agreed. "But responsibility shared is responsibility halved."

He almost smiled at her practical wisdom. "Are you offering to lead the wagon train, Miss Wilson?"

"Hardly," she replied. "But I am offering to listen when the weight becomes too much. And to remind you that not every decision rests solely on your shoulders."

A commotion at the far side of the camp drew their attention. Voices raised in alarm, a shuffle of movement in the darkness. Weston was on his feet immediately, every sense alert.

"Stay here," he instructed, striding toward the disturbance.

He found a small crowd gathered around the Croft's wagon. Silas was on the ground supporting his wife Martha, who appeared to have collapsed.

"What happened?" Weston demanded, pushing through.

"She just went down," Silas explained, his voice tight with worry. "One minute standing, the next on the ground."

Martha's face was alarmingly pale, her breathing shallow. Reverend Holloway knelt beside her, his expression grave.

"Might be the altitude," someone suggested. "Affects some folks worse than others."

"Or exhaustion," another voice added.

Weston looked back toward his wagon, and saw Emily already approaching, medical satchel in hand. He felt a surge of gratitude for her instinctive response.

"Give her room to breathe," Emily instructed, kneeling beside Martha. She placed a hand on the older woman's forehead, checked the pulse at her wrist. "How long has she been feeling unwell?"

"Said she was lightheaded this morning," Silas admitted reluctantly. "But she insisted it was nothing."

Emily's examination was thorough, but gentle. "Her heart's racing, and she's feverish. Altitude sickness is possible, but so is exhaustion and dehydration." She looked up at Silas. "Has she been drinking enough water?"

The older man hesitated. "She's been giving some of her share to Caleb. Said he needed it more."

A tremor of concern passed through the watching crowd. Water was already carefully rationed. If Martha had been taking less than her share...

"We need to get her into the wagon," Emily directed. "Elevated feet, cool compresses if possible. And water, a little at a time but regularly."

"We can spare some," Liz Billings offered immediately.

"Us too," Mercy Holloway added.

Others nodded in agreement. Weston felt a swell of pride in these people who, despite their own hardships, didn't hesitate to help one of their own.

Chapter 21

Sleep eluded Weston that night. Every creak of wagon wood, every snort from the restless livestock, every whisper of wind through the rocky crags kept him alert. He lay on his bedroll beside the wagon. The hard ground pressed against his back, but physical discomfort was the least of his concerns.

Martha's collapse was a stark warning. The mountains were exacting a toll even before the truly difficult passages. What would happen when they faced the steepest climbs, the narrowest ledges?

He rose quietly, needing movement. The night air was bitterly cold, the stars overhead piercingly bright in the thin mountain atmosphere. Most fires had died to embers. The guards nodded to him as he made a slow circuit of the camp.

At the eastern edge, he paused, looking back down the trail they had climbed that day. In the moonlight, the route seemed even more treacherous—a pale ribbon winding through dark masses of stone. Their progress, so hard-won, appeared insignificant against the massive scale of the mountains.

A soft footstep behind him broke his reverie. He turned to find Barnaby.

"Can't sleep either, Reynolds?" Cobb asked, his voice as weathered as his face.

"Too much thinking," Weston admitted.

Cobb nodded, producing a pipe which he did not light. "Mountains'll do that to a man. Make him feel small."

"Three days to the pass, if we're lucky," Weston said, more to himself than to Cobb.

The older man nodded again, slowly. "If we're lucky," he echoed. "Crossed these peaks before. Never gets easier."

"Any grand words of advice?" Weston asked, respecting the man's experience.

Cobb chewed thoughtfully on his unlit pipe stem. "Watch the sky more than the trail. Weather changes fast up here. Clear morning can be blinding snow by noon."

"I've witnessed that snow before," Weston said, remembering previous crossings.

"And watch Vance. Don't let his poison spread," Cobb added unexpectedly. "A man like that can turn fear into something ugly, tear a train apart from inside."

Weston glanced at him sharply. "You've seen it happen?"

"Once." Cobb's craggy face hardened at the memory. "Lost eight people. Not to the mountains. To panic. To turning on each other." He removed the pipe, pointing its stem at Weston. "You're doing right, keeping us together. Don't doubt it, regardless of what Vance says."

Weston nodded. "The man is truly testing my patience."

Cobb grunted, returning the pipe to his mouth. "Get some sleep, Reynolds. Mountain'll still be here in the morning."

As the older man shuffled away, Weston remained at the edge of camp, his gaze drawn to the towering peaks silhouetted against the starry sky. So much uncertainty lay ahead. So many factors were beyond his control.

"Lord," he whispered into the cold night air, "guide our steps. Keep us safe through this. Please."

The word, please, emerged with unexpected urgency, revealing the depth of his fear. Not for himself, but for those in his care. For Matthew, whose trusting prayers touched him more deeply than the boy could know. For Emily, whose quiet strength had become essential to him in ways he hadn't anticipated.

"I cannot lose either of them," the thought formed unbidden. "They both mean so much to me."

He stood a while longer in the cold, wrestling with his thoughts. Then, with a deep breath of the thin mountain air, he turned back toward camp, toward the wagon where Emily and Matthew slept, protected for the moment by canvas walls and his constant vigilance.

***

The following days proved Barnaby and Weston right about the fickleness of mountain weather. They woke to clear skies that rapidly clouded over by mid-morning. Cold rains began shortly after, turning the already difficult trail into a treacherous slide of mud and loose stone.

The oxen struggled for footing, their progress painfully slow. Wagons that had weathered months on the trail now groaned under the strain of the incline and the weight of sodden canvas. Men walked beside their teams, faces grim with effort, clothes plastered to their bodies by the relentless downpour.

Weston rode constantly between the front and rear of the train, soaked to the skin, directing wagons around the worst spots, helping to free wheels from sudden ruts, rallying spirits with calm authority. His exhaustion was a distant concern, pushed aside by immediate needs.

Despite his vigilance, disaster nearly struck when the Finch wagon slipped sideways on a particularly steep section. Young Sarah's scream cut through the drumming rain as her wagon tilted precariously toward the drop-off, her infant clutched desperately to her chest as her father drove the wagon.

Weston was there in moments, leaping from his horse to the high side of the wagon. "Hold on!" he shouted. "Don't move!"

Other men rushed to help—Silas, George, and Samson, with his blacksmith's strength. They threw their weight against the wagon, fighting gravity and mud, as the team of oxen bawled in confusion.

For a terrible moment, the outcome hung in balance. The wagon continued to slide, the men's boots finding little purchase in the mud. Then, with a collective roar of effort, they halted its movement long enough for Samson to jam rocks behind the wheels.

Sarah sat frozen in terror on the wagon seat, her baby wailing against her chest. Weston reached for her. "Come now, quickly," he urged. "The wagon's not safe."

She allowed herself and the infant to be helped down, legs barely supporting her as she was guided to solid ground. The wagon would have to be unloaded, its weight reduced, before it could be righted and moved forward.

"Take her to our wagon," Emily directed, appearing suddenly beside Weston, a blanket held over her head against the rain. "I'll look after her and the baby."

Mercy Holloway stepped forward to help, and together they led the shaken young widow toward the relative shelter of Weston's wagon.

The incident cast a shadow over the already dispirited train. As men worked to salvage the Finch wagon, Ezekiel Vance's voice rose above the rain.

"This is madness!" he shouted. "We're risking everything on this death trap of a trail when there are safer routes!"

Weston turned slowly, the rain streaming down his face. "Not now, Vance."

"Oh, it's never the right time, is it?" Vance sneered, approaching.

A dangerous stillness came over Weston. The gathered men fell silent, sensing the tension.

"You're frightening people who are already scared," Weston said, his voice low and controlled. "You're causing division when we need unity more than ever."

"I'm speaking the truth when others are too afraid to," Vance shot back. "How many more near-disasters before you admit this route was a mistake?"

"There is no perfect route through these mountains," Weston replied evenly. "Every path has its dangers. The difference is whether we face them together or let fear tear us apart."

Vance's eyes narrowed. "Pretty words. They won't mean much if a wagon goes over the edge with a family inside."

A murmur went through the soaked onlookers. Weston felt the weight of their fear, and their doubt. Ezekiel was sowing seeds that found fertile ground in exhausted and frightened minds.

"We move forward," Weston stated firmly. "Together. One wagon, one train. That was our agreement from Independence, and it stands now when it matters most."

"And if someone disagrees?" Vance challenged.

"Then they can make their choice," Weston replied, meeting his gaze steadily. "But splitting this train, taking separate routes… that leads to greater danger, not less."

The confrontation might have escalated further if not for Reverend Holloway's intervention. The minister stepped between the two men, his usual gentle demeanor hardened by the crisis.

"Ezekiel," he said, "your concerns are noted. But this is not the time or place. We have a wagon to right and people who need help."

For a moment, it seemed Vance might continue his tirade. Then, with a disgusted snort, he turned away. "Your funeral," he muttered, stalking back to his wagon.

The fragile unity held, but Weston knew the damage was done. Doubt had been planted. Fear had been stoked. He would need to be more vigilant than ever, not just against the physical dangers of the mountains, but against the human tendency to fracture under pressure.

By nightfall, they had managed to move only a mile further up the trail. The rain continued unabated, turning the planned camp into a miserable collection of dripping canvas and mud. Fires were nearly impossible to start with the sodden wood. Cold rations were distributed, eaten quickly by people desperate to retreat to whatever shelter their wagons provided.

Weston completed his rounds, checking on those most affected by the day's ordeal. Sarah and her baby were still with Emily. Sarah's father, Harold, remained with their wagon. Martha was slightly improved, but still weak. The Calkins were shaken but unharmed. The Billings' youngest had developed a cough that worried Liz.

Finally, drenched and bone-weary, he returned to his own wagon. Inside, he found Emily tending to baby Hope. Sarah was asleep, exhaustion having overcome her fear. Matthew sat beside her, his small face solemn as he watched over her in a touching imitation of Emily's care.

"How is she?" Weston asked quietly, water pooling at his feet from his sodden clothes.

"Terrified, but physically unharmed," Emily replied, her voice equally low. "The baby's cold, but not dangerously so."

She looked at him, concern evident in her eyes. "You're soaked through. You need to change before you fall ill, too."

He nodded, too tired to argue. Moving to the corner where his spare clothes were stored, he said, "I'll sleep outside."

"Nonsense," Emily countered practically. "It's pouring. Change behind the partition. I'll see to some hot coffee."

He did as she suggested, grateful beyond words for dry clothes when he emerged.

Emily handed him a steaming cup of coffee. "Drink this. Then rest. You've done all you can for today."

"I should check on—"

"The guards are posted, the camp is settled, and you can barely stand," she interrupted gently but firmly. "Rest now, Weston. Tomorrow needs you strong."

He accepted the cup; the warmth seeping into his cold-numbed fingers. "Thank you."

Matthew left his self-appointed watch over Sarah and came to sit beside Weston on the floor of the wagon.

"Papa, Mrs. Finch was real scared today," the boy whispered, his eyes wide. "I told her you wouldn't let anything bad happen to her or baby Hope."

Weston's heart contracted painfully at his son's unwavering faith in him. "That was kind of you, Matt."

"I said you always pray for the whole train, so God is watching over us special," Matthew continued with the absolute certainty of childhood. "Miss Emily said that was right."

Weston glanced at Emily. She met his gaze briefly, a slight flush coloring her cheeks.

"It seemed to comfort him," she explained softly. "And her."

They sat in comfortable silence for a while; the rain drumming on the canvas above them. Despite the cold and damp that had seeped into every corner of existence, the small space felt like a sanctuary.

When Matthew's eyes began to droop, Emily helped him to his sleeping place, tucking blankets around him with practiced gentleness. The boy whispered his prayers, asking specifically for God to help his father find the safe path tomorrow, to watch over Mrs. Finch and baby Hope, and to make the rain stop.

After Matthew had fallen asleep, Emily returned to sit near Weston.

"Vance is becoming dangerous," she said.

Weston nodded, staring into his empty cup. "It's fear."

"It's more than fear with him," Emily countered. "There's something... spiteful about it. He almost seems to want failure, to prove himself right."

"Some men are like that," Weston agreed wearily. "Would rather be right in disaster than wrong in success."

He set the cup aside, running a hand over his face. "The next stretch is worse than today's. Narrower trail, steeper climb."

"We'll face it when it comes," Emily said. "Not before."

"You sound like me."

"Heaven forbid," she replied dryly, but her eyes held warmth.

A sudden gust of wind shook the wagon, driving rain against the canvas with increased fury. Sarah stirred in her sleep, murmuring anxiously. Emily moved to check on her, adjusting blankets, soothing with a gentle touch.

Watching her, Weston was struck again by her transformation. The withdrawn, grief-paralyzed woman from Richmond was gone, replaced by someone who moved with purpose, whose hands brought comfort, and whose very presence created a sense of stability in chaos.

"You should rest too," he said when she returned to her seat.

Emily nodded. "Soon."

Another gust rattled the wagon. Beyond the canvas walls, the mountain storm continued unabated, a reminder of how exposed they were, how much still lay ahead.

"Do you think we'll make it?" she asked. "Through the mountains?"

Weston pondered his answer. He could offer empty reassurance, but Emily deserved honesty.

"I believe we can. But it will demand everything from us—courage, perseverance, and sacrifice. And faith, most of all."

"You're afraid."

"Yes," Weston admitted, the confession easier in the dim light, with the storm masking their voices. "Not of the mountains themselves. But of failing those who trust me."

Emily's hand found his in the shadows, her fingers cool and slender but surprisingly strong. "You won't fail, Weston. Not because you're perfect or because the path is clear. But because your heart is set on bringing us through safely, whatever it takes."

Weston nodded. "God will see us through this."

Chapter 22

Emily gripped the sideboard of the wagon until her knuckles turned white, her breath forming wispy clouds in the thin mountain air as Barnaby drove the wagon. Another jolt sent a sharp pain through her wrists as the left wheel dropped into a hidden crevice. The oxen strained, muscles rippling beneath their hides, as they pulled the wagon free.

The narrow trail wound between towering walls of granite that seemed to press inward from both sides. Above them, the sky had narrowed to a pale blue ribbon, distant and unreachable. Emily gazed upward at the sheer rock faces surrounding them, feeling as though the mountains themselves were closing in, trapping them within their stiff embrace.

"Careful there!" Weston's voice carried from somewhere ahead, followed by the steady clop of his horse's hooves on stone. "Keep tight to the inside of the trail!"

Emily steadied herself as Matthew, huddled against her side beneath a thick woolen blanket, stirred in his sleep. The boy had grown silent over the past days, his usual chatter replaced by wide-eyed watchfulness. She drew him closer, feeling his small body relax again as his breathing steadied.

The wagon lurched again. Emily heard Martha Croft exclaim sharply from the vehicle behind them, followed by Silas's rumbling reassurances. The entire train moved with painful slowness.

Further ahead in the distance, Weston had dismounted, leading his horse by the reins as he scouted the trail ahead. Emily watched the set of his shoulders, the deliberate, careful placement of each step. His usual confidence seemed tempered by the same wariness that had settled over the entire company.

The cold bit through Emily's woolen shawl. The mountain air carried a strange scent—something mineral and sharp, mixed with the faint sweetness of pine. It filled her lungs with each breath, reminding her how far they'd come from the warm, dusty plains.

"The Lord is my shepherd," Barnaby murmured. "I shall not want..."

The familiar psalm carried a thread of comfort. But beneath the comfort lurked a dark current of doubt. Would God lead them through this wilderness? Or had they come this far only to be trapped within the merciless embrace of stone?

Matthew stirred again, his small hand clutching at the fabric of her dress.

"It's all right," she whispered, brushing back a lock of hair from his forehead. "We're going to be fine."

The words felt hollow even as they left her lips.

Ahead, Emily saw Weston pause, his body gone suddenly rigid. Then he turned, waving an arm in a sharp, urgent gesture.

"Hold!" His voice carried, edged with something that made Emily's heart skip. "Everyone, stop where you are!"

The command rippled back through the line of wagons. Emily felt their wagon lurch to a halt as Barnaby pulled back on the reins, the oxen snorting in confusion.

"What is it?" Barnaby called, his weathered face creased with concern as he peered ahead.

Emily carefully shifted Matthew and climbed down, her boots meeting the stony ground with a thud that jarred her ankles. She stepped carefully on the uneven surface.

What she saw when she was within a few feet of Weston made her blood run cold.

Twenty yards beyond where Weston stood, the narrow pass simply ended. A massive wall of newly fallen rock completely blocked the way forward—boulders larger than the wagons themselves tumbled together in an impenetrable barrier. Small stones still occasionally tumbled down from above, evidence of how recent the slide had been.

"Lord have mercy," Reverend Holloway breathed from beside her, having moved forward as well.

For several heartbeats, no one spoke. The wind whistled through the narrow gap of sky above them, a lonely, desolate sound that seemed to underscore the gravity of their situation.

"That will be impossible to clear," Silas's voice broke the silence.

Weston was already examining the slide, moving carefully across the loose stone at its base. He placed a hand on one of the massive boulders, as if testing its weight, then stepped back, shaking his head.

"We cannot clear this with what we have," he said, voice tight with controlled emotion. "This would take dozens of men with proper tools, maybe black powder. Even then..."

He let the words trail off, but the implication was clear. They were trapped.

Emily felt a terrible familiarity in the sinking sensation that spread through her chest. There was nothing she could do now to help in this situation.

Trapped in the mountains.

No way forward.

No way back.

The narrow walls of the pass seemed to press closer. Emily forced herself to breathe, to keep her composure as more people began to emerge from their wagons, gathering in small, uncertain clusters.

"What about turning back?" Liz Billings suggested, her arms wrapped tightly around her middle. "Going back the way we came?"

Barnaby shook his grizzled head. "Trail's too narrow. No place to turn the wagons." His voice was grim, matter-of-fact. "Could unhitch the teams, maybe, try to back them out, but it'd be a devil of a job."

"There must be another way," George insisted, though his voice lacked conviction.

Ezekiel Vance pushed forward, his tall frame rigid with anger. "I told you this was madness, Reynolds! Taking us through this death trap instead of following the main trail!"

"The main trail was flooded out," Weston replied evenly, though Emily could see the tension in his jaw. "You know that as well as I do."

"Well, your shortcut has done us in proper, hasn't it?" Vance's voice rose, tinged with panic. "Look at us! Trapped like rats!" He spun in place, addressing the gathered pioneers. "We're going to die in these mountains because of his incompetence!"

"That's enough, Vance," Silas said sharply.

But the damage was done. Emily could see the fear spreading across faces, could hear the rising murmur of panic. A child began to cry somewhere in the back of the line.

Matthew appeared at her side, having climbed down from the wagon on his own. His small hand found hers, cold fingers curling around her palm. His eyes were wide, frightened.

"Are we stuck, Miss Emily?" he asked quietly.

Weston approached, his expression carefully controlled as he knelt before his son.

"For now," he said. "But we'll figure something out, Matthew. I promise."

The boy nodded solemnly, trusting his father absolutely. The sight sent a sharp pang through Emily's chest.

Weston rose, meeting Emily's gaze. For a brief moment, she saw past his carefully maintained façade and saw the weight of responsibility, the fear, and the desperate calculation happening behind his eyes. Then his expression steadied again.

"We need to make camp," he announced, raising his voice to be heard over the growing murmur. "Right here, best we can. Then I'll scout for another route."

"Camp?" Vance's voice was incredulous. "In this death trap?"

"Unless you'd prefer to stand all night," Weston replied, his tone leaving no room for argument. He turned to the group. "We've got shelter, supplies, and each other. We'll weather this and find a way forward."

His words carried a confidence Emily knew he didn't entirely feel, but they had the desired effect. The immediate panic subsided as people began the routine of setting up camp, though the movements were mechanical, laden with dread.

Emily moved among the wagons, helping where she could. The narrow confines of the pass meant the wagons remained in a line, with barely enough room between them for people to move. There would be no circling for protection tonight—just a vulnerable string of vehicles pressed against the mountain walls.

As darkness began to fall, the temperature plummeted. Stars appeared in the narrow strip of sky above, cold and distant. Small fires were lit between the wagons, offering meager warmth and pools of flickering light that barely pushed back against the surrounding blackness.

Emily helped Mercy, Martha, and Liz prepare a simple meal, their breaths visible in the firelight. None of them spoke much. What was there to say? The reality of their situation pressed down on all of them, heavier than the mountains themselves.

Weston had disappeared shortly after giving his orders, climbing up a nearby slope to scout, returning only as the light was failing entirely. Emily watched him approach the central fire, noting his careful, measured steps.

"Any luck?" Reverend Holloway asked, as Weston accepted a tin cup of coffee.

"Nothing clear," Weston answered, his voice low. "There might be another pass to the north, but it's hard to tell in this light. I'll try again at first light."

His eyes met Emily's briefly across the fire, and in that moment of unguarded connection, she saw what he wouldn't say aloud—that he'd found nothing promising, and they were trapped. She held his gaze, wishing she could offer some comfort, some solution. But there was nothing.

The evening meal passed in subdued silence. Matthew ate a little, pressing against Weston's side. Most of the children had already been put to bed in the wagons, exhausted parents preferring they sleep through this frightening uncertainty.

As the final cups were being collected, Reverend Holloway rose from his place by the fire. His tall form cast a long shadow in the flickering light, but his face, usually so serene, was etched with the same worry that gripped them all.

"Friends," he said, "I think it might do us well to pray together."

No one objected. Even Ezekiel, who sat apart from the others, didn't voice his usual skepticism. One by one, people moved closer to the fire, drawn by the simple comfort of proximity and shared faith.

Emily stood between Weston and Sarah, who held baby Hope swaddled against the cold. In the firelight, Sarah's young face looked drawn and exhausted. Emily gently placed a hand on the young mother's arm, receiving a grateful glance in return.

"Lord God," Reverend Holloway began, his voice gaining strength as he spoke, "we come before You this night as Your children, lost in the wilderness."

Emily closed her eyes, and let the Reverend's words wash over her.

"We acknowledge that we have reached the end of our own strength," the Reverend continued, his voice cracking slightly. "We stand before a barrier we cannot overcome through our own power or wisdom."

"We ask, Lord, not because we deserve Your help, but because we need it," Holloway's voice grew more fervent, more raw. "Because we have nowhere else to turn. Because our children and our future rest in Your hands."

Emily felt her throat tighten as she looked up at. In the firelight, she could see tears tracking silently down Mercy's weathered cheeks. Nearby, Martha clutched her husband's hand, so tightly her knuckles were white.

"Show us Your mercy, Father. Guide us through this wilderness as You guided Your people of old. Provide a way where there seems to be no way."

The final words hung in the cold air, a desperate plea echoing against indifferent stone. The silence that followed was profound, broken only by the crackling of the fire and the distant whistle of wind through the heights.

Emily opened her eyes again, surprised to find tears threatening. Not tears of faith or comfort—but of frustration. She had prayed just as fervently as her family died, one by one. Had begged for mercy that never came.

And now here they were, trapped in the mountains, facing slow starvation or the elements, with nothing but desperate prayers between them and death.

"Amen," Weston murmured beside her, his voice low but steady.

"Amen," echoed through the group, a whisper of hope against the darkness.

People began to move back toward their wagons, shoulders hunched against the cold and the weight of their circumstances. Emily remained by the fire, unwilling to return to the confines of the wagon just yet.

"You should try to rest," Weston said.

Emily nodded, watching the flames. "And you?"

A faint smile touched his lips, though it didn't reach his eyes. "Someone needs to keep watch."

"For what?" The words came out more bitterly than she'd intended.

He didn't answer immediately, poking at the fire with a stick, sending a shower of sparks upward. "For whatever might come," he said finally.

"Nothing's coming, Weston," she said softly. "No one knows where we are. No one can help us."

He looked at her then, the firelight casting shadows across his face. "I have to believe that's not true."

"Because of faith?"

"Because of experience," he replied, surprising her. "I've seen too many last-minute rescues, too many unexpected turns on this trail to give up hope before we've exhausted every possibility."

Emily wrapped her arms around herself, cold despite the fire's proximity. "And if those possibilities are exhausted? If there is no way out?"

"Then we'll face that when it comes." His voice was quiet but firm. "But not before."

She wanted to argue, to point out the futility of false hope, but the certainty in his voice gave her pause. It wasn't blind faith—it was the hard-earned conviction of a man who had faced the wilderness and survived, time and again.

"Get some rest, Emily," he said gently.

Reluctantly, she rose, making her way back to the wagon. Matthew was already asleep, curled in his small bed, wrapped in blankets against the cold. Emily watched him for a moment, his face peaceful in sleep, unburdened by the reality of their situation.

How many times had she faced death on this journey? The river crossing, the fever that swept through the camp, the countless daily dangers of the trail. Each time, they had survived, through miracles, skill, determination, and yes, perhaps sometimes luck.

But this felt different. Final. The mountain itself had closed around them, cutting off any path forward or back.

She lay down on her pallet, pulling the blankets tight around her.

Sleep, when it finally came, was fitful and filled with dreams of dark, closing spaces.

Chapter 23

Emily woke to the sound of voices—urgent, confused, and carrying a note she couldn't immediately identify. For a moment, she lay perfectly still, disoriented in the gray pre-dawn light filtering through the wagon cover.

Matthew was still asleep beside her. She rose carefully, pulling her shawl around her shoulders against the biting cold, and moved to the wagon opening.

Outside, people were emerging from their vehicles, looking upward with expressions of bewilderment and—was that hope?

Emily followed their gaze.

Two figures stood on the ridge above them, silhouetted against the lightening sky. One tall and lean, the other smaller, more compact. Both were dressed in buckskins, with long dark hair visible even from this distance.

"Spotted Elk," Weston's voice came from nearby, filled with a disbelief. "And Prairie Rose."

The Lakota man and woman regarded the trapped wagon train with calm appraisal.

Every eye was fixed on the pair as they began to descend, moving with a casual grace that made the treacherous slope seem like a gentle hill. Their feet found footholds invisible to Emily's eye, their balance never wavering as they navigated the steep terrain.

"How is this possible?" Mercy said, giving voice to the thought that echoed in Emily's mind. "How could they have found us?"

No one answered. There was no answer that made sense.

Spotted Elk reached the bottom of the slope first, followed closely by Prairie Rose. Up close, Emily was struck by their presence—a quiet dignity and composure that contrasted sharply with the pioneers' desperate state.

Spotted Elk was tall and lean, with a deeply lined face that spoke of years under the open sky. His dark hair, streaked with gray at the temples, was braided with small beads and feathers. Prairie Rose was shorter, but carried herself with equal confidence. Her face was younger, though weathered by the elements, her eyes sharp and assessing as they took in the stranded wagons.

Weston stepped forward, extending a hand, which Spotted Elk clasped in greeting.

"My friend," Weston said, his voice thick with emotion. "How did you find us?"

"We did not look for you," Spotted Elk replied, his English clear but lilting with the cadence of his native tongue. "We travel to the northern hunting grounds and heard voices in the pass last night." A faint smile touched his lips. "White men are not quiet travelers."

There was a ripple of nervous laughter from the gathered pioneers, the first sound of mirth Emily had heard since they'd been trapped.

"As you can see, we have a problem," Weston said.

He gestured toward the rock slide, blocking the pass. Spotted Elk nodded, unsurprised.

"The mountain has closed this path," he said simply. "The spring melt and rains make the high places unstable."

"Do you know another way?" Reverend Holloway asked, stepping forward. "Any path that might take these wagons through?"

Spotted Elk and Prairie Rose exchanged a quick glance, a wordless communication passing between them.

"There is a way," Prairie Rose said, speaking for the first time. Her voice was musical, softer than her husband's, but no less assured. "An old path, not on your maps."

"Why not?" Vance demanded, pushing his way forward. "What's wrong with it?"

"It is difficult," Spotted Elk answered calmly, unruffled by Vance's abrupt manner. "Narrow, winding. It goes high before it goes down. But it is the only way through these mountains from here."

"Can wagons make it?" Weston asked.

Spotted Elk considered, his gaze traveling the length of the wagon train. "If the drivers are skilled. If the animals are strong. If you are willing to work very hard." He nodded slowly. "Yes, it is possible."

A murmur ran through the gathered pioneers.

"And you would guide us?" Weston pressed.

"We would not leave you here to die," Prairie Rose said simply.

The words, so direct, sent a shiver through Emily. That was indeed what they had been facing—a slow death, trapped by stone and circumstance.

Emily stood rooted to the spot, her mind struggling to make sense of what was happening. Just hours ago, they had been utterly trapped, abandoned to a slow, terrible fate. Now, salvation appeared in the form of two people who had no reason to help them, who had simply been passing by at the precise moment when hope seemed lost.

The timing was too perfect. The coincidence was too great.

Her thoughts turned to Reverend Holloway's prayer the night before. "Provide a way where there seems to be no way."

And now, here stood that way, embodied in Spotted Elk and Prairie Rose.

It wasn't chance. It was Providence.

Spotted Elk was gesturing toward a nearly invisible passage in the distance, something Emily would never have noticed on her own.

"There is a path there," he said quietly to Weston. "Not for many. Hard. But it is open. We will show you."

Emily watched, her breath catching in her throat, feeling a tremor of hope.

"Emily?" Sarah appeared at her elbow, baby Hope bundled against her chest. The young widow's eyes were bright. "Isn't it remarkable? Just when we thought all was lost."

Emily managed a nod, unable to find words.

"Reverend Holloway says it's Providence," Sarah continued, adjusting her hold on Hope. "An answer to prayer."

"It is," Emily replied.

Emily watched the easy confidence with which the Lakota spoke and moved, their intimate understanding of the land that had so nearly become the pioneers' grave. Their appearance had been timely and so utterly miraculous.

"Miss Emily!" Matthew's voice cut through her thoughts. He was hurrying toward her from the direction of the wagon, his small face alight with excitement. "Is it true? Did Indians come to help us?"

Emily knelt at his level, grateful for the distraction from her troubling thoughts. "Yes, Matthew. Their names are Spotted Elk and

Prairie Rose. They're going to show us another way through the mountains."

Matthew's eyes widened as he took in the two figures in their buckskin clothing. "Did God send them to help us?"

"I believe he did, Matthew."

"That's what Papa says God does. He sends help when we need it most, not always how we think it should come."

"From the mouths of babes." Emily thought.

"Your father is a wise man," she said.

"He says I'm gonna be wise too someday. But first I gotta learn to tie my boots proper by myself."

Despite everything—the cold, the danger still ahead, the tumult in her heart—Emily found herself smiling genuinely. "One step at a time," she agreed, helping him straighten his coat. "And speaking of steps, we need to get ready to move along."

They returned to the wagon together, Emily helping Matthew gather his few belongings while Barnaby readied the oxen. Around them, the camp was quickly being dismantled, the routine of packing up happening with an energy and purpose that had been absent the night before.

Emily worked methodically, her body moving through tasks while her mind continued to wrestle with this unexpected salvation.

She climbed back into the wagon as Weston approached, his face drawn with fatigue, but his eyes clearer than they had been since they entered the mountains.

"We'll be moving out soon," he said. "Spotted Elk says the path is difficult but passable. We'll need to go single file, very carefully."

Emily nodded, securing the last of their belongings. "Do you trust them?"

"With my life," Weston answered without hesitation. "And with Matthew's. And yours."

The certainty in his voice was compelling. This man, who measured each word, each action with such care, was placing absolute faith in these unexpected guides.

"How do you know them?" she asked, curious about the evident friendship and trust between Weston and the Lakota couple.

"I met them three seasons back when I was scouting for a timber company," Weston replied. "I got caught in an early blizzard. Matthew and I would have died for certain if they hadn't found us." A shadow of memory crossed his face. "They took us in, nursed me back from a fever that nearly claimed me, and watched after Matthew as I recovered. They taught me things about this land I'd never have learned otherwise."

Emily absorbed this, seeing yet another layer of the man she had come to rely on. "So they saved your life before."

"They did." His eyes met hers, steady and sure. "And now they'll save all of us if we listen and follow their guidance."

"We're ready," she said.

Weston nodded. "Barnaby will stay close to the wagon ahead of you. The path is narrow but clear. If you feel better walking, just say the word." He hesitated, then added, "And Emily? Whatever happens, we face it together."

"Together," she repeated, the word somehow both frightening and comforting.

Within the hour, they were following Spotted Elk into the hidden cleft in the rock. The passage was indeed narrow—so narrow that in places the wagon wheels seemed to scrape both sides simultaneously. It twisted and climbed, following an unimaginable route.

From her perch on the wagon seat beside Barnaby, Emily watched Spotted Elk's confident progress ahead, the way he occasionally paused to indicate a particular turn or hazard. Prairie Rose walked sometimes beside him, sometimes dropping back to check on the progress of the wagons behind.

The path climbed steadily, the air growing colder and thinner as they ascended. The oxen strained with the effort, their breath forming clouds in the frigid air. Barnaby muttered encouragement to them, his gnarled hands steady on the reins.

"Remarkable, ain't it?" he said after they'd successfully navigated a particularly tight turn. "I plain couldn't see this path yesterday and neither did Weston, and here we are, moving through like it was meant for us all along."

"It's fortunate," Emily said.

Barnaby chuckled, a dry sound that matched his weathered face. "Call it what you will, miss. I'm just grateful we ain't sitting back there waiting to die."

Emily couldn't argue with that sentiment. Whatever had brought Spotted Elk and Prairie Rose to them, the simple fact remained—they now had hope where before there had been none.

As they climbed higher, the narrow walls of the pass occasionally opened to reveal breathtaking vistas. Towering peaks stretching to the horizon and valleys falling away in dizzying drops. The beauty was both terrifying and exhilarating. Emily found herself holding her breath at these moments, struck by the sheer scale and grandeur around them.

"Look, Miss Emily!" Matthew exclaimed from inside the wagon, poking his head out at one such opening. "We're up in the clouds!"

Indeed, wispy tendrils of mist swirled around them, caught in the mountain currents. For a moment, it seemed as though they traveled through the sky itself, suspended between earth and heaven.

The image stirred an unexpected thought: this was what faith felt like.

This precarious journey. This narrow path, visible only to those who knew where to look. This tentative movement forward despite the very real dangers on either side.

Not blind certainty, but a trembling step into the unknown, guided by a God who could see what was hidden from her own limited perspective.

The thought was both frightening and strangely liberating.

As the day progressed, the worst of the climb began to ease. The path, while still narrow, grew slightly less treacherous. Emily noticed Spotted Elk and Prairie Rose exchanging satisfied glances, a sense that they were past the most dangerous section.

The wagon train continued its slow, careful progress, each vehicle clearing another difficult stretch with cautious triumph. The mood, though still serious, had shifted subtly from desperate fear to focused determination.

Late in the afternoon, they reached a small plateau where the path widened enough to allow the wagons to pull abreast of one another. Spotted Elk called a halt, suggesting they rest the animals before continuing.

Emily climbed down from the wagon, stretching her cramped limbs. The plateau offered a commanding view of the path they had traveled—a seemingly impossible route through sheer rock faces and dizzying heights.

"Hard to believe we came through that," Sarah said, appearing beside Emily with Hope bundled against her chest.

Emily nodded, still processing the journey. "If you'd shown me that path yesterday and told me wagons would pass through, I'd have thought you mad."

"Yet here we stand," Sarah replied with a small smile. "It makes me wonder what other impossible paths might be before us."

Weston approached, his face lined with exhaustion, but his eyes clear.

"Spotted Elk says we've cleared the worst of it," he reported. "The path widens from here and begins to descend. We should reach the other side of the range by tomorrow evening."

"That's wonderful news," Sarah exclaimed.

"It is," Weston agreed, his gaze meeting Emily's. "You and Matthew holding up all right?"

"We're fine," Emily assured him, touched by his concern despite his own obvious fatigue. "Matthew's been braver than most of the adults."

A smile briefly lit Weston's weary features. "That's my boy."

The simple pride in his voice touched Emily's heart. This man, this father, had faced the possibility of losing everything, of failing in his duty to protect those in his care. Yet here he stood, steady and determined, his faith neither shaken nor smug.

She looked past him to where Spotted Elk and Prairie Rose stood at the edge of the plateau, their figures silhouetted against the vast landscape beyond. Something about their presence here, at this moment, continued to gnaw at the edges of her certainty.

"Why do you think they came?" she asked Weston softly. "Spotted Elk and Prairie Rose. What brought them here just when we needed them most?"

Weston followed her gaze, considering the question. "Spotted Elk would probably say it was the wind, or the mountain spirits." He paused, then added, "But I believe God guides even those who don't recognize His hand."

"And if it was just coincidence?" Emily pressed. "Just luck?"

"Then it was the most remarkable coincidence I've ever witnessed," Weston replied. "And I've seen my share." His eyes met hers, serious but gentle. "What do you believe, Emily?"

"I believe God just led us to safety," she answered honestly.

Chapter 24

The wagon train inched forward, a ragged line of exhausted people and animals.

Spotted Elk and Prairie Rose led them with quiet assurance.

"How much farther?" Weston asked, his voice low as he caught up to them at a narrow bend.

The Lakota man's dark eyes met his. "The path opens soon. Beyond lies what you seek."

Weston nodded, swallowing his frustration at the cryptic answer. The guides had been steadfast in their assistance but sparing with details, speaking of a place beyond the mountains in terms that seemed more spiritual than geographic.

The ragged line of pioneers stretched behind him—men, women, and children who had trusted his leadership. Some were walking, others riding in their wagons. Their faces were drawn with exhaustion, clothes worn threadbare, eyes hollowed by hardship.

Weston turned and found Emily some twenty paces back, her hand steadying Sarah Finch's elbow as they navigated a particularly uneven stretch. Emily's face was smudged with trail dust, her hair partially escaping its practical knot, but the set of her jaw revealed the quiet determination that had become so familiar to him. So necessary to them all.

Matthew trailed just behind her, one small hand gripping a fold of her skirt. The boy had taken to Emily completely during their months on the trail—her quiet strength and precious smiles drawing him like a moth to a flame.

Their eyes met briefly across the distance, and Weston felt the familiar tightening in his chest, a complex knot of emotion he did not dare to fully unravel just yet.

"Weston!" Reverend Holloway's voice carried from further back. "How much longer must we continue this way? May we take a break soon?"

"Not far now," Weston called back with more confidence than he felt. He turned to Spotted Elk. "Tell me true—are we near the end of this pass?"

The Lakota nodded once, gesturing forward. "The path widens ahead. Come."

They continued in strained silence for another quarter-hour. The faint sounds of labored breathing, the scrape of boots on stone, and the occasional whinny of a nervous horse or grunts from the oxen echoed around them.

Then, without warning, the path bent sharply, and Spotted Elk disappeared around the corner.

Weston followed, and suddenly—

The world opened up.

The constricting path and rock walls fell away on either side. The path widened into a broad ledge, and beyond it...

Weston stopped dead in his tracks, his breath caught in his throat.

Stretching before him was a valley unlike anything he had ever seen. A vast, verdant expanse cradled within the surrounding mountain peaks, vibrant with life and color, that seemed impossible after the barren stone and thin vegetation they'd endured for days.

The late afternoon sun illuminated the scene with clarity, revealing meadows of waving grass interspersed with groves of pines and aspens. A ribbon of water wound through the center of the valley, reflecting the clear sky above. And near the far side, barely visible at this distance, rose faint wisps of what looked like steam or mist.

For several heartbeats, Weston simply stood frozen, his mind struggling to comprehend what his eyes beheld. This expanse of verdant life, this hidden paradise, was so utterly contrary to everything he had expected to find, to everything he knew of the terrain beyond the mountains from his years as a guide. It felt like stepping into a dream.

The stark contrast to the harsh, unforgiving terrain they'd just traversed was so complete, so utterly disorienting, that a single thought crystallized with absolute clarity: This was not chance. No fortunate accident of geology or climate could explain this. In that moment of stunned revelation, Weston felt the unmistakable touch of providence—a divine hand reaching down to deliver them precisely when all human effort had failed.

"What..." he began, but the words died on his lips.

Spotted Elk stood silently beside him, his expression serene and knowing. Prairie Rose emerged from the pass behind them, her movements graceful despite the difficult journey, and came to stand at her companion's side. Neither seemed surprised by the vista before them.

"You knew," Weston said finally, his voice barely above a whisper. "You knew this was here."

Spotted Elk nodded once. "This has been known to my people for many generations. A place of healing. A place where the land gives freely."

Behind him, pioneers began emerging from the pass, their weary footsteps faltering as they beheld what lay before them. Gasps of astonishment rose from the group, followed by murmurs of disbelief and wonder.

"Merciful heavens," Reverend Holloway breathed as he stepped up beside Weston, his gaunt face transformed by awe. "What is this place?"

Weston shook his head slowly, still struggling to reconcile what his eyes were seeing with what his mind had expected. "It's not on any map I've studied," he said, the implications of that fact spinning through his thoughts. "This isn't the territory we expected. This isn't..."

"Oregon," the reverend finished softly.

"No," Weston agreed, his mind racing. "We should be facing more mountains, more difficult passes before the descent. Not..." He gestured helplessly at the improbable paradise before them.

The reverend's eyes widened with sudden understanding, and Weston saw the exact moment the spiritual significance struck the older man. "The Lord has brought us here," Holloway whispered, his voice thick with emotion. "When all seemed darkest, when our own strength and wisdom failed us completely..."

Weston was unable to dismiss the reverend's words. After everything they'd endured, after the seemingly miraculous appearance of Spotted Elk and Prairie Rose at their moment of deepest need, after being led through a hidden pass no white man had mapped, to emerge into... this. What else could it be but divine intervention?

The Crofts emerged next, Silas supporting his wife by the elbow. Martha's tired face crumpled with emotion at the sight.

"Oh, Silas," she whispered. "Look at it."

One by one, the pioneers emerged from the confines of the pass onto the wide ledge. Some stumbled to their knees, overcome by relief or exhaustion or both. Others stood slack-jawed, staring at the valley as though afraid it might vanish if they blinked.

Emily appeared with Matthew still clutching her skirt, Sarah and baby Hope just behind them. The young widow's pale face showed a flicker of hope. But it was Emily's reaction that Weston found himself watching most intently.

She stopped abruptly when the valley came into view, her lips parting slightly, eyes widening. The careful composure she had maintained through even the worst hardships of their journey slipped momentarily, revealing naked wonder and disbelief. The sight stirred something deep within him.

Matthew released her skirt and darted forward, his small face alight with wonder.

"Papa!" he called, pointing with unrestrained excitement. "Look at all the flowers! And trees! It's like a picture book!"

Emily moved forward slowly, as though in a daze, stopping at Weston's side. Her eyes, so often guarded and shadowed with pain, were wide with astonishment. He watched as she took in the expansive view, her gaze traveling across the verdant meadows, the shimmering water, and the distant rising steam.

"What is this?" she asked.

Weston shook his head slightly. "I don't know. It's not on any map. It's not where we're supposed to be."

Prairie Rose spoke then, her voice soft but clear. "The springs bring healing. They have called to those in need for many seasons."

"Springs?" Sarah asked, her voice trembling as she clutched baby Hope tighter.

Prairie Rose nodded, gesturing toward the distant wisps of steam. "Water that comes from deep within the earth. Warm even when snow covers the ground. It carries medicine."

Ezekiel Vance pushed his way forward, his perpetual scowl deepening as he surveyed the valley. "This ain't Oregon," he said flatly, voicing the obvious with characteristic bitterness. "This ain't what we set out for."

"No," Weston agreed, forcing himself to think practically despite the wonder tugging at him. "It's not Oregon. But it might be our salvation."

The descent from the ledge proved less arduous than the pass itself. Spotted Elk and Prairie Rose guided them down the steep but navigable path that switch backed down the mountainside.

With each step downward, the air changed—growing warmer, richer, carrying scents of grass and soil and growing things instead of the thin, sterile atmosphere of the high passes. The sounds changed too, from the hollow echo of boot on stone to the subtle symphony of a living landscape—rustling grass, bird calls, the distant murmur of water over rock.

Matthew had raced ahead with a child's boundless energy, his earlier exhaustion forgotten in the face of discovery. Weston watched him dart between clumps of wildflowers, laughing with delight at a butterfly, calling back excitedly about each new treasure.

"He seems to have found his second wind," Emily observed, walking beside Weston.

"He's resilient," Weston replied, feeling a swell of pride mixed with lingering guilt. The journey had demanded too much of the boy, asked him to endure hardships no child should face. "Children often are."

"Yes, they are."

Weston studied her profile, wondering what thoughts moved behind her composed expression.

"What do you make of this place?" he asked after a moment.

She glanced at him, a flash of vulnerability crossing her face before her natural caution reasserted itself. "I don't know what to make of it. It seems... impossible."

"I know what you mean." Weston looked out over the valley, stretching before them as far as the eye could see. "I've crossed these mountains before. I knew what to expect. Or thought I did." He shook his head slightly. "In all my journeys, I've never seen anything like this. Never even heard whispers of it."

"The Lakota knew," Emily said, glancing ahead to where Spotted Elk and Prairie Rose stood. "They spoke of it as a place of healing."

"Yes. That's what troubles me."

"Troubles you?" Emily looked at him in surprise. "Why would healing trouble you?"

He struggled to articulate the unease threading through his wonder. "Not the healing itself. The secrecy. If this place is as remarkable as it appears, why isn't it marked on any map? Why haven't settlers claimed it?"

"Perhaps because it's hidden," Emily suggested. "We'd never have found it without Spotted Elk's guidance."

"Maybe." Weston wasn't convinced. "Or perhaps there's something about it that's kept people away."

They continued downward in thoughtful silence, the path gradually leveling as they neared the valley floor. The late afternoon light stretched long shadows across the waving grass, creating patterns of light and dark that emphasized the contours of the land.

As many began to reach level ground, Weston called for a brief halt, allowing the stragglers to catch up and the animals to rest. The pioneers collapsed gratefully onto the soft grass, many lying back with expressions of disbelieving relief.

"Ain't never felt nothing like this," Clarence Hodge murmured, his weathered hand stroking the grass beside him. "Like God himself laid out a carpet for us."

"It is remarkable," Reverend Holloway agreed, lowering himself stiffly to sit beside his wife. The minister's face was drawn with exhaustion but alight with something Weston recognized as spiritual fervor. "After such hardship, such desperate straits... to find this place. It cannot be a simple chance."

Ezekiel Vance snorted derisively. "It's a valley, Reverend. Pretty enough, I'll grant you, but it ain't the promised land. And it certainly ain't Oregon, which is what we all paid good money and risked our lives to reach."

"No one's suggesting we abandon our destination, Mr. Vance," Weston said carefully, though the thought had already begun to form in the back of his mind.

Ezekiel's gaze swept over the group accusingly. "I see the looks on your faces. All of you are ready to call it quits just because we found a pretty meadow."

"It's more than a meadow," Sarah said unexpectedly, her voice soft but steady. Baby Hope cooed in her arms, looking more content than Weston had seen the infant in weeks. "Can't you feel it? There's something... different about this place."

Vance rolled his eyes. "Woman's fancies. I didn't sell everything I owned and trudge halfway across the continent to stop short of the prize."

"Perhaps," Reverend Holloway said thoughtfully, "we should consider whether the prize we sought is the one the Lord intended for us to find."

A tense silence followed his words.

Weston needed time to think, to plan. They all did.

"We'll camp here tonight," he announced, his tone brooking no argument. "No one's making any decisions before we've rested, eaten, and explored this place properly."

The familiar routine of making camp provided a welcome distraction from the overwhelming questions that hung in the air. Tents were erected, fires kindled, and the remaining provisions unpacked. The animals grazed on the lush grass, their quiet munching a peaceful counterpoint to the murmured conversations of the pioneers.

Weston organized scouting parties—Silas and George to check the game trails for signs of wildlife; Clarence and Samson to assess the nearby timber; and he himself would investigate the water source with Spotted Elk.

Before departing, he found Emily helping Sarah set up her tent, the two women working in comfortable tandem.

"I'm going to scout the stream and those springs," he told her. "Will you keep an eye on Matthew?"

"Of course," she replied, adjusting a tent rope. "Though I doubt he'll stray far from this flower field. He's been gathering a bouquet for the past half hour."

Weston glanced to where his son crouched amidst a patch of vibrant wildflowers, his small face a study in concentration as he selected blooms with careful deliberation.

"Be careful," she added, a fleeting touch on his arm accompanying her words. The brief contact sent warmth spreading through him.

"Always am," he replied, the corner of his mouth pulling up in a half-smile.

He joined Spotted Elk at the edge of camp, and together they set out across the meadow toward the line of trees that bordered the stream. The grass reached nearly to Weston's knees in places, thick and vibrant in a way that spoke of deep, rich soil.

"This land is fertile," he remarked as they walked.

Spotted Elk nodded. "The valley catches the water from the mountains. The soil is fed by it."

They reached the tree line. A mixture of aspens with their white trunks and quivering leaves, and pines that provided deeper shade. The ground beneath was carpeted with fallen needles and moss, soft underfoot after months of hard-packed dirt and stone.

The stream itself was a revelation, clear water flowing over smooth stones, deep enough in the middle to reach a man's knees. Fish darted in the deeper pools, their sleek forms visible even from the bank.

"Trout," Weston said, crouching to watch their movement. "Good eating."

"The water brings many gifts," Spotted Elk agreed. "Game comes to drink. Plants grow strong along the banks."

They followed the meandering course of the stream for perhaps half a mile, Weston taking mental notes of the terrain, the resources, and the potential. It was everything a settler could hope for: water, timber, game, and fertile soil, all nestled within the protective embrace of the surrounding mountains.

As they continued, the scent in the air changed subtly, taking on a mineral quality that reminded Weston of the hot springs he'd encountered in his previous travels. The pleasant, earthy smell grew stronger as they approached a slight rise in the terrain.

Cresting the rise, Weston stopped in his tracks.

Before him lay a series of pools, some as small as a washtub, others large enough for several people, their surfaces steaming gently in the late afternoon air. The water was crystalline, revealing smooth stones at the bottom of the shallower pools, and disappearing into mysterious depths in the larger ones. Around them grew lush vegetation, including plants Weston had never seen before.

"The healing springs," Spotted Elk said simply.

Weston approached cautiously, kneeling beside one of the smaller pools. He dipped his fingers into the water, finding it pleasantly warm, not scalding like some hot springs, but comfortably heated.

"These waters come from deep within the earth," Spotted Elk explained. "They carry the medicine of the mountain's heart."

"Is this why your people kept this place secret?" he asked, looking up at his companion.

Spotted Elk's face remained impassive, but his eyes held ancient wisdom. "Some places are not meant to be found by those who would take without giving back. Some healing is only for those who need it most."

Weston considered this cryptic response. "And you believe we need it? Need this place?"

"I have watched your people struggle. I have seen the sickness and sorrow you carry." The Lakota man glanced back in the direction of their camp. "The woman with the child in her arms. The quiet one with sadness in her eyes. The little one who runs today but has known hunger. The old ones whose body's ache from the journey." He looked back at Weston. "Even you, who carries the weight of all their lives."

"And you brought us here," he said slowly. "Why?"

"The path you traveled was blocked. You would have died in the high country." Spotted Elk looked out over the steaming pools.

"Prairie Rose had a vision which led us to find you. In her vision, she saw your people here, by these waters. She saw healing."

Weston fell silent, absorbing this. He wasn't sure how much stock to put in visions and spiritual intuitions, but he couldn't deny the extraordinary circumstances that had brought them to this hidden paradise just when all hope seemed lost.

They explored the spring area thoroughly, Spotted Elk pointing out plants used for medicine and explaining how his people had long come to these waters for healing of body and spirit. As they completed their circuit, Weston found himself both awed and troubled by the discovery. This place was a gift. There was no other way to describe it, but gifts came with responsibility.

They returned to camp as the sun dipped toward the western mountains; the sky deepening from blue to violet overhead. The other scouting parties had returned as well, their reports confirming what Weston had already begun to suspect: the valley was extraordinary in its abundance. Game trails crisscrossed the woodlands, promising deer and elk. The timber was strong and plentiful. Even wild berries and edible plants seemed to grow in unusual profusion.

The mood in camp had lifted considerably. Faces that had been drawn with exhaustion now looked animated, invigorated by the proper rest and the promise of their surroundings. A substantial meal was being prepared and children played at the edge of camp, their laughter a sound that made Weston smile.

He found Emily sitting beside Sarah, both women watching as Matthew proudly presented his wildflower bouquet to little Hope, who waved pudgy hands in delight at the bright colors.

"For the smallest lady," Matthew announced with an exaggerated gallantry that made both women smile. "Papa says gentlemen always bring flowers to ladies."

"That's very kind of you," Sarah said. "Hope certainly appreciates it, don't you, my sweet?"

The baby gurgled happily, reaching for a particularly vivid purple bloom.

Emily glanced up as Weston approached, a question in her eyes. "What did you find?"

"More than I expected," he admitted, lowering himself to sit beside them. "The stream is full of trout. The springs are... remarkable." He hesitated, still processing what he'd seen. "Spotted Elk says they have healing properties. I'm not sure what to make of that claim, but the water is unusually clear and warm."

"Healing properties?" Sarah echoed.

"So they say." Weston wasn't one to fuel false hopes. "At the very least, they'd make for a comfortable bath, which is more luxury than we've had in months."

"What else did you discover?" Emily pressed her practical mind, always seeking facts.

"Game is plentiful. Timber is good. Soil seems rich." He shook his head slightly, still marveling at their fortune. "It's everything settlers look for, all in one place. Protected by the mountains, with natural resources in abundance."

"It sounds too good to be true," Emily said softly, voicing the doubt that had niggled at the back of his own mind.

"That's what I thought at first." Weston glanced across the camp to where Spotted Elk and Prairie Rose sat slightly apart, conversing quietly.

Sarah looked down at Hope, who had fallen asleep. "Do you think... could we stay here? Just for a while at least, to rest and recover? Before continuing to Oregon?"

Weston considered his response carefully.

"That's a decision for the whole company," he said finally. "We'd need to discuss it together. But yes, I think a rest here would be wise. Beyond that..." He trailed off, unwilling to commit to more.

Emily studied his face, her perceptive gaze catching what he left unsaid. "You're considering something more permanent, aren't you?"

He met her eyes, seeing no judgment there, only keen insight. "The thought has crossed my mind," he admitted quietly. "This place offers everything we all hoped to find in Oregon, and we've already endured the worst of the journey to reach it."

"What about land claims?" Sarah asked. "In Oregon, there's the promise of legal ownership."

"True," Weston acknowledged. "But this area isn't claimed by any government that I know of. It's outside the established territories. In some ways, that could be an advantage."

Their conversation was interrupted by Reverend Holloway approaching.

"Mr. Reynolds," he called, his face alight with a spiritual fervor that seemed stronger than before. "Might I have a word?"

Weston nodded, rising to meet him. "Of course, Reverend."

The minister led him a short distance away, his manner betraying barely contained excitement. "I've been exploring the valley's edge," he began, his voice low but intense. "And consulting with Prairie Rose about its properties."

"And what have you found?" Weston asked, curious about the man's obvious enthusiasm.

The reverend clasped his hands together, his eyes bright. "I believe we have been led here by divine providence, Mr. Reynolds. This valley, hidden from all maps and knowledge, revealed to us in our darkest hour of need—can you not see the hand of God in this?"

"It's certainly remarkable timing," he allowed.

"More than remarkable!" Holloway insisted. "Think of it—we were trapped, with no way forward or back. Our supplies dwindling, our spirits at their lowest ebb. And then, guidance appears in the form of your Lakota friends, leading us to a place of safety and abundance that no white man has recorded." His voice dropped reverently. "Is this not like the Israelites, led through the wilderness to a promised land?"

The comparison hadn't occurred to Weston, but he couldn't entirely dismiss it, either. Their journey had taken on aspects of a biblical exodus—hardship, loss, moments of divine intervention, and now, this unexpected sanctuary.

"What are you suggesting, Reverend?" he asked.

"I am suggesting, Mr. Reynolds, that we consider the possibility that Oregon was never our true destination." Holloway's eyes shone with conviction. "That God has brought us here for a purpose."

The words struck Weston with force. All these months, he had viewed Oregon as the clear, fixed point on the horizon, the goal toward which every step, every decision, and every sacrifice had been directed. The notion that their true destination might have been this unmapped valley, revealed only through near-disaster and mysterious guidance, challenged his understanding of their entire journey.

Yet, he couldn't deny the profound sense of rightness that had settled over him since they descended into the valley. A feeling that went beyond appreciation of its resources or relief at finding shelter. Something deeper, more fundamental. Like coming home to a place he'd never known existed.

Before Weston could respond, a shout from the edge of the camp drew their attention. Ezekiel Vance was gesturing angrily, his voice rising as he argued with George Billings about something. The confrontation was drawing stares.

"Excuse me, Reverend," Weston said, moving quickly toward the disturbance. "We'll continue this discussion later."

He reached the pair as their argument escalated, stepping between them with practiced authority. "What's the problem here?"

"This fool is talking about staying put," Vance spat, his face flushed with anger. "Abandoning Oregon altogether for this—this detour."

George, normally mild-mannered, stood his ground. "I'm saying we should consider it, Ezekiel. The women, children, and animals are exhausted. And this place—it has everything we hoped to find."

"It ain't got legal claim papers," Vance sneered. "It ain't got established trade routes. It ain't got the protection of American law. It's a pretty prison, that's all."

"Enough," Weston said firmly, noting that the commotion had drawn most of the camp's attention. "This isn't the time or place for this discussion. We're all tired. We've had a remarkable day. Let's eat, rest, and approach this with clear heads tomorrow."

"There's nothing to discuss," Vance insisted, glaring at the assembled pioneers. "We set out for Oregon. That's where we're bound."

"Ezekiel," Reverend Holloway intervened, his voice gentle but firm. "Surely you can see that this place deserves consideration. After all we've endured, is it not possible that the Lord has guided us here for a purpose?"

Vance scoffed openly. "Don't bring religion into this, Reverend. We got lost. These Indians showed us a way out. There's no divine hand in it."

A murmur of disapproval rippled through the onlookers at his dismissive tone. For all the hardships they'd faced, the majority of the wagon train held to their faith, finding solace in prayer and scripture when all else failed.

"You're entitled to your opinion, Mr. Vance," Weston said evenly, "as is everyone here. But this decision affects us all, and it will be made carefully, with proper deliberation." He raised his voice to address the whole camp. "Tomorrow, after we've rested and had a chance to explore further, we'll hold a proper council. Until then, I ask everyone to reflect on what we've found here, and what it might mean for our future."

The crowd dispersed slowly, breaking into small groups that continued the discussion in hushed tones. Vance stalked off alone, his disapproval evident in every line of his body.

Weston found himself standing beside Emily, who had approached during the confrontation with Matthew at her side.

"That man..."

"He has been challenging my leadership since Independence," Weston replied, keeping his voice low. "But he has a point. Abandoning our original destination is no small decision."

Matthew tugged at Weston's hand, his small face serious. "Papa, are we not going to Oregon anymore?"

Weston crouched to his son's level, struck anew by how much the boy resembled his mother. The same thoughtful eyes, the same delicate curve of nose and cheek. "I don't know yet, Matthew. We need to think carefully about what's best for everyone."

"I like it here," the boy said earnestly. "There're flowers for Hope, and I saw a rabbit, and Miss Emily says there are berries we can pick tomorrow."

"Does she now?" Weston glanced up at Emily, who met his look with a smile.

"I may have made some promises about berry-picking expeditions," she admitted.

"Well, we'll see what tomorrow brings." Weston straightened, ruffling Matthew's hair. "For now, it's about time for supper and bed. You've had a big day."

"Can Miss Emily tell me a story tonight?" Matthew asked, his expression hopeful. The bedtime stories had become a ritual during their months of shared travel—one of many small, domestic routines that had grown to feel natural despite the unusual circumstances.

"If she's not too tired," Weston hedged.

"I think I can manage one story," Emily said, her expression softening as it always did when Matthew looked at her with those earnest eyes. "After we've eaten."

The camp settled into evening routines, the meal more generous than usual thanks to the successful fishing expedition that had returned with a string of fat trout. The atmosphere was subdued but not somber, a thoughtful quiet rather than the desperate exhaustion of previous weeks.

As darkness fell, stars appeared overhead, brilliant, and numerous in the clear mountain air. A few lanterns dotted the camp, but most families retired early, the day's revelations and exertions taking their toll.

Weston completed his usual circuit of the camp perimeter, checking that all was secure, though the valley felt safer than any place they'd camped in months. When he returned to his tent, he found Matthew already asleep on his bedroll, his face peaceful in the soft light of the single lantern.

Emily sat beside him, her back straight, hands folded in her lap. She looked up as Weston entered, her expression thoughtful.

"He fell asleep before I even finished the story," she said. "I'm not sure whether to be offended or relieved."

"He was exhausted," Weston replied, lowering himself to sit on his bedroll. "The excitement of the day caught up with him."

"With all of us, I think." Emily said as she tucked a strand of hair behind her ear. "This place... it's remarkable."

"That's one word for it." Weston leaned back against his pack, stretching his legs out before him. His muscles ached from the day's journey, but it was a clean pain, honest and earned. "Revolutionary might be another."

"You're considering it seriously, aren't you?" she asked. "Staying here instead of continuing to Oregon."

He studied her face in the lantern light, trying to read her thoughts on the matter. "I'm considering it. There are practical advantages. The resources are abundant. The location is defensible."

"And the disadvantages?"

"No established governance. No legal claim process. No guarantee of trade or supplies. Isolation." He ticked them off methodically. "Though some might see those as advantages, depending on their perspective."

Emily was silent for a moment, her gaze drifting to Matthew's sleeping form. "What does your instinct tell you, Weston?"

He considered how to answer.

"My instinct tells me this place is... significant," he said finally, choosing his words with care. "Whether by chance or providence, finding it when we did, as we did, feels important. Like something we should heed."

She nodded slowly. "I feel it too. This sense that we're standing at a crossroads. That what we decide will shape everything that follows."

"You've been quiet about your own thoughts," he observed. "What do you think we should do?"

Emily's gaze lifted to meet his, direct and clear. "When I left Richmond, I wasn't looking for a home. I was looking for... an end. Or at least a place so removed from everything I'd lost that the pain might finally dull." Her voice was steady, but he could hear the cost of such honesty. "Oregon represented that for me. Distance. Isolation. A clean slate."

Weston nodded, understanding better than most the desire to put physical space between oneself and the site of overwhelming loss.

"But now... this place feels different. Not like an escape. More like..."

"A beginning," Weston supplied when she faltered.

"Yes. Exactly that. A beginning for all of us who've lost so much. A place where the land itself seems to offer healing, not just survival."

The lantern flame wavered slightly, casting shifting shadows across her face. In that moment, Weston was struck by how far they had both come from the guarded strangers who had met in Independence. The journey had stripped away pretenses, leaving bare the essential truth of who they were—two people marked by loss but still standing, still capable of seeing beauty and possibility in an unexpected future.

"Whatever we decide," he said quietly, "I value your counsel, Emily. Your perspective."

She rose gracefully, smoothing her skirts.

"I should return to my tent," she said. "Tomorrow will be...significant."

Weston nodded. "Rest well."

"And you."

She slipped out into the night, leaving him alone with his sleeping son and the weight of decisions to come.

Weston extinguished the lantern and lay back on his bedroll, staring up at the darkness. Outside, the night sounds of the valley created a gentle symphony, the distant murmur of the stream, the soft rustle of wind through grass, and the occasional call of a night bird.

His mind replayed the day's events, still marveling at the stark contrast between despair and discovery. The blocked pass that had seemed a death sentence. The unexpected arrival of Spotted Elk and Prairie Rose, like figures from a parable. The arduous journey through the hidden pass. And then... this valley. This impossible, beautiful valley that had appeared just when all hope seemed lost.

Reverend Holloway's words echoed in his thoughts: Is this not like the Israelites led through the wilderness to a promised land?

Chapter 25

Weston watched Ezekiel's wagon and three others grow smaller against the eastern sky, retreating toward the mountain pass they'd conquered together. The wooden wagon wheels kicked up dust that hung in the air like a statement. Beside him, several members of the wagon train stood in silence, their faces reflecting a mixture of resolution and uncertainty as they watched members of their community disappear.

"They won't make it," Silas said quietly, crossing his arms over his chest.

"They might," Weston replied, though he harbored the same doubts. "Vance is stubborn and skilled enough. And he's taking three capable families with him."

Reverend Holloway stepped forward, his Bible clutched in one weathered hand. "We should pray for their safe passage, regardless of our disagreements."

Weston nodded, removing his hat as the Reverend spoke a brief prayer for protection over those departing. When he finished, the small gathering dispersed, each person turning back toward the valley that had unexpectedly become their destination.

The valley stretched before them, vibrant with colors that seemed almost unreal after months of dust and hardship.

"It doesn't seem right, watching them leave," Martha said as she turned away.

"Each person must follow their own conviction," Weston replied, placing his hat back on his head. "Vance and the other families that left us believe Oregon is still the promised land. But I believe we've already found it."

The words settled in his chest with unexpected certainty. After months of driving toward Oregon, after years of planning to build a life there for Matthew and himself, the sudden change in destination and plans should have felt jarring. Instead, it felt right, like arriving home after a long absence.

"We've much to do," he said, his mind already cataloging the tasks ahead. "If we're to make this valley our home."

***

By mid-afternoon, the valley buzzed with purposeful activity. The decision to stay had transformed the weary travelers into builders and planners. Weston moved between groups, organizing and advising, his years of frontier knowledge suddenly repurposed for settlement rather than travel.

Near the largest spring, several men had gathered to discuss the layout of the future settlement. George, a carpenter by trade before joining the wagon train, spread a crude map drawn on a scrap of canvas.

"Water access is critical," he said, tapping the sketch. "We'll want the cabins within reasonable distance of the springs, but not so close we contaminate them."

Silas nodded, squinting against the sunlight. "We need to think about winter, too. That ridge to the north will block the worst winds if we build in its lee."

Weston knelt beside them, studying the map. "The soil here and here," he pointed to areas he'd examined earlier, "is good for planting. We'll need fields cleared before winter if we're to have crops next season."

Samson, the blacksmith whose powerful arms had saved more than one wagon on the journey, rubbed his beard thoughtfully. "My forge'll need to be set somewhat apart... for the fire danger. But not too far. Everyone will need tools, nails."

The practical considerations anchored Weston, giving him solid ground as the magnitude of their decision continued to settle around him. This wasn't just a temporary camp. This was the foundation of a community that might stand for generations.

"What about you, Weston?" George asked, looking up from the map. "Where will you and Matthew be setting down roots?"

"I was thinking near that stand of pines overlooking the mainspring," he said after a moment. "Good protection, good view, close enough to water."

As the words left his mouth, an image formed unbidden in his mind—not just a cabin for himself and Matthew, but a home with Emily there too. He saw her tending herbs in a garden, Matthew playing in the yard, and lamplight glowing from windows on a winter evening. The vision was so vivid, so complete, that it startled him. And with it came the familiar tightening in his chest, the old fear rising, warning him against hoping for too much.

"Well," George said, returning his attention to the map, "we'll need to start felling trees soon. The sooner we have shelter built, the better."

The conversation returned to practicalities, timber sources, how many cabins they would need immediately, and which families might share quarters through the first winter. Weston's mind occasionally drifted to Emily. Since making the decision to stay, she'd seemed different—lighter and purposeful.

"Weston?" Samson's deep voice pulled him back to the present.

"Sorry," he said, refocusing. "What was that?"

"I asked if you think the springs have any peculiar properties. For the forge, I mean. Some mineral waters can affect metal work."

Clarence Hodge, who had been quietly listening nearby, spoke up. "They have healing properties, that's certain." The man rolled up his sleeve, revealing an inflamed cut that had worried him for weeks on the trail. "Soaked it this morning after Prairie Rose showed me which spring to use. The pain's lessened quite a bit."

The men leaned in to examine the wound, which did indeed look less angry than it had the previous day.

"Could be coincidence," Samson said skeptically.

"Or providence," Reverend Holloway added, approaching the group.

Weston nodded slowly. "Providence," he repeated quietly.

Providence that had brought Emily into his life when he needed her most, though he hadn't known it then.

The realization lodged in his chest like a physical thing, impossible to ignore.

***

Weston found Emily near the eastern spring later that afternoon. She knelt beside Prairie Rose, the two women examining plants growing along the water's edge. Matthew sat nearby, carefully placing stones in a pattern only he understood, his tongue poking out in concentration.

Weston paused, taking in the scene. The late afternoon light caught in Emily's hair, bringing out auburn highlights he'd never noticed during their dusty journey. Her face was animated as she spoke with Prairie Rose, pointing to different plants, and nodding at the older woman's explanations. There was no trace of the withdrawn, grief-stricken woman who had joined their wagon train months ago. This Emily was alive, engaged, her natural curiosity and compassion no longer buried beneath layers of sorrow.

The sight of her this way, vital and present, made something twist in Weston's chest, a mixture of joy and the old, persistent fear.

"See this one?" he heard Emily say as he approached. "In Virginia, we used it for fever. Do your people use it the same way?"

Prairie Rose nodded, her weathered face creasing in a smile. "Yes, good medicine. Good for children's fevers, especially."

Matthew looked up at Weston's approach, his face lighting up. "Papa! Look what I made!" He gestured proudly to his stone arrangement, which Weston now saw formed a crude but recognizable letter M.

"That's fine work," Weston said, crouching beside his son. "Did Miss Emily teach you that?"

Matthew nodded vigorously. "She says I can learn all my letters, and then I can read the Bible stories myself instead of having her read them to me!"

"That would be something," Weston agreed, ruffling the boy's hair. He glanced up to find Emily watching them, a soft smile playing on her lips.

"Miss Emily knows lots of plants," Matthew continued, oblivious to the exchange. "And Prairie Rose knows even more!"

"I'm learning," Emily said, rising to her feet. "Prairie Rose has been kind enough to show me which local plants might be useful for medicine." She brushed her skirts, suddenly self-conscious under Weston's gaze.

Prairie Rose gathered several sprigs of herbs into a small pouch. "She learns quick," the older woman said, her dark eyes wise and knowing as they moved between Weston and Emily. "Good for a healer to know the land's medicine."

"The land is so generous," Weston said. "More than I could ever imagine a place being."

"This valley has been sacred to my people for many generations," Prairie Rose said. "We come here for healing, for peace. Now it will be your home. Treat the land wisely and do not abuse it." She handed the pouch of herbs to Emily. "Use these wisely. I will show you more before we leave."

"You're leaving?" Emily asked, a note of disappointment in her voice.

Prairie Rose nodded. "Soon. Spotted Elk and I must return to our people. But we will visit when the seasons change." She looked at Weston. "This is a good place for new beginnings, Weston... remember this."

Weston felt her words settle on his shoulders—not as a burden, but as a blessing. Yet with it came the nagging whisper of doubt, of fear—was he worthy of a new beginning? Could he bear the risk of opening his heart again, knowing the pain that might follow?

"Thank you," he said. "For everything."

Prairie Rose inclined her head slightly, then moved away toward the main encampment, leaving the three of them alone by the spring.

Matthew immediately resumed his stone arrangement, adding more pebbles, while Emily turned to Weston, her expression curious.

"How are the plans progressing?" she asked.

"Well enough," he replied. "We've mapped out where the settlement should lie, areas for planting, where Samson can set up his forge. George thinks we can have at least basic shelter before the weather turns."

Emily nodded, glancing around the valley. "It feels strange, doesn't it? Planning to stay in one place after being on the move for so long."

"Strange, but right."

"Yes," she said softly. "Right." She hesitated, then added, "Have you chosen a spot? For you and Matthew?"

Weston cleared his throat. "I was thinking near that stand of pines," he said, pointing to the elevated area overlooking the main spring. "Good protection from weather, close to water."

Emily followed his gaze. "It's beautiful," she said after a moment. "You can see the whole valley from there."

"I thought so too." He paused, searching for words. "There's... room enough for a good-sized cabin."

Her eyes returned to his, questioning, a flicker of hope visible beneath her cautious expression.

Matthew tugged at Emily's skirt. "Miss Emily! I made another letter!"

The moment broke as Emily turned her attention to the boy, praising his crude 'E' formed in stones. Weston watched them together. Emily's gentle patience, Matthew's adoring response, and felt the fear rise in his chest. The fear of loving and losing again. The fear that had kept him isolated even among companions, that had defined his life since Susannah's death.

But alongside it, stronger with each passing day, grew something else—the undeniable certainty that Emily belonged with them, that the life ahead would be incomplete without her.

Was he brave enough to acknowledge it? To risk his heart again?

Chapter 26

The valley held a quietness unlike anything Emily had known before. Not the heavy stillness of empty Richmond rooms that once rang with her sisters' laughter. Not the false peace of numbed grief. Something altogether different.

Emily stood at the edge of the bubbling springs, their mineral scent hanging in the cool evening air. The western sky blazed as the sun dipped below the ridge, painting the clouds in shades that reminded her of her mother's prized rose garden. Her mother would have loved this valley, she thought. Both her parents would have seen God's hand in a place like this, clear water erupting from stone, verdant life flourishing against all expectations, and warmth and abundance cradled by mountains.

She closed her eyes, letting the gentle sounds wash over her—water bubbling from the earth, birds settling into evening song, and the distant voices of the settlers preparing evening meals. Sounds of life. Of the future.

Three weeks had passed since the wagon train's momentous decision. Three weeks of watching Weston organize the first tentative steps of settlement—mapping cabin sites, assessing timber stands with Silas, and planning fields with George. Three weeks of seeing Matthew run freely through meadows dotted with wildflowers, his laughter no longer confined to brief stops along a grueling trail. Three weeks of finding herself smiling without reason, of catching Weston's eyes across the busy camp and feeling her heart bloom within her chest, something that she'd thought had forever withered.

She bent down, trailing her fingers through the warm water. It never ceased to amaze her how the springs emerged from the earth already heated, as if the mountain itself had warmed them. Perhaps there was a sermon in that, Reverend Holloway might say. How even the hardest, coldest places could yield something healing.

"Even the waters here don't behave as expected," she murmured to herself.

Much like her heart.

When she'd fled Richmond, she'd sought only emptiness—vast, endless plains where her grief might spread thin enough to bear. She'd longed for a desolate horizon where she might disappear into insignificance. She'd wanted Oregon precisely because it promised nothing but hardship and distance.

What she'd found instead, first on the trail and now in this valley, was a connection. Community. Matthew's sunny persistence. Weston's quiet strength. Sarah resilient grace with baby Hope. The Crofts' steadfast kindness. The Holloway's unwavering faith.

And her heart, stubbornly insisting on beating with purpose again.

The decision to stay in the valley had come with startling clarity. When Reverend Holloway spoke of God's unexpected paths, and unexpected grace, his words had resonated within her. This valley wasn't what any of them had planned. It wasn't what she had sought. It wasn't Oregon. It was better. It was—

"Beautiful evening, isn't it?"

Emily turned to find Weston approaching, his broad-shouldered silhouette outlined against the darkening eastern ridgeline. Her pulse quickened involuntarily. He moved with the measured confidence she'd come to associate with him—deliberate steps, shoulders squared against whatever challenges might arise, and yet a gentleness in his bearing that had emerged more fully since they'd discovered the valley.

"It is," she agreed. "You know.... every day I keep expecting to wake up and find myself back on the trail, bouncing along in your wagon with Matthew asking if we're 'there yet.'"

Weston's lips curved into a smile as he came to stand beside her. "He's asked that very question every day since we stopped. Only now it's 'is our cabin built yet?'"

They stood watching the springs bubble. The evening light softened the angles of Weston's face, catching in the strands of hair that had escaped his hat. Without the constant vigilance required by the trail, tension had eased from his expression, though the responsibility of leadership still rested visibly upon his shoulders.

"You've been busy," Emily said, thinking of the countless decisions, the organizing, and the planning he'd undertaken since they'd arrived. "I've hardly seen you these past few days."

"Settling a community takes almost as much work as moving one," he replied. Then he turned to look at her fully, his eyes serious. "But I've been remiss. I should have made time."

"I understand. There's so much to be done. Everyone needs your attention."

"Not everyone." His voice was quiet, almost reverent in the gathering dusk. "Just Matthew. And you."

He took a step closer. Emily became acutely aware of the space between them, less than an arm's length now, and the profound meaning contained in that small distance.

"Emily." He spoke her name with such care, as if it were something precious. "I need to tell you something."

Her hands trembled slightly. She clasped them together to steady herself. "What is it?"

Weston removed his hat, holding it before him. The gesture struck her as deeply vulnerable, exposing his face fully to her gaze. His eyes, those striking blue eyes that had first registered her existence with wary assessment back in Independence, but now held emotions so complex and deep that Emily found herself without words.

"I've spent six years guarding my heart," he began, his voice low and textured with emotion. "After Susannah... after losing her, I convinced myself that my only purpose was Matthew. That love was... too dangerous. Too painful to risk again."

The evening breeze stirred around them, carrying the sweet scent of valley grasses and the mineral tang of the springs. Emily didn't move, barely breathed, afraid any response might disrupt the moment unfolding between them.

"I've told myself that," Weston continued, "every day since she died. Told myself that Matthew was enough reason to wake up each morning. That keeping him safe, giving him a future, was all I needed to concern myself with."

He took another step forward, closing more of the distance between them.

"And then you stepped into my life in Independence. Looking like you'd lost everything. And I recognized that look because I'd worn it myself."

Emily's throat tightened with emotion. "Weston—"

He shook his head gently. "Let me finish. I need to say this, Emily."

She nodded, waiting.

"I didn't want to see you," he admitted. "I didn't want to know your grief, or let you know mine. I had my walls built, and my path set." A rueful smile crossed his face. "And then the wagon you were riding in overturned in the river."

Emily felt a small smile tug at her lips, remembering that chaotic day that had changed everything.

"You came into our wagon, into our lives, and everything changed." His voice strengthened with conviction. "I watched you with Matthew... how you listened to him, told him stories, and tucked him in at night. I saw how you fought to save lives on the trail. I witnessed how you comforted Sarah through her grief and the struggles of being a new mother alone without her husband. I saw how you never stopped trying, even when it would have been easier to retreat back into your grief."

He paused, drawing a deep breath.

"I watched you have no faith and then find it again. But most of all, Emily, I watched you choose to live again. To feel again. And in watching you, I found myself doing the same."

The air seemed to still around them, as if the entire valley held its breath. The last light of sunset reflected in the springs at their feet, rippling with the continuous bubbling motion.

"When we found this valley," Weston continued, gesturing at the surrounding landscape, "I knew it wasn't a mistake or a detour. It was a gift. A second chance. Not just for the settlement, but for me. For us." He met her eyes, his own shining with emotion in the fading light. "Emily Grace Wilson, I love you with everything in me."

The simple words, spoken with such depth and certainty, washed over Emily like a balm. Her eyes filled with tears that she made no attempt to hide.

"I thought I'd never say those words again to anyone," he continued, his voice rough with feeling. "I thought that part of me died with Susannah. But it didn't. It was just waiting. Waiting for you."

He reached out, taking both her hands in his. His palms were warm and calloused from months of labor, his grip steady and secure.

"Matthew loves you, too. You've become the mother he never had the chance to know. And I..." He paused, his thumbs gently caressing her knuckles. "I can't imagine building a life here without you beside me. I don't want to."

Emily felt as though her heart might burst from her chest. She looked down at their joined hands, then back up to his face.

"Are you asking what I think you're asking?" she whispered, hardly trusting her voice.

Weston nodded, a mixture of vulnerability and certainty in his expression. "I'm asking you to be my wife, Emily. To build a life with me and Matthew in this valley. To make a home together. To face whatever comes... joys and hardships alike... as a family."

The word "family" sent a tremor through Emily's entire being. Family, what she had lost so completely in Richmond. What she had been certain she would never have again.

Yet here it was, offered with such tender hope by this man who had known his own devastating loss, and who understood the cost of opening his heart again.

"I know it's not what either of us planned," Weston said, misinterpreting her silence. "When we set out for Oregon—"

"Oregon was never my destination," Emily interrupted softly, finding her voice at last. "Not really. It was just a place I chose because it was far away from Richmond."

She turned slightly, gazing out at the valley stretching below them. The first evening stars had appeared in the eastern sky, pinpricks of light against the deepening blue.

"I wasn't looking for a home when I left Richmond," she continued. "I was looking for... emptiness. For a place vast enough to hold my grief. For hardship hard enough to make me forget, even for a moment." She looked back at him, her heart in her eyes. "I never expected to find life again. To find... love."

The word felt strange and wonderful on her tongue after so long. Love—not the aching memory of love lost, but the living, breathing presence of it, here and now.

"My family died, and I thought that was the end of me, too. I couldn't imagine surviving it, let alone finding joy again. I was so angry at God, so convinced He'd abandoned me."

Weston's hands tightened gently around hers, understanding in his eyes.

"But He hadn't," she continued. "He led me to that wagon train. To you and Matthew. Through the wilderness, not to Oregon, but here. To this valley. To... healing. He led me back to living again."

She took a deep breath, gathering courage for words she had never expected to say again.

"I love you, Weston Reynolds," she said, her voice clear and certain, despite the tears that spilled down her cheeks. "I love the man who leads with quiet strength and unfailing principle. Who loves his son so fiercely I can feel it? Who makes terrible coffee but always shares it, anyway?"

A smile broke across Weston's face, transforming his features in the fading light.

"I love you," she repeated, savoring the words, "and I love Matthew as if he were my own. And yes... yes, I will be your wife. It would be my honor to be your wife."

The space between them vanished as Weston drew her into his embrace. His arms encircled her, strong and sure, as if he'd been waiting a lifetime to hold her this way. Emily felt the solid warmth of him, the steady beat of his heart against hers, and knew with absolute certainty that she had found her place in the world.

When he finally drew back enough to look at her, his eyes shone with a joy so pure it took her breath away.

"Thank you," he whispered, his voice thick with emotion.

Emily reached up, resting her palm against his cheek. "For what?"

"For finding the courage to love again," he answered.

She nodded. They had both walked through fire, both lost what they had thought was their entire world. That they had found each other amidst the ashes seemed nothing short of miraculous.

"Not courage," she corrected gently. "Grace. God's unexpected grace."

The words transported her back to Reverend Holloway's sermon after they'd discovered the valley. How he had spoken of God's paths being not what we plan or expect, but often exactly what we need.

"Grace it is." He glanced around at the valley, now bathed in the soft purple light of dusk. "This whole place feels like grace, doesn't it? As if God kept it hidden, waiting just for us, until the moment we needed it most."

"Like the manna in the wilderness," Emily murmured. "Provided exactly when needed, not before."

"Just so," Weston agreed, his smile deepening. "Though I hope our stay here lasts considerably longer than forty years of wandering."

Emily laughed, the sound bubbling up from a well of joy she'd thought forever dry. "I've had quite enough wandering, thank you very much."

As dusk deepened around them, Weston's expression grew tender. His hand came up to brush a strand of hair from her face, his touch light against her cheek. His eyes asked a silent question, and Emily's heart answered without hesitation.

When his lips met hers, the kiss was gentle. A promise rather than a demand. Emily closed her eyes, letting herself be fully present in the moment. The warmth of his nearness. The gentle pressure of his hand at her waist, steadying her.

When they parted, Emily felt light-headed, and breathless with the wonder of this moment she had never expected to experience again.

"Should we tell Matthew tonight?" she asked, her voice soft in the gathering darkness.

Weston's expression softened at the mention of his son. "I think we should. He'll be over the moon." He chuckled. "He's been asking me for weeks when I was going to 'make Miss Emily stay forever.'"

"Has he now? And what did you tell him?"

"That some things can't be rushed. That the best and most important decisions take time and certainty." His voice lowered. "That when you love someone, you want to be sure they're ready."

"I'm ready now. I've been ready since the moment we crested that final mountain pass and saw this valley spread before us. I just... needed to be certain it was real. That I wasn't dreaming."

"Not dreaming, Emily. Very real." His gaze held hers, steady and true.

Hand in hand, they turned from the springs and walked toward the cluster of temporary shelters and tents that would soon give way to permanent cabins. A slight breeze had picked up, cool against her flushed cheeks, bringing with it the mingled scents of campfires and cooking food.

As they approached the clearing, Emily spotted Matthew sitting with Caleb Croft and Luke Billings. The three boys were engaged in some game involving sticks and pebbles, their faces intent with concentration in the glow of a nearby fire.

It was Matthew who spotted them first, his head lifting like a deer sensing movement. His expression brightened instantly. "Papa! Miss Emily!" He scrambled to his feet, abandoning the game without a backward glance, and ran towards them.

Weston released Emily's hand just in time to catch Matthew in a bear hug, lifting him high. "There's my boy," he said, his voice warm with affection. "Having a good time with your friends?"

Matthew nodded enthusiastically as Weston set him back on his feet. "We're playing settlers and Indians, but the good kind of Indians like Spotted Elk who help people, not the scary kind."

"That sounds like a fine game," Weston said, resting his hand on Matthew's shoulder. "Miss Emily and I have something important to talk to you about."

Matthew's eyes widened, darting between them. A hopeful expression dawned on his face. "Is it about our cabin? Is it about Miss Emily staying with us forever?"

Weston chuckled, tousling his son's already unruly hair. "You're too smart for your own good, Matthew Reynolds. Let's go sit by our fire, and we'll tell you properly."

Matthew reached for Emily's hand without hesitation, tugging her along as if he couldn't bear to wait another moment. "Come on, Miss Emily! Papa says important talks happen by the fire."

Emily allowed herself to be pulled along, her heart so full she could scarcely contain it. The simple trust in Matthew's grip, the unquestioning way he included her, the eager anticipation in his step. It was a gift beyond measure.

Their temporary camp was modest but comfortable, with a small fire burning in a ring of stones. Weston had constructed a simple bench from a fallen log, and Matthew immediately pulled Emily towards it, positioning himself between her and his father as they sat.

"Now," he demanded, looking up at Weston expectantly. "Tell me the important thing."

Weston cleared his throat, his expression suddenly serious, though Emily could see the joy dancing behind his eyes. "Matthew, you know that I've always told you that the most important decisions shouldn't be rushed. That they require thought, and prayer, and certainty."

Matthew nodded solemnly.

"Well, Miss Emily and I have made an important decision. The most important one since we found this valley."

"What did you decide?"

Weston met Emily's eyes over Matthew's head, a silent question in his gaze. She nodded, encouraging him to continue.

"We've decided," Weston said, his voice gentle, "that we want to be a family together. Miss Emily has agreed to become my wife, and—" his voice caught slightly, "—your mama. If that would be alright with you."

For a moment, Matthew sat frozen, his eyes enormous in his small face. Then, with a cry that seemed to contain every ounce of his six-year-old joy, he flung his arms around Emily's waist.

"Really?" he asked, his voice muffled against her dress. "Really, truly forever?"

Emily cradled him close, her own eyes filling with tears. "Really, truly forever. If that's what you want, Matthew."

He pulled back, his face alight with happiness. "It's what I asked God for! Every night in my prayers. I asked Him to let you be my mama, and He did it! He really did it!"

The simple, absolute faith in the child's face struck Emily to her core. While she and Weston had navigated their complex journey of grief and healing, Matthew had simply asked God for what his heart desired most, trusting completely that it would be provided.

"You've been praying for that?" Weston asked.

Matthew nodded vigorously. "Ever since the river, when you told Miss Emily she could stay in our wagon. I prayed real quiet, so I wouldn't wake anybody up every night, but God hears quiet prayers, too. That's what Reverend Holloway says."

"He certainly does," Emily managed, brushing away a tear. "And sometimes He answers them in ways we never expected."

"Like the valley!" Matthew exclaimed, making the connection instantly. "We didn't expect the valley, but God knew it was here all along, waiting for us!"

"Just like that," Weston agreed, reaching out to include both Matthew and Emily in his embrace. "God had plans for us we couldn't see, but He led us right where we needed to be."

The three of them sat together on the simple log bench, encircled in each other's arms as the fire crackled quietly before them. Emily closed her eyes, memorizing the moment—the solid warmth of Weston beside her, the trusting weight of Matthew against her side, the profound sense of belonging that came with being precisely where she was meant to be.

"When will you be my mama for real?" Matthew asked after a long, contented silence. "Tomorrow?"

Weston chuckled, the sound rumbling beneath Emily's ear where her head rested against his shoulder. "These things take a bit of planning, son. Reverend Holloway will need to perform a proper ceremony."

"Like the one for Mr. and Mrs. Billings when they renewed their vowels before we left on the wagon train?"

"Vows," Weston corrected gently. "And yes, something like that, but it will be our first wedding, not a renewal."

Matthew considered this, his brow furrowed in concentration. "Can I stand up with you, Papa? Mr. Billings had Luke stand with him."

"I wouldn't have it any other way. You'll be right beside me as I make my promises to Miss Emily."

"And I'll make promises to you too, Matthew," Emily added. "Because I'll be promising to be a mama to you, not just a wife to your papa."

Matthew's smile could have illuminated the darkest night. "And then I can call you Mama? Not Miss Emily anymore?"

"Yes," she whispered, gathering him close. "Then you can call me Mama. I would be honored."

"Best day ever," Matthew declared with absolute conviction.

Chapter 27

"Hold still now," Martha murmured, her fingers working deftly through Emily's dark curls. "This ribbon Sarah gave you is perfect. Something borrowed and blue."

Emily's hands trembled slightly as she touched the locket on her chest. "I never thought..." she began, then stopped, emotion catching in her throat.

Martha's hands paused in their work. "None of ever do, dear. That's the beauty of it. God's paths aren't always the ones we set out to follow."

Outside, Emily could hear the settlement alive with purpose, the quiet murmur of voices, footsteps in the soft earth, and someone humming a hymn. These people, strangers just months ago when the wagon train formed, had become her family, forged in the shared crucible of the trail.

"Reverend Holloway is ready whenever you are," Sarah said, entering the tent with baby Hope balanced on her hip. The infant, growing plumper and more alert each day, reached toward Emily with pudgy fingers and a gummy smile.

Emily touched Hope's tiny hand.

"How are you feeling?" Sarah asked.

Emily took a measured breath. "Like I've been wandering through a wilderness and finally found my way home."

Martha smoothed the simple cream-colored dress Emily wore—her best, not a wedding gown, but it would serve. "Every journey has its purpose, even when the destination isn't what we expected."

Emily nodded, her hand returning to the locket around her neck. She had considered leaving it behind today, afraid to mingle past grief with present joy. But as she opened it one last time, studying the beloved faces that had once surrounded her in Richmond, love settled within her heart.

"They would be happy for me," she whispered.

Martha placed a warm hand on Emily's shoulders. "Of course they would. They loved you."

Liz peered inside the tent, her arms full of wildflowers gathered from the valley floor—purple lupine, golden balsam root, and delicate white yarrow.

"These are for you," she said. "The children helped me gather them."

Emily accepted the bouquet, burying her nose in its fresh scent. The faint sweetness of lupine mingled with the earthy fragrance of yarrow and the more subtle wildflowers. "They're beautiful."

"As are you," Liz replied, her eyes suddenly moist. She glanced away, embarrassed by the display of emotion. "Well, I should go and help with the final preparations."

As she ducked back outside, Emily caught a glimpse of the activity beyond—the community moving with shared purpose, preparing for the simple celebration that would mark this day. The same people who had toiled together, suffered together, and ultimately chosen to stay together in this unexpected valley of grace.

"It's time," Martha said gently, adjusting the ribbon one final time and stepping back to assess her work. "Are you ready?"

Emily tucked the locket beneath her dress, where it rested against her heart. She reached for her mother's handkerchief and gently tucked it into the wildflower bouquet.

"I am," she said.

***

The path to the healing springs had been worn smooth by daily use in the weeks since they'd decided to make the valley their home. Emily walked it now with measured steps, Silas Croft at her side, his weathered hand steady under her elbow. The afternoon light bathed the valley in clarity, turning the mountains to sentinels of purple and gray against the vast sky. Birds called from the trees that ringed the valley floor. The air was cool and still.

The community had gathered in a loose half-circle near the largest of the healing springs, where the warm, mineral-rich water bubbled up from beneath the earth. Simple benches fashioned from split logs had been arranged for those who wanted to sit. Wildflowers tied with scraps of ribbon marked the way.

And there at the center, standing beside Reverend Holloway, was Weston.

Emily's heart caught at the sight of him. He stood tall in his best shirt, freshly washed and pressed, his dark hair combed neatly back from his forehead. His eyes found hers across the gathering, and the expression that crossed his face, a mixture of awe, tenderness, and gratitude, made her breath catch.

Beside him stood Matthew, scrubbed clean, and practically bouncing in place with excitement. When he spotted Emily, he waved enthusiastically, earning a gentle, steadying hand on his shoulder from his father.

The small crowd parted as Emily approached, faces turned toward her with smiles of genuine warmth. Their eyes reflected not just happiness for the occasion, but a shared understanding of the journey that had brought them all to this moment.

As Silas guided her to stand before Reverend Holloway, Emily felt the love of every individual present.

Reverend Holloway's voice carried clearly in the afternoon air as he began.

"Dearly beloved, we are gathered together in the sight of God and in the presence of these witnesses to join Weston Clay Reynolds and Emily Grace Wilson in holy matrimony."

His kind eyes moved between them, then swept across the gathered community.

"This union we celebrate today holds special meaning, not just for Weston and Emily, but for all of us who have journeyed together and found our way to this valley. Like the Israelites of old who wandered the wilderness before finding their promised land, we have traveled far, faced hardship, and discovered that God's plan often leads us to unexpected places of blessing."

Emily smiled as Weston's eyes focused on her, steady and warm.

Reverend Holloway continued, "I am reminded of the words in Jeremiah: For I know the plans I have for you, declares the Lord, plans to prosper you and not to harm you, plans to give you hope and a future. Through the most difficult trials of our journey, when the path seemed uncertain and the destination unknown, God was leading us to this place of hope and new beginnings."

Emily's mind flashed back to those first desperate days on the trail, when she had been so certain she wanted only to escape her pain, to find oblivion in the hardship of the journey westward. How far she had come from that desolate woman who boarded a wagon in Independence with no expectation of finding joy again.

"Marriage," Reverend Holloway continued, addressing the gathering, "is like this valley itself, a covenant of promise and possibility. As it says in the book of Ruth: Where you go I will go, and where you stay, I will stay. Your people will be my people, and your God my God. Today, Weston and Emily pledge not merely to weather life's storms together, but to build something lasting and beautiful from whatever materials God provides."

He turned to Weston. "Weston, you embarked on this journey as a guide, responsible for leading others safely to their destination. Along the way, God had another purpose—bringing healing not just to others, but to your own heart. In Emily, He has provided a companion for your journey and a mother for Matthew."

Weston's throat worked visibly as he nodded, his gaze never leaving Emily's face.

"And Emily," Reverend Holloway said, his voice gentling, "you joined this expedition, seeking only distance from your pain. Instead, God drew you close to Himself again through the unexpected gift of love and community. In Weston and Matthew, He has provided a family when you believed all family was lost to you."

Emily blinked back tears, feeling the truth of his words settle deep in her heart.

"Marriage," Reverend Holloway continued, addressing the gathering again, "is a sacred covenant reflecting Christ's faithful love for His church. It is a journey undertaken together, through joys and sorrows, abundance and want, health and sickness. Just as we have supported one another on the trail, we now pledge to support Weston and Emily as they build their life together."

He nodded to Weston, whose hands were steady as he reached for Emily's.

"Weston and Emily have prepared their vows, promises they will make before God and this community of faithful witnesses."

Emily felt the warm, callused strength of Weston's hands enfolding hers. Those hands that had led them safely across rivers and mountains now held hers with reverent care.

"Emily," Weston began, his deep voice unwavering despite the emotion she saw gathered in his eyes. "I never expected to find love again."

He paused, his thumbs brushing lightly over her knuckles. "But God had different plans. He brought you into my life. You... this remarkable woman of courage and compassion, whose heart is so much bigger than the grief that tried to claim it. I promise to cherish you, Emily Grace, all the days of my life. To build with you a home filled with laughter, love, and faith. To stand beside you through whatever joys or trials God brings our way. To honor the memories of those you've lost by helping you create new memories of joy."

He reached into his pocket and withdrew a simple band of gold. Emily's mother's wedding band that she had tucked away in her trunk before leaving Richmond.

"With this ring, and with my whole heart," Weston said, sliding it onto her finger, "I promise you my love, my life, and my future. Always."

The ring, warm from his pocket, settled against her skin. Emily looked down at their joined hands, at the simple band that had once been on her mother's hand, and she smiled. When she spoke, her voice was clear and steady, carrying across the quiet gathering.

"Weston, when I set out on the Oregon Trail, I was running away from everything. I thought I wanted solitude. I thought I deserved it. Then God placed you and Matthew in my life. Your quiet strength became my shelter, Weston. Your steadfast faith challenged my despair. Your son's innocent love reminded me how to laugh again."

She glanced at Matthew, whose small face was solemn with the importance of the moment, though his eyes danced with excitement.

"I promise to love you both with all that I am," she continued. "To build our life in this valley that God has provided. To be a wife to you, Weston, and a mama to Matthew. To face whatever comes with the same courage and faith you've shown me."

She felt the emotion rising in her throat as she slipped her father's gold wedding band on his finger. "I love you, Weston. Forever. God has blessed me beyond measure."

Reverend Holloway's voice rose again, resonant with joy. "What God has joined together, let no one separate. By the authority vested in me, I now pronounce you husband and wife."

He smiled at Weston. "You may kiss your bride."

Weston's hands released hers to gently frame her face. His eyes held nothing but open tenderness as he bent to brush his lips against hers—a kiss of promise, of profound gratitude, and of undeniable love.

The gathered community erupted in cheers and applause. Matthew, unable to contain his excitement any longer, threw his arms around both of them.

"We're a family now!" he exclaimed, his voice bright with certainty. "Forever and ever!"

Emily knelt to embrace him, her heart so full it threatened to over-flow. "Yes, we are," she whispered against his hair. "God has made us a family."

Weston's hand rested on her shoulder, strong and steady, as the community gathered around them with congratulations and bless-ings.

"Praise be to God," Reverend Holloway pronounced, raising his hands. "Who brings beauty from ashes, joy from mourning, and makes all things new."

***

The celebration that followed was simple but joyful. A testament to the creativity and generosity of their community. Tables had been fashioned from salvaged wagon boards set across barrels, and covered with the cleanest linens available. Food gathered and prepared with care by many hands was spread for all to share.

The air filled with the savory scents of roasted venison and rabbit, the yeasty smell of bread baked in the communal clay oven they had constructed, and the sweetness of wild berries the children had gath-ered. Every family had contributed something, a special dish, a skill, or a helping hand, making the feast a true communion of their shared resources and goodwill.

Emily moved through the gathering, accepting embraces and well-wishes. Her mother's simple gold band on her finger caught the light when she gestured, still unfamiliar but so precious.

"You've done wonders for that boy," Silas said, nodding toward Matthew, who was playing an improvised game with Luke and Caleb. "And for his father. Weston's always been a good man, but he carries himself different now. Lighter."

"They've done wonders for me as well," Emily replied, watching as Weston approached the children, crouching down to speak with them at eye level.

As twilight softened, the valley, lamps, and candles were lit around the gathering space. Zach surprised everyone by pulling out his fiddle, and soon the air filled with music that drew people to dance on the grassy ground near the springs.

"May I have this dance, Mrs. Reynolds?" Weston asked, appearing at her side and extending his hand with formal grace.

The name—her new name—sent a thrill through her. "You may, Mr. Reynolds," she replied, placing her hand in his.

He led her to the patch of ground that had become the impromptu dance floor. His hand settled at her waist, warm and secure through the fabric of her dress, as they began to move in time with the music.

"Happy?" Weston asked, his eyes never leaving hers.

"Completely," she replied. Then, with a smile that reached her eyes, she added, "Happier than I believed possible."

He pulled her closer. "I have something to show you later," he murmured. "When the celebration winds down."

His mysterious tone sparked her curiosity. "What is it?"

"Patience, Mrs. Reynolds," he teased gently. "It's a surprise."

As they moved together, the warmth of his hand on her waist, the strength of his shoulder beneath her palm, and the rhythm of their steps in perfect synchrony, Emily felt a sense of belonging that went beyond the moment. This man knew her and still loved her. He had seen her at her lowest, had witnessed her struggles, and had walked beside her through the wilderness. And still, he had chosen her, as she had chosen him.

Later, as the stars appeared in the vast dome of sky above the valley, Emily watched Matthew, who had fallen asleep on a blanket near the fire, exhausted from excitement and dancing. His small face was peaceful in sleep, one arm flung out, his hair tousled against his forehead.

"He's been waiting for you, you know," Martha said, as she joined Emily.

Emily looked at the older woman, whose wise eyes had seen so much of life's joys and sorrows. "What do you mean?"

"A child needs a mother's love," Martha said simply. "Weston did his best, and a fine job he did, but there was always something missing. Until you." She patted Emily's hand. "You've brought our Weston back to life. We've known him for several years. We were his neighbors back when he lived in St. Louis with Susannah. We witnessed the severe sorrow he experienced when he lost her. We crossed paths with him through the years. He did his duty, and took care of that boy, but Weston.... well, he never really lived. Now he laughs again."

"He brought me back to life too," Emily replied, her voice thick with emotion. "I didn't want to be saved. I wanted to disappear. But God knew better."

Martha nodded, her eyes crinkling. "He always does, dear. He always does."

A presence at her side drew Emily's attention away from the conversation. Weston stood there, his expression unreadable in the flickering firelight.

"Ready for that surprise?" he asked quietly.

Emily nodded, turning back to Martha. "Would you..."

"I'll keep an eye on him," the older woman assured her, gesturing toward Matthew. "Take your time."

Weston took Emily's hand, his fingers twining naturally with hers as he led her away from the celebration. They walked along a path that wound toward the edge of the springs. The sound of music and laughter receded behind them, replaced by the gentle bubbling of the warm water and the night chorus of crickets.

He stopped at a particular spot overlooking the valley. Emily recognized it immediately as the place where he had proposed weeks earlier.

"I wanted to show you something," Weston said, his voice low and intimate in the darkness.

He guided her gaze upward, to where the Milky Way stretched across the vast expanse of night sky, a river of stars partially obscured by the rising moon.

"On the trail," he said, "I used to watch the stars every night. They were my compass, my constant. Sometimes, when the weight of responsibility felt too heavy, they reminded me how small my troubles were in God's grand design."

Emily leaned against him, feeling the solid warmth of his body beside hers. "And now?"

"Now," he murmured, his hand finding hers, "I still see God's design in them. But I no longer feel small. I feel..." he searched for the words, "precisely where I'm meant to be."

He turned to face her, his features half-illuminated by moonlight, his eyes holding hers with quiet intensity.

"I thought I understood God's plan for me. To be Matthew's father, to keep him safe, to lead others through the wilderness. To be alone." He lifted his hand to lightly trace the line of her cheek. "I never imagined God would bring me you, Emily Grace. A woman strong enough to face her darkest fears, brave enough to open her heart again after unimaginable loss. Compassionate enough to love a little boy who desperately needed a mama."

Emily's throat tightened with emotion. "You make me sound much braver than I am," she whispered.

"No," he said firmly. "I see you clearly. I've watched you fight your way back to life. I've seen your faith rekindled. I've witnessed your capacity for love even when you thought it was gone forever."

His hand settled warmly at the curve of her neck. "Emily Reynolds," he said, "my wife. My heart's companion. The mother of our son."

Our son.

The words settled deep in Emily's soul, a missing piece finally falling into place.

"I never thought I'd feel this way again," she admitted. "When I lost everyone in Richmond, I believed that was the end of my story. That I would just...continue, somehow. Exist. But not really live."

She shook her head slightly, still amazed at the journey that had brought them here. "Then you offered me space in your wagon."

A smile tugged at his mouth. "Not entirely willingly, as I recall."

She laughed softly. "No. You were quite clear about the temporary nature of the arrangement."

His expression sobered. "And now it's permanent. For as long as God grants us."

The reminder of life's fragility might have frightened her once. Now it only deepened her gratitude for the present moment—for this man, for Matthew, for the valley, for the community they were building together.

"For as long as God grants," she agreed. "And I will treasure every day."

In the distance, Zach's fiddle began a slow, sweet melody—a waltz that drifted across the valley like a benediction.

Weston stepped back slightly, extending his hand with formal grace. "Mrs. Reynolds, may I have this dance?"

Emily placed her hand in his, a smile blooming across her face. "You may, Mr. Reynolds."

Under the canopy of stars, beside the healing springs that had drawn them to this unexpected home, they danced. His arm was steady around her waist, her hand resting on his shoulder. They moved together in perfect rhythm, as if they had been doing so all their lives.

"I love you, Emily Reynolds," Weston murmured against her hair as they swayed to the distant music.

The words, once unimaginable, now felt like coming home. "And I love you, Weston Reynolds," she replied. "With all my heart."

Leave A Review

If you enjoyed this book, please consider leaving an honest review on Amazon

Visit Our Website:

www.vivianbelle.com

Visit Our Amazon Author Page HERE

Find Us On Social Media:

Facebook

Facebook Author Page

Instagram